Yes, THE RIVER KNOWS

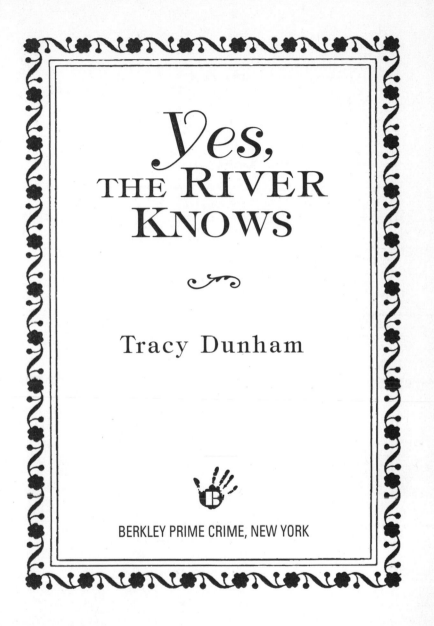

Yes, THE RIVER KNOWS

Tracy Dunham

BERKLEY PRIME CRIME, NEW YORK

THE BERKLEY PUBLISHING GROUP
Published by the Penguin Group
Penguin Group (USA) Inc.
375 Hudson Street, New York, New York 10014, USA
Penguin Group (Canada), 90 Eglinton Avenue East, Suite 700, Toronto, Ontario M4P 2Y3, Canada
(a division of Pearson Penguin Canada Inc.)
Penguin Books Ltd., 80 Strand, London WC2R 0RL, England
Penguin Group Ireland, 25 St. Stephen's Green, Dublin 2, Ireland (a division of Penguin Books Ltd.)
Penguin Group (Australia), 250 Camberwell Road, Camberwell, Victoria 3124, Australia
(a division of Pearson Australia Group Pty. Ltd.)
Penguin Books India Pvt. Ltd., 11 Community Centre, Panchsheel Park, New Delhi—110 017, India
Penguin Group (NZ), Cnr. Airborne and Rosedale Roads, Albany, Auckland 1310, New Zealand
(a division of Pearson New Zealand Ltd.)
Penguin Books (South Africa) (Pty.) Ltd., 24 Sturdee Avenue, Rosebank, Johannesburg 2196, South
Africa

Penguin Books Ltd., Registered Offices: 80 Strand, London WC2R 0RL, England

This book is an original publication of The Berkley Publishing Group.

This is a work of fiction. Names, characters, places, and incidents either are the product of the author's imagination or are used fictitiously, and any resemblance to actual persons, living or dead, business establishments, events, or locales is entirely coincidental. The publisher does not have any control over and does not assume any responsibility for author or third-party websites or their content.

First edition: December 2005

Library of Congress Cataloging-in-Publication Data

Dunham, Tracy.
    Yes, the river knows / Tracy Dunham.—1st ed.
        p. cm.
    ISBN 0-425-20577-0
    1. Women lawyers—Fiction. 2. South Carolina—Fiction. 3. Attorney and client—Fiction. 4. Divorced men—Crimes against—Fiction. 5. Secretaries—Fiction. I. Title.

PS3554.U4686Y47 2005
813'.54—dc22

2005053626

PRINTED IN THE UNITED STATES OF AMERICA

10   9   8   7   6   5   4   3   2   1

To Bill, Dianne, Kim, Kyle, and John—good people and great friends

Chapter 1

THE river flowed through Wynnton, South Carolina, like some muddy antediluvian, inching its way toward the millennium on feet mired in the past. I loved that river. The defining moments of my life had occurred there, well most of them. I mean, I wasn't born on the river bank, or thrown into it in a boat of bulrushes or anything like that. But I'd left my virginity behind on its grassy knoll, and more times than I could count, promised myself while sitting beside it that I'd find a way out of Wynnton.

I had. I'm Talbot Jefferson, formerly of a big city law firm partnership, now scratching by on traffic cases and small wills and trusts in a sleepy little town that could still be used for a movie set for the 1950s. But like the river that pulled the clay from the shores, I found my way back to the town I'd left like some crazed road freak, hell-bent on living hard, flying fast, burning like some comet into the stratosphere of the real world outside its narrow Southern confines. I'd come home to Wynnton a woman with no self-respect and very little interest in anything that wasn't distilled in Kentucky.

The river pulled me to it today like some old lover who still has the cutest butt in town. I'd been dragged back into the practice of law by Crystal Walker, a girl I'd known since grade school. While I'd fallen into representing other clients, albeit with some trepidation, like an alcoholic who's not sure she can walk by a bar without giving into temptation, I hadn't yet decided to give my life and soul to these people who seemed to think I could straighten out their tangled legal problems. I'd made that mistake only once, but then, it had been too late. Parnell Moses had already faced that needle laced with drugs that stopped his heart like a second baseman making a lightening-fast double play.

The flotsam of Wynnton's finer folks drifted by—a plastic-webbed lawn chair caught in some sticks, the top to a styrofoam cooler, probably lost by some fisherman, a red sock. I got a kick out of wondering how these twentieth-century artifacts fell into their watery graves. Would they someday become layered in sediment, sandstone fossils to be discovered hundreds of years from now, revered for sacred objects of a long-dead people? Or would the microbes of the river, polluted still despite the best efforts of the EPA, chew them down to size, leaving nothing but future food for the pfiesteria that left welts on fish and oozing sores on human flesh?

"Hey there."

I just about tumbled off the riverbank into the mud. "God bless, Travis, you scared me out of a year's growth."

Folding himself onto his haunches like some Middle Eastern guru, Travis Whitlock looked like an extinct crane settling onto a nest. Like me, Travis had come home to roost after a foray into the big, bad world. Unlike me, he'd been successful.

"Didn't mean to. Thought for sure you heard me trampin' through the brush like an elephant." His freckled face split wide with a grin that hadn't grown up.

"Been thinking." I always liked Travis. He'd been one of those open-faced boys I could read, and there'd been no harm in him.

We'd been through school together, but never in the same crowd. Travis Whitlock, even back then, set himself apart. No midnight raids on the corner convenience store to buy beer, no deer season license. Sketchbook in hand, he drew and painted, smudged and frowned at his work whenever he wasn't forced to go to class. I'd admired his complete self-knowledge at sixteen, that elusive air of knowing what he'd been created to do in life. But I didn't know him, not the boy nor the man. He'd never made a move on me, never written my name on a bathroom wall, so he was beyond my early years of contempt for most adolescent males.

"Bad thing to do. Leads to trouble for sure." He frowned at the river. "Looks particularly lethal today. You weren't planning a swim, were you?"

I laughed. "I'm not suicidal, if that's what you're thinking."

Rocking back on his heels, Travis studied me as if I were one of his subjects. He'd painted portraits all over the world, had been sought out by the rich and famous who wanted to be preserved in oils as if they'd been John Singer Sargent subjects. I'd seen some of Travis's work in an Atlanta art gallery once, and he was good. No matter how lavish the clothing, how rich the colors he used, the sitter's soul poured out of his eyes like a dirty little secret. I wondered how many of his wealthy clients really understood what Travis had done when he'd immortalized their likenesses on canvas.

He didn't answer me. Growing uncomfortable under his scrutiny, I turned my face to the river.

"Why're you here, Travis? Can't say as you've said two words to me since I've been back." I was being truthful. We'd said hello at Becky's Cafe, nothing more—just a nodding acquaintance with an old classmate.

"June said I could find you here."

She would. June, my secretary and a future lawyer, disapproved of what she called my wool-gathering. Entrusted by Henry Rolfe, her cousin's husband and my oldest friend, to keep me away from the bottle, she had her spies everywhere. Using someone like Travis to do her spying wasn't her usual technique, however.

"She did, did she?" Mentally trying to knock some of the chips off my shoulder, I forced myself to be more pleasant. "So what can I do for you, Travis?"

He had a face like a crane, I realized. Beak-nosed, long in the jaw, fading red hair swept away from his forehead like some aging hippie, he wasn't a handsome man. But his blue eyes, truly an aquamarine, could mesmerize. He focused them full-bore at me.

"I want to paint you."

The laugh roared out of me before I could shut my mouth. "You've gotta be kidding."

"Nope. Just finished a particularly lucrative commission, want to do something for myself for a change. I've always wanted to do you."

If he'd blown on my back, I'd have tumbled into the river.

"The bloom of youth is long gone, Travis, and I wasn't exactly a beauty in my prime. What on God's green earth do you want to paint me for?" The whole idea of sitting still and posing made me more than uncomfortable. Enforced idleness was what made prison the hell it was, and I knew I'd kill before I'd sit still for hours on end. Besides, I wasn't sure I wanted my skinny face and wild hair immortalized in oil paints.

"I just want to. You've your grandmother's cheekbones, you know. Now Miss Ena, I wish I'd been able to capture her . . ."

Staring at the river, he wasn't seeing the murky water. With surprise, I realized he was seeing my dead grandmother.

"So what do you say?" Turning the full charm of those eyes back to me, Travis smiled like a cat about to feast on the fish bowl. "I've got just a few more bits to finish on my Epps portrait, then I'd like to get right on it with you. Preliminary sketches, that sort of thing. You don't mind wearing a costume I've chosen, do you?"

Shaking my head, I was amazed he never considered the possibility I'd say no. "I have a life, Travis, in case you didn't notice. A house to renovate, a law practice, the whole nine yards."

"June told me you weren't especially busy. Said she could carry what you couldn't while you sat for me." Wiggling his eyebrows like Groucho Marx, he forced a smile from me.

"June has a big mouth, and someday I'm going to stuff a sock in it."

June had been right. I wasn't busy because I didn't want to be. We were doing some wills and trusts work, sent over mostly from the bank where I still owned inherited stock from Miss Ena. I did traffic cases on Monday mornings, some

DUIs, and the occasional shoplifter. My biggest client was former Judge Linwood Jordan. Him, I was representing before the Joint Legislative Audit and Review Commission as well as the State Bar on ethics charges. I knew quite a bit about ethics, most of it from personal failings.

"So, what do you say?" He brushed his long, paint-stained fingers through the wild tangles of his hair, impatient to get my commitment, impatient with my reluctance. I liked that. I sensed that if I said no, he'd hound me like a dog after a raccoon. Self-interest asserted itself.

"I'll do it, on one condition. You tell me why you came back to Wynnton."

He didn't smile this time. "Drive a hard bargain, Tal."

"That I do. I was known as a killer shark of a lawyer at one time." I wasn't exaggerating, and he knew it.

"Okay, but while I'm painting you. Not until then." He was deadly serious. Spitting in his palm, he held it out to me in the time-honored tradition of kids making an oath.

I slapped my palm to his. "Deal. But no nude posing. The boobs have drooped too much." Waving my spit-marked hand at the front of my shirt, I laughed.

"Oh, I think you'll be happy with what I've picked out for you to wear." Again, he had that faraway look that said he was seeing something I couldn't imagine. "As soon as I saw it, I knew you were the one to wear it for your portrait."

I groaned. "You and June. Why can't the two of you leave me to my jeans?"

Touching my shoulder gently, he used his single finger to balance himself as he unfolded like an origami bird. "Because there's more to you, my lovely model." With a light kiss on the top of my head, he started to leave me.

"Travis," I called after him, not knowing what I wanted to say, loath to be left alone, "wait a sec, I'll come with you."

Reaching back with his hand to pull me up, he suddenly jerked his fingers from mine. Startled, I looked up to see him frowning past my shoulder.

"Good God," he muttered, sliding past me down the embankment.

"Travis," I called after him, annoyed that he'd broken off his attentions to me. Hussy, I chided myself. You're flattered he's noticed you after all these years, and you're already miffed he's found something more interesting. "What're you doing?"

"Don't you see it?" His feet sank in the silt at the river's edge, Travis grabbed a water-soaked stick and jabbed.

I followed his gesture. Something bobbed at the water's edge, caught in the debris that had snarled around a half-submerged stump. Dark and ball-like, it was snagged.

"It's nothing, just some junk. Leave it be." I didn't want any dirty trash from the Wynnton landing at my feet.

"Tal, come here," Travis commanded. "Hold onto me."

"Travis," I protested, sliding down the embankment to stand beside him, "don't be an idiot. You'll catch all manner of diseases from this sewer."

"But I saw something. Look, there."

Ignoring me, Travis fastened my hands onto his belt and leaned over, scooping up the ball. Water flew in clay-colored spirals and I instinctively recoiled. I wouldn't dare swim in the river now, though I'd done it often when I was a kid.

"Oh God." Travis turned to me, holding the ball in his hands as if he wanted nothing more than to drop it back into the river, but it had fused itself into his flesh and he couldn't.

It wasn't a ball, but a head with dark hair.

"It's what I saw, a face."

The water had added a waxy, opalescent glow to the skin, but Travis was right. The eyeballs had been eaten by something, I didn't want to think what, and the lips and ears were severely nibbled. The hair, however, was cut short and tightly curled. A *black man,* I thought. Definitely African-American, with a raggedly chopped neck. My mind was as clear as it had been in weeks.

"Put it down carefully, Travis." I scrambled to pull off my shirt and drape it over the head. I was wearing a sports bra underneath, more decent than a bikini top.

He dropped it like a lead weight, his face pale, freckles standing out like liver spots. "I didn't really think I'd seen it, thought I was just imagining things."

The confident, smooth voice I'd heard a minute ago was gone. He was frightened, deeply so. Painting society portraits didn't prepare you to stare into the face of violent death.

"Did you drive down here, Travis?" He wasn't looking at me, but at the severed head. "Travis," I shook his arm like a rat terrier, "listen to me."

Like a gawker at a horrific accident site, he could barely pull his eyes away to notice me.

"Get in your car, drive to the sheriff's office, have them get out here. I'll stay with . . . it." I swallowed hard.

He was still staring at me as if I'd jumped off the moon and landed in his lap.

"Travis, go now." I didn't relish being left alone with this grisly bit of jetsam, but Travis wasn't up to it, that much was sure. "Go!" I commanded.

"Okay," he finally mumbled. "Get the sheriff."

"Yes, Travis." I prodded him away, my finger poking him in the small of the back. "I'll stay here."

"I thought it was something else," he mumbled. "Thought my eyes were playing tricks on me."

I wanted to tell him that an artist's eyes didn't play tricks. I envied him his acuity of vision, his perception, the clarity that let him see death where I'd seen lawn chairs. But I didn't think he'd appreciate it at the moment.

Travis Whitlock had just risen in my estimation. He finally started jogging for wherever he'd parked, swearing he'd be right back with the authorities. I settled down to swat biting flies away from the head, figuring it was the least I could do to show my respect for the dead.

Death held little horror for me. The coils and tangles of the living are what terrify me. Not a good reaction for a lawyer to possess, I admit. But sitting guard beside the head of a man who'd met his end violently, I half-envied him. He didn't have to go through the farce of existence any longer. I wondered who he was, how he ended up in the Wynnton River, and how I was going to explain all this to June without sounding mentally deranged. My own thoughts kept me company as I knelt in the clay and did my best to preserve the evidence.

I should have known the dead man claimed me that day, like a devil tapping me on the shoulder and whispering in wily tones, "I choose you, Talbot Jefferson."

I should have known I have more affinity for the dead than the living.

Chapter 2

FRANK Bonnet, Wynnton's sheriff, acted as if he thought the head at my feet was all my fault. In a way, I guess it was. If I hadn't been river-watching, Travis wouldn't have tracked me down, and then seen the thing in the water. So it was, in a manner of speaking, my fault.

Travis didn't return once Frank told him to take his green face and go home. Kneeling in the dirt, Frank gave the head with its greasy sheen a solid look. I had to give him credit.

"Seen this guy before, Frank?"

I'd be damned if I'd stand there with my skinny arms wrapped around my chest like an adolescent hiding her boobs from a lecherous old man. So I parked my hands on my hips and gave him my tough-girl imitation.

His dark glasses reflected the sun like the back of a beetle. "Guess the real question is, you know him, Tal?"

I shook my head. "You sure it's a man? I mean, some black women cut their hair pretty short like that."

"Hell no, I'm not sure of anything except you're a pain in the ass. Get on outta here, Tal, this here's a crime scene."

"That's my shirt," I pointed out. "When can I get it back?"

His smile said he'd like to wrap it around my throat and pull tight. Frank and I had never been friends, even as kids, but we were working on getting past those days.

"Soon as the lab's through with it."

One of my favorite shirts down the drain. Now I'd have to scrounge through the Episcopalian Thrift Store to find another one as soft and friendly as the blue one holding the head. I took his unsubtle hint and wandered back to my '66 Mustang. I bet myself that Travis called off the portrait session because every time he looked at me, he'd see that severed head.

In a way, I was thankful to the dead man. I certainly didn't relish having Travis dissect my soul on canvas.

Pulling up in front of my office/house, I wondered if the Wynnton grapevine had sprung into action already. Pretending nothing had happened, I ducked into the first floor where we kept the office.

"Back," I waved at June, perched precisely on her chair as she typed away at the keyboard, her eyes focused on the monitor.

She spared me the barest of glances. "That guy find you? Tivis or something?"

"Yep, no thanks to you. He wants to paint my portrait." I knew that would get her attention. "Why'd you tell him I had the time?" I didn't correct her pronunciation of Travis's name.

"Figured you'd have fun giving him the brush-off.

Anyway, he's hard up if he thinks you'll sit still. . . ." She noticed, for the first time, my half-undress. "Land's sake, what happened to you? I know you were decent when you stepped out that door."

She sounded just like my grandmother, Miss Ena, scolding after finding I'd destroyed a dress or a pair of patent leather shoes just before we had to leave for church.

"Nothing happened to me. Travis found something in the river, and I had to use my top to . . ."

She wasn't interested. "Good riddance. That shirt was a disgrace. I'll have to ask your painter friend if he can get rid of the rest of your clothes," she muttered, turning back to her keyboard.

June dressed as if she were about to audition for Miss America every day. My lack of concern with what covered my back was driving her to distraction. The fact that most of my wardrobe, except what she put together for me to wear to court, came from thrift stores, was the bane of her existence.

"I don't want you running downtown now, and spending your hard-earned fifty cents on something from that place you think is the only shop in town." June was just beginning to warm up when there was brisk knock at the front door of the house.

Henry Rolfe, my black childhood friend, didn't wait for an invitation, he breezed in. Whenever Henry showed up on my doorstep, I knew I'd get a scolding before he told me why he was there. So when he had on his county-pathologist face as he charged through the front hall, heading for my office like the four horsemen were on his tail, I didn't think he was looking for refuge. The fact that his face froze when he saw June, his wife's cousin, told me he wanted to talk to me alone.

Sighing, I put aside my remaining plans to tease June. Clearly, she hadn't gotten any calls about the head, and I was looking forward to grossing her out. June grossed out so easily, it was almost no fun.

"Yes, Henry? How're you today?" Quickly, I filed through my copious list of possible transgressions. I hadn't had a drink, I refrained from parading nude down Main Street, I hadn't even pissed off Frank, the town sheriff, by the river. I'd been sorely tempted, but I hadn't.

Closing the double glass doors to my office, Henry pressed his face against the frame.

"This isn't good, Tal."

I'd known Henry all my life. If he thought whatever it was was bad, it had to be very bad indeed.

"Nothing's happened to Grace?" Panic welled up from my gut, and I feverishly prayed Henry's smart, beautiful wife was okay. If she wasn't, I didn't think Henry would survive. Grace wore her hair long, not like the head pulled from the river, I reminded myself. Besides, Grace was lovely, and the head I'd seen had never come close. Just the thought that Grace could have been the victim sent me reaching for my desk chair.

Turning slowly, he adjusted his glasses. The skin on his face seemed too tight for his bones. Tall like me but built for football, he was uncomfortable in his skin today. My flesh crawled at what he must have to tell me.

"I need June to identify a body. I got here before Frank— he'd make a mess of it. Can you come with us?"

I couldn't imagine who was dead that June needed to ID. "Talk to me, Henry. What's this about?"

Twisting the glasses from his face, Henry proceeded to polish them slowly with the tip of his tie. "Her husband. I think his head's in my lab. Darryl Henshaw."

Darryl Henshaw had been out of June's life when we first met. I'd assumed they were divorced, and June had taken back her maiden name of Atkins. So Henry knew the name that belonged to the head Travis had rescued. Very interesting, I mused.

"Wait a sec. Isn't he her ex-husband?" I didn't see any need to drag June into a former spouse's doo-doo pile. If he had people, let them identify him.

"Evidently not. Darryl was in the Marines, you know. I don't think June could afford to pay the legal fees it takes to divorce a service man. She'd left him but didn't do the paperwork, from what Grace told me. I called her at work to ask."

June and Grace were first cousins.

"Oh." I couldn't think of anything else to say.

"So I need a positive ID. I only saw him that one time, at the wedding. But I think it's Henshaw." Henry was still polishing those damn glasses, as if he could wear away the prescription until he couldn't see what needed seeing.

"Hold on." I shoved Henry aside and took a peek out the door. June had a habit of listening around corners when she thought I was up to something. At the moment, however, she was nowhere in sight.

"Tell me what the hell Darryl Henshaw is doing in Wynnton. I thought she'd dumped him in Atlanta?"

Henry shook his head. "That, I don't know. Maybe he was stationed at the post."

The old army post was home to a transportation corps. Every year Congress threatened to close it down, but there were no wealthy buyers interested in the property, so it stayed open.

"I thought Darryl was a Marine. There're no Marines on base."

"He was. I don't know what the hell's going on, all I know is, I think it's Darryl's head. I can get dental records from the Marines, but it'll take a while. Help me tell June."

This was one of the reasons I'd retreated to Wynnton after my career had crashed and burned in Atlanta. I'd lived alone, had minimal contacts with other humans, and drunk myself into a stupor. Friends meant responsibilities. Clients meant responsibilities. Life meant responsibilities. I hadn't wanted any of it.

"Let's get it over with." I felt the Miss Ena in my DNA take over. Straightening my shoulders, I pulled Henry with me into June's office.

She wasn't around. Probably, she was upstairs in my closet, throwing away every pair of jeans I owned.

"June?" I shouted from the bottom of the old oak staircase.

I'd been restoring my grandmother's house for about two years now, and the balustrade was the last thing I planned on tackling. Layers of varnish had left it dark and cracked like old china. I studied the intricate webs as I waited for June to answer. Maybe I'd undertake burning off the layers tonight.

"Keep your britches on," June snapped from the kitchen. "Henry, you want something to drink, you come out here and get it yourself."

Henry stared at me as if a viper had nipped his heel.

"All right, I'll do it." Henry was hopeless in the midst of feminine tears, but I thought he had June all wrong. If I knew June, she'd dance on the bastard's grave. From the bits and pieces she'd dropped over the months we'd worked together, I knew the marriage hadn't been even close to perfect.

Propping myself in the kitchen door, I watched as June quickly and efficiently fixed a sandwich.

"Tell Henry I'll fix him one if he's not in too much of a hurry." Turning, she thrust the plate into my hand. "Eat. You skipped breakfast, I can tell. You always get testy when you don't eat."

"June," I set the plate on the counter. "Henry's here on business. He needs you to identify a body in the morgue." I swallowed hard, my throat suddenly dry. I couldn't imagine how grisly the scene must be in the cooler at Henry's office. The antiseptic surroundings couldn't disguise a horrible death. Ex-husband, estranged husband, Henshaw had still been a man.

"Actually, it's a head. Just a head."

June stared at me like a bull that's been pole-axed. "Who on earth could it be? Why me?"

I turned to see if Henry was going to give me any help here, but he'd stayed in the hallway, his face hidden in the shadow of the stairs.

"He thinks it's Darryl Henshaw, but he can't be sure. That's why he needs you."

The woman was going to make a hell of a trial lawyer. The muscle at the corner of her eyes had twitched, but only I would have noticed it.

"That's impossible."

I fumbled with the light switch, thinking I should cut the overhead off. I didn't want to see her face as she thought about what I'd just said.

"Henry's waiting. I'll go, too."

Carefully and with great precision, June screwed the top on the mayonnaise jar. "Let me clean up. I'll be with him in a sec. You go get dressed. Honestly, you look like some cheap hooker."

"No." I stepped forward and took the jar from her hands. "Don't worry with this. Let's get it over with, then we can get back to work. I need you to draft some documents for the Stinson trust." I hoped the mention of legal work would keep June focused.

Her eyes were somewhere else. They stared at me, but she wasn't seeing anything in her present. I imagined she was watching Darryl, alive and as she'd last seen him.

She took the mayonnaise jar from me and walked to the ice box without knowing what she was doing.

Gently, I pried her hand off the refrigerator door. "Let's just do it. I saw the head already, by the river. To be honest, I wasn't sure it was a man. Henry's as upset as you, but he's got a job to do."

Her heart-shaped face seemed pinched at the edges, as if the sublayer of fat that held the shape of cheeks, above her jawline, had collapsed inward. "You saw it? This morning?"

I nodded. "Travis fished it out of the river."

She squirmed somewhere deep inside of herself, as if she'd leave her body behind like some cocoon that had housed her for only so long before she was ready to fly. "Darryl hated water. He was a bad swimmer."

I didn't want to remind her that he didn't have a chance to swim, that probably only his head had made it into the river. Leading her out to Henry, I grabbed my keys on the credenza in the hallway and ran upstairs for a clean shirt.

"I'll drive her," I told Henry. At least he'd stopped rubbing those damned glasses.

"Good," was all he could manage. "This won't take a minute."

I got June into the car, lifting her legs inside like a polio victim. Her skin was cold. She may have hated the bastard and let everyone know it, but she was still attached to Darryl in some way I couldn't fathom. Actually, I did understand. I'd kept an old flame burning for an ancient love, before I learned not long ago that old flames are nothing but memories that have nothing to do with the truth or any genuine heat.

I pulled my Mustang out of the driveway and onto Woolfolk Avenue, driving slowly as if I were transporting someone ill in body. The trip to Henry's office didn't take five minutes. Parking, I hurried to open June's door and helped her out.

She shook me off. The old June was back, I noted gratefully.

"Tal?"

"Yes, June?"

"They investigate the wife, don't they?"

My stomach balled into a knot. "That's where they start."

"And everyone knew he was a no-good, no-count, lying son of a bitch, because I told them so. Right?"

"Guess so." I wondered where this was going.

"He wasn't all bad, Tal. He had his moments. He could be a good man." She sounded so sad, I felt close to tears. Her eyes glittered for the first time since I'd told her.

"But truth to tell, I'm not sorry he's dead. I'm sorry for the way it sounds like he died, and I sure as hell don't want to have to defend myself to Frank Bonnet, but this saved me a lot of grief. He'd never have given me the divorce. He'd have used lawyers to stall me every way he could."

"If you say so, June." I was glad the town sheriff wasn't

hearing this. June was giving a hell of a good reason for murder.

Henry pulled into the lot beside us. Wearing his official face, he unlocked the office door, and waited for June and me to enter first. A medical doctor who could have practiced anywhere, he was a part-time coroner for the county. Not many murders happened in Wynnton. Why so many had occurred since I'd returned was a mystery.

"I'll get it ready, June, if you and Tal will wait here," Henry ordered.

I really didn't want to see this. I'd seen enough misery to last me for six lifetimes. Sitting beside the head, waiting for Frank, had been sufficient for me.

After what seemed seconds, Henry gestured from the green door that marked the entrance to his small morgue. My feet felt like I was wearing concrete sneakers, but June glided in first as if she were Cinderella dancing on a waxed floor in glass slippers. She took up her position beside Henry, chin up, her glittering eyes unblinking.

Henry flipped back a blue, blood-stained cloth hiding a lump in the middle of an autopsy table.

The face was as unreal as it had been beside the river when I swatted flies from its tortured expression.

"That's him," June spit from between clenched lips. "As I live and breathe, that's Darryl."

Henry covered the head and took June by the arm to lead her to me. But June was having none of it. Jerking back the covering, she leaned over until she was eye-level with her dead husband's head.

"Told you, you'd push it too far one of these days. Shoulda listened to me, Darryl. Told you, I did." Her face wore a sadness her words didn't express.

I was more than grateful that Frank Bonnet wasn't hearing this. Her rant could have been made to sound incriminating even by a first-year prosecutor.

I'd given her credit for holding it together a second too long.

"Oh God." June's eyes flooded as she balled her fists at her mouth. A long, low wailing erupted from her like a fire alarm. "Oh God, Darryl," she sobbed.

I shoved Henry out of the way and took her in my arms. She'd never forgive me for giving her comfort, but it was a risk I had to take.

I'd never heard anyone cry like that.

Chapter 3

DENTAL records confirmed the identification. June was checking on whether Darryl could be buried in Arlington, but it was going to be hard for her to do a casket without a body. Despite her misgivings about cremation, she settled on it as the only decent thing to do. Only problem was, she couldn't bury Darryl until Henry was finished with him.

"Why didn't you tell me you two were still married?"

June and I were rocking in wrought-iron chairs, the sort that bounce backward when you plunk into them. We'd retreated to Henry and Grace's porch, me with a glass of iced tea, forcing the others into foregoing anything stronger. The three of them looked as if they needed a strong belt of Kentucky's finest more than I did.

"You told me you were getting divorced as soon as you

could afford it," Grace complained. "Why didn't Tal get the paperwork going?"

I instantly felt as if I'd let Grace down, something I planned on avoiding the rest of my life. Grace was not a woman to let down. Long-legged, stunningly beautiful, and aristocratic in manners as well as substance, she had more brains than Henry and I put together. Working for the government space program on a consulting basis, she was often gone for weeks at a time. She and Henry, with their combined brains and income, could have decided to live anywhere in the country. Henry, however, had wanted to come home to Wynnton to be close to his widowed mother, my grandmother's friend. However, not too many years back, Mrs. Rolfe had gone west and taken up the wicked life of a gay widow in a retirement community. Henry and I were still in shock over the image of her playing golf. Mrs. Rolfe had never taken time for games and such "frivolities," as she called them, while we were growing up.

"Never did," June shot back. "All I said was, I'd left him."

"You haven't answered my question," I noted. I was getting accustomed to drinking sweet tea again. Southerners have been adding a substantial dollop of corn syrup to their tea pitchers for years, probably as an overreaction to the shortage of sugar during the War of Northern Aggression. The practice had stuck. For years, it had made my teeth ache and my blood sugar do weird things. But it was growing on me now that I'd cut out all alcohol.

I studied my tea glass, waiting for June to quit ignoring me.

"Well? I think we both deserve an answer." Grace could get more from her than I. If she'd spoken to me in that tone of voice, I'd have prostrated myself at her feet and spilled my guts.

"None of your business, is why." June's heart-shaped face was tight with defiance. "Besides," she whispered softly, "I guess I always hoped he'd straighten out, come back to me a changed man."

I couldn't help myself, I snorted like a cat with a furball. June gave me one of her freezer looks.

"You're smart enough to know men don't change." Grace rescued me from my faux pas. "Especially guys like Darryl who live to fight, and they don't care with whom."

I loved Grace's precise diction, her impeccable grammar. While I was admiring Henry's choice of wife, he reappeared, a tray of snacks in his hands.

"Now Grace, don't be hard on her," Henry chastened. "She's had a rough day."

"They're going to get rougher." I loved summer nights like this—the cicadas singing their little hearts out, the sun lingering on the horizon as if it didn't want to leave us.

"Heard from that new prosecutor, Braidwood, I think his name is." I wiped the bottom of my glass on my jeans.

Henry nodded. "Guy Braidwood. Replaced Owen . . ." He trailed off.

He meant Owen Amos, the prior prosecutor who'd killed several people to keep quiet his military record in Vietnam. I'd been attracted to him, and everyone assumed I was still embarrassed by my extremely poor taste in men. They didn't know me well, not at all. I had bigger things in my life to humiliate me.

"Whatever. He wants June to come in for a formal

interview. I'm not too happy about it, but if we don't, they can make life very unpleasant."

I'd held off telling June, but I knew she'd been expecting something like this. She was, after all, Darryl's wife, and logically, the first person the police should take a serious look at for motive.

"Anyone find out what Darryl was doing here?" Henry was trying to deflect me, but June wasn't having any of it.

"When?" She looked as if she'd swallowed a lemon.

"Tomorrow morning. I said we'd be in around nine." I was a morning person, but June wasn't. The prosecutor had wanted to see her at eight.

"You know the drill. Wait before you answer a question to see if I'm going to stop you. Don't jump into any explanations, and keep whatever you do say short and sweet." I felt strange, prepping June to face the verbal shotguns of a prosecutor.

"I've heard stories about Braidwood." June was once again trying to change the subject. "Mae Ellen Roberts says he's gay."

"Why? Because he isn't married?" Grace scoffed.

"No, more than that. You know how some men are who are like that. They try to act more macho. But Mae Ellen says she can tell one a mile away, after her great uncle Hunter and his 'companion.'" June wiggled her little finger. "Mae Ellen says she's never been wrong."

"Who cares." I hadn't met the man yet; he'd only been around a couple of weeks.

His had been the only name submitted to the Circuit Court judges for our jurisdiction for appointment to fulfill Owen's unexpired term. All I knew about him was that he'd been practicing law about five years with one of the bigger law firms in town, and he didn't do traffic cases. He was also younger than I was, and ordered chili to go from Becky's for lunch. Sometimes the lack of breadth of my knowledge astounded even me.

"I'll bet he hates women." June was looking for excuses already. We were in trouble.

"Don't be an idiot. This is a formality. You have to be interviewed, you know that." I was going to need something stronger than iced tea to get me through this.

"Well, I don't have to like it. I may have married the jerk, but I didn't kill him."

"That's not the issue here." I noticed that Grace and Henry were staring at the two of us as if we were exotic animals in the zoo. "You have to get scratched off their list. So just be cool."

June acting uncool was a prime example of the stars out of alignment, the heavens about to fall. June was the ultimate cool lady. I was the one who had trouble hanging onto my sanity by my fingernails.

"What if I don't get scratched off their list?" June was giving far too much attention to her French tips.

"What do you mean?" I'd been planning on half an hour at the most in Braidwood's office. I was beginning to have an inkling that I was way off in my calculations as to June's importance in this investigation.

"What if, for example, I'd seen Darryl recently? Like, maybe, a month ago, maybe a couple of weeks?"

She didn't have the guts to face me, I noted, with an urge to strangle her right there and then.

"It all depends. Did you two have a knock-down-drag-out

in public? Or, the gods willing, a romantic interlude?" I
wished Grace would help me out here. Henry, I knew, was
hopeless.

"I think Henry and I should leave you two alone." Rising
like a model from her chair, Grace grasped Henry's hand in
hers and tugged. "Come on, sweetie, we need to get to the
store."

"But I went yester . . ." Henry began to protest.

Sometimes, Henry wasn't swift on the uptake. Grace
gave him the lifted-eyebrows wiggle, and another pull to
haul him out of his chair. Henry's a big man, it takes the
strength of a linebacker to move him when he doesn't want
to be moved. Grace got him going, however.

"You two stay as long as you want," Grace added in a
thick, honeyed drawl as she shepherded Henry out the porch
door toward the garage. "I'll talk to you later, June."

I pitied June. But at the moment, I needed to know more
about this meeting between her and Darryl.

"So spill it. The whole enchilada." In the back of my
mind, I was wondering if I should get her another lawyer,
one who could see her through a trial. Every warning bell
told me she was going to need a hell of a criminal attorney
and it shouldn't be me. What if I failed her?

June hesitated, pushing at a cuticle, sighing copiously. I
waited.

"He called me up, said he was coming to town, had some
leave he was taking. He'd had his tour in Germany cut
short. Something about troop cutbacks."

I was remembering what she'd told me in Henry's
morgue, and this didn't sound a bit like that story.

"And?" I was getting impatient.

"And he showed up, like he said he would. First time in

his life he's ever kept a date on time with me. He was even late to our wedding." Her voice was bitter.

"Where did he show up?" Not where half the town saw them together, please Lord.

"You know that truck stop on Route 11? The big one, with the restaurant? There."

I knew the place. Rumor had it that prostitution and drug dealing were as available as gasoline, but Frank had kept his hands off it. As long as it catered to the transient and not the good folk of Wynnton, he didn't care.

"He was doing smaller weapons shows, then headed to Richmond, for that big gun deal at the Fairgrounds. You know the one, there's always a billboard up for it this time of year?"

I did indeed. I'd bought a gun at a similar show in Greensville myself not too long ago. The show, filled with dealers with modern and antique weapons, was an easy way to get around a records check, and you could take your purchase home that day. As a lawyer, I tried to avoid forms and registrations whenever I could.

I'd wanted a small caliber number, a vintage model classified as an antique, to feel a little safer after the murder attempts when Owen Amos had been out to get me. Like all Southern women, I had a healthy respect for the business end of a gun. Henry and I had started out on air rifles and progressed to pinging tin cans by the river by the time we were ten.

The cicadas sang louder, as if their voices could help them escape their ugly bodies. The smooth night air was beginning to raise goosebumps on my arms. I didn't think I wanted to hear this from June, but there was no way around it.

"Anyway, we met. Had a hamburger. He was driving a van, I asked if it was his, he said yes, he'd saved some money in Germany." June didn't like this any more than I did.

"And what importance does this van have?"

June flared. "You don't understand, he'd never saved up for anything in his life. When we were together, I paid for everything. If I didn't have the cash, he'd go find a game or something, and don't ask me what that something was."

"I can guess." Darryl sounded like one of those men who "liberated" military equipment for sale to civilians.

"So there he was, looking as fine as the first day I saw him." She sighed, her voice trembling. "You see a man in full dress uniform, Tal, Lord Almighty, it'll take your breath away. That's how I first saw Darryl, and it was all over after that."

"Was he in his uniform when you met him at the truck stop?"

June gave a very unladylike snort. "Not hardly. But he gave me a present, and we talked, and I started to think maybe he'd finally grown up, and that we might work it out, you know. All that dumb stuff."

I knew. I'd done a few divorces when I'd begun practicing law, and the capacity of women to forgive and take back into the family bosom the most obnoxious of men was truly astounding.

"What kind of present?" This wasn't sounding too awful. I had a feeling I knew what Darryl had been up to, if he wanted to stop any possible divorce. I began to wonder why, until I remembered the allowances made in the military for married personnel exceeded those received by single men.

"A ring." Reluctantly, June extended her right hand.

I'd been a dolt not to notice it. Miss Ena had left me several nice family pieces, but only a few compared with this little number. Three diamonds, perfect ones, I'd have bet, marched across a decorative white gold band. Smaller diamonds trailed down the sides of the band. The ring looked old and very expensive. I guessed it was a turn-of-the-century dinner ring.

"Wow." I whistled my respect for a man with that kind of taste.

"Yeah, that's what I said. When we got married, I bought my own band. Nothing fancy. Now he's dropping diamonds on me, promising me he's changed."

I knew what was coming next. A ring like that had a price.

"We spent the night in the motel at the truck stop. When I woke up the next morning, he was gone. He'd already paid the bill, at least. Guess I was a fool, huh?"

I'd never dare call June a fool. "Did you hear from him again?"

"Nope. It was like he dropped back into the hole he crawled out of. I expected to see him, but part of me wondered."

That night must have been good. I'd never understand what Darryl Henshaw had had that made a smart woman like June lose any vestige of common sense she'd ever possessed.

"You think of trying to find him at the weapons show?"

June reared back and gave me her withering look. "What sort of fool do you think I am? Man does me like that, I don't go crawling after him."

"Wonder what he was planning on doing there? You think he was buying or showing?"

June shrugged. "Probably a bit of both. He said he had a fancy alarm on the van to keep his stuff safe outside the motel."

"Was he a collector while you guys were together?"

"Nothing much. Got all his jollies with the stuff the Marines gave him to play with. Plenty of that going around." She sniffed.

"And you never heard from him again?"

"Will you quit asking me that? I'm not exactly proud of what I did, sleeping with him at that motel. But he was my husband, after all."

She had a good point. "You do know, by sleeping together, you ruined your chances of getting a divorce without waiting another year? I assume he didn't sign any property settlement agreement while you had him under your spell?" Not that it mattered now.

Cocking one eyebrow, June stared at me as if I were a stink bug. "You've never been married, may I remind you, Miss Jefferson? Don't you go judging me and my relationship with Darryl."

Well, I thought, I'd been put in my place by a master at the game. "No ma'am. But you think I'm nosy, wait until you sit down with Guy Braidwood and one of his investigators. I understand the ex-army types Owen Amos brought in are still on the job. And boy howdy, do those ex-army types know their business."

They were trained in the same techniques used by the FBI. I hated to think how June would handle them. I'd probably have to represent her on an assault charge, at a minimum. If she'd have me, that is.

"I'll tell 'em the truth. I'm sorry Darryl's dead. He was one hell of a man when he wanted to charm you. Rest of the time, he deserved what he got."

"Please don't say that. Please." I was accustomed to June's brutal honesty. I was betting the investigator assigned to the case would listen to June and rub his hands in glee at how easy his case would be to make.

Crossing her arms on her chest, June looked like a petulant child. "Maybe I should do this alone."

I squawked. "Not on your life. Literally. You don't want me, say so. I'll find you another lawyer. I probably should anyway."

Truth to tell, I'd be hurt to no end if she said yes, she wanted other counsel. I thought we'd progressed some in our relationship, enough to trust one another so far. Maybe no further, but at least this far.

She was taking her own sweet time about answering me. I listened for the sound of neighborhood children at play on a long summer's evening. When I was a kid, we'd have been out for hours, long past our bedtimes, playing hide-and-seek or hopscotch. Now, I heard nothing. Everyone was probably glued to a TV set, and the poorer for it. Thank God Miss Ena had rationed television. I'd spent my youth with books, and I thanked her spirit even now.

"All right. But I still don't think I need you."

"Yeah, right," I muttered. "It'll be hard to get your law license with a felony conviction, you know."

June was a big girl, I reminded myself. She'd been taking care of herself before she walked into my office and announced she was commandeering it. She'd done a far better job of self-preservation than I had.

At least I'd never married a creep like Darryl Henshaw. For the first time, I felt I'd won the upper hand.

I knew it was a transitory victory and thoroughly hollow. I wished I'd just learned how to love enough to take such a huge step. June trumped me on that one.

Shoving my ruins of a life from my mind, I followed June out the porch door. I'd try to sleep tonight, even though the old longing for the bottle I no longer stashed in the kitchen was marching through my gut like Sherman through Georgia.

Chapter 4

I didn't see him on the porch swing. Parking my Mustang on the street, I was intent on fighting my demons as I fumbled for the door key.

"Hey, Tal," he said as if he'd spent half his life swinging on Miss Ena's porch.

I have to admit, I squeaked. "Pete's sake, what're you doing here?"

Hands crammed in his jeans pockets, Travis shuffled closer to the door. The swing creaked as it rocked in response to his standing. He was wearing a paint-spattered T-shirt dominated by reds. The colors clashed with his hair.

"Just wanted to talk. That's all." He held up his hands as if showing he didn't hold a weapon.

What did he think I thought, I wondered. That he was a mad rapist? I was tired and worried, not in the best of moods to make Travis feel better about Darryl Henshaw's demise. I knew that was what he was looking for—comfort and solace. I was fresh out.

"Tell the truth, Travis, I'm about talked out tonight. Can it wait?"

I'd left the hall light on. The door now open, the yellow glow from the overhead fixture splashed his face, cutting it into Picassoesque lines. I didn't hold the screen open for him to follow me in.

"I just wanted to see if you could tell me, um, you know, about what we found today?"

Slouching against the door frame, he reminded me of boys from my youth, shy but unwilling to give up on a girl, hanging around the front door but reluctant to force their way inside. I always wondered if their shoulders hurt from leaning on them like that.

I thought about it for half a second. The whole town would know soon enough. "It was a guy named Darryl Henshaw. He was married to my secretary."

His Adam's apple bobbed. "Wow. That's a coincidence, huh?"

"Travis, you and I are old enough to know there are no coincidences in this life. Now, is there anything else I can do for you? I'm sorry about posing for your painting, but until I get June through this . . ."

Shaking his head, he looked shocked I'd even think of mentioning it. "Actually, I figured you'd be pretty much bummed out by that, you know, thing."

"I'm not." I felt like Miss Ena trying to explain the facts of life and failing miserably. Henry's mother had had to do the job for me.

"And I wanted you to know, I feel badly about leaving you alone with it." His eyes on mine, not pleading, but asking for something from me, he was still. I wasn't good at giving people what they wanted.

Maybe I'd underestimated him. The aura of danger I'd been feeling from him heightened, like ozone in the air before a thunderstorm. *Well, well,* I mused, *Travis Whitlock might have some admirable qualities after all.* I'd always had a high opinion of his talent, but didn't know enough about the real him behind the artist to judge whether or not he fit into my very narrow criteria of people fit to know well.

"That's okay. I've seen death before. This was a new one, for sure, but it's nothing I can't handle." At least, I hoped so.

"I should have stayed." He looked angry, like a boy who'd lost his first girl or the big football game and felt foolish. I didn't know artists had such doubts about their macho status.

"Ah, hell, Travis, let it go. I'll fix you something to drink." I was a sucker for men questioning their masculinity.

"Don't want to bother you," he protested. "It's just that I can't work, can't do anything without seeing it, the head, that is. Never happened to me before." He slipped through my front door, still talking.

"What's never happened before?" I led the way down the hall to the kitchen at the back of the house. A large room, it held an oak table and chairs, the regular kitchen appliances, albeit about a zillion years old, and a pantry where Miss Ena's silver serving pieces were stashed behind the cans and crackers. She'd used it for her hiding place, and I'd seen no reason to change it.

I jerked open the ice box door. In the South of my roots, the refrigerator will always be an ice box, even though blocks of ice are never delivered to the back door these days. I studied the ancient Frigidair's empty interior, wondering what I'd offer Travis in the way of hospitality. More than that was probably beyond my ability, but a cold drink wasn't impossible.

In the best of times, I don't have a lot hanging around in there. I found some cans of root beer, however, and pulled them out. Without asking Travis what he preferred, I handed him one.

He stared at the can as if he'd never seen one before. "I've never been able not to find that zone, you know, that place where I can freeze it all out and focus on my work. Just leave it behind and get to what matters."

Whistling softly, I seated myself at the table and watched to see what he did. He followed, almost as if he didn't see me or anything else, but his body knew what to do.

"It'd be a shock for anyone, Travis. Don't be so hard on yourself." I kicked back a slug and pretended it was a name-brand beer.

I didn't see his gaze shift to me. "You pretend you're so hard, so immune, Tal. But you're not. You're marshmallow on the inside, just like I am. Takes one to know one."

I don't like pop psychology, don't think delving into the depths of what makes us tick is constructive. "Maybe you're right. But death is death, Travis. We'll find out when we get there if we guessed right. Nothing can hurt Darryl Henshaw anymore. He's not part of your life, your existence. His death should mean nothing to you." I was calling it as I saw it.

Travis was studying me as if he'd never seen me before.

"What?" I demanded to know. "What's the matter?"

"I think I've changed my mind. I'm going to pose you differently than I first thought. Got a pencil around here?"

I didn't know what to say, so I got up and dug a pencil

out of the junk drawer. Pulling a small pad of paper from his back pocket, Travis took over.

"Here, hold this can like this." He posed my hand. "Stare at it as if it holds the meaning of life."

"Hard to do," I laughed. "It's not potent enough for that."

"Pretend," he commanded. He was all business, he who must be obeyed. I'd heard judges speak like that.

I stopped laughing.

"Now bend your head like this." He tucked a piece of hair behind my right ear. "No, bent more, like this." His hand was warm on my neck. "Good, now don't move."

I started to ask him how long he was going to torture me like this, but he shushed me before I could get the words out.

"Don't talk. I want your lips just as they are now."

I'd never felt so naked in my life.

"Travis," I began to protest.

"Hush." I was his underling, his hired hand. "You mustn't move your mouth until I've got it right."

I shushed. Slowly, his fingers slid the pencil across the page, smudged a line, redrew it. Watching him from the corner of my eye, I saw his face transformed. For a second, the look frightened me, it was so intense, so focused. A man with that much concentration was capable of doing anything he set his mind to.

"Always wanted to ask you," he began slowly, as if the words interfered with how his mind was working and were being dredged up out of some other part of his psyche, "what you ever saw in Jack Bland."

I jumped.

"Don't answer that. I'll tell you. You liked the idea of a

nonintellectual, someone who couldn't challenge your mind. You were, my dear Tal, taking the easy way out. You wanted his body, you didn't care if he was dumb as dirt."

I almost protested that Jack had been the love of my life, but I knew that wasn't true. I'd gotten over him recently, during my defense of Crystal Walker. The past was a bitter-sweet memory, but just that.

"Did you know I used to watch you, back in high school? In English, senior year, you looked like a hunted criminal. As if you had dark and dirty secrets, and you'd take them to your grave. I sometimes wondered what sins I could see in your face, and believe me, in my mind, they were pretty cool."

I started to laugh, then remembered his interdiction. I didn't think he'd appreciate my finding his musings humorous, anyway.

"I could tell from your eyes you were sleeping with Jack. Did you know, I always envied him?"

I must have started, because he leaned over and pressed his hand to the nape of my neck, bending it lower again. *This,* I thought, *is getting weird.* Then part of me was flattered.

"But you know how it is, awkward adolescent boy mooning over the class star. I didn't have the guts back then to do more than say hello. Believe me, that took every ounce of courage I had."

I wanted to ask him how and when that boy had acquired the aplomb and polish to hobnob with the rich and famous while he did their portraits. I wondered if he chatted them up, flattered them as he exposed them on canvas as if they were unclothed.

He continued talking, his face bent to the sketch pad, then lifting, staring at me intently, then back to the pad.

"You had a face like a lioness then. All pointed angles,

wild hair, fierce gaze. Someday I'll paint you as I remember you. But now, your face has changed. The planes are harder now, you look skinnier than you did when you were seventeen. Funny huh? Most women get rounder, more filled out as they age. The majority of the women I paint are fighting the bulge, paying plastic surgeons to lift eyelids and firm up their jaws. It always shows, a certain tightness in their skin, as if they're trying to cover up who they really are.

"You're different, though, Tal. It's as if your skin has given up trying to make you softer, more womanly, and shrunk until your soul is crawling out of your pores. You haven't had a good life, have you?"

My lungs were refusing to work properly. Staring at Travis despite his command, I was ready to knock him from here to Sunday. But I couldn't. I'd always admired honesty. This was what I'd been afraid of, and sure enough, I'd fallen into his trap.

"Bet you don't insult the people who pay your commissions."

He didn't order me into silence. "I do, but they don't know it."

So I'd been correct about his work. "So why insult me? I'm not paying you."

"It's not an insult. You wouldn't have me lie to you. You'd take me off at the knees if I did."

The day had been longer than twenty-four hours as far as I was concerned, and the hour was certainly too late for this kind of analysis. I couldn't hide from Henry, he knew me too well. But I didn't relish exposing myself to Travis's critical eye. Not at this hour.

"It's late, I'm tired, and you're upset over today. Why don't we call it a night?" I should have nipped this in the bud.

Standing, I swept the root beer cans into the trash. "I'll see you out."

Gazing at his sketch pad with a satisfied smile, Travis flipped the cover down and stuffed it back in his pocket. "That's fine. I've got enough done now to start some serious sketching. It'll keep me busy until you're free to sit again."

"Who says there's going to be any more of these little sessions?" I was playing it tough and hoping it would work. Usually, I could scatter a room full of men with the tone of voice I was using now.

"There will be. You won't be able to wait to see the finished portrait." He sounded like a man having entirely too much fun at my expense.

I led the way to the front door, expecting him to protest a bit more for effect. He didn't, slipping through the screen door as I held it open. With a wave of his hand, almost a dismissal of me in my own home, he trotted down the stairs. Clearly, he was a happier man now than he'd been when he showed up on my doorstep.

"Hey, Travis." I couldn't resist.

"Yeah?" He still had that happy, goofy expression, as if he'd struck paydirt but couldn't go shouting about it in the streets.

"Why didn't you say anything to me back in high school? About wanting to be with me?"

He shook his head. "I was saving it for the right time."

"Tonight was it?" I was incredulous. "Of all the rotten timing, you've got it, Travis Whitlock."

"Never said I didn't." He threw me a happy little wave. "Thanks, Tal. I'm feeling better. I'll let you know when I need you to sit again."

"Glad to be of help," I muttered, angry at him for disturbing the peaceful, albeit boring, tenor of my existence.

I wasn't attracted to Travis, but I had to admit I was intrigued. The man sure wasn't the boy, that much was as clear as the markings on a copperhead.

I'd have to be fast on my feet if I didn't want to get bitten.

Chapter 5

❦

G UY Braidwood was so wet behind the ears he almost dripped. At least ten years younger than I, he was still fighting pimples and a baby face that must have made him furious. Men like that in prosecutorial positions could be very dangerous. Being five years out of law school had given him a confidence he hadn't yet earned.

The investigator he was using was one of Owen Amos's ex-military types. The haircut and blank expression gave him away. I wondered why Frank wasn't present.

I shook hands, introducing myself and June to Braidwood. He gave the investigator a brief nod, saying "This is Watson."

I almost laughed and asked where Sherlock was today. But I was in my somber navy blue suit and trying to play it straight. June was looking a bit peaked around the eyes, but was her impeccable self in a silk pantsuit and perfect makeup. I'd remembered lipstick, which was a step forward in my personal style.

We sat around the far end of a huge conference table in a tiny office in the old county building. The air-conditioning must have been running like a mouse on a treadmill all night, because it was cold enough to make me wish I'd worn a padded bra.

"We have a few questions to ask Mrs. Henshaw."

"Good, because a few is all I can handle this morning. I've got the ten o'clock docket with Judge DeShazo." I was letting him know that June and I were there voluntarily, and I wasn't going to let him grill her like a hot dog on Saturday afternoon.

Watson evidently decided I'd said enough and he wasn't going to wait for Braidwood to get into the fray.

"Mrs. Henshaw, when was the last time you saw your husband?"

I wanted to give June time to collect herself. Admitting to a one-nighter at a truck stop motel wasn't going to be easy for her.

"It's Ms. Atkins. Ms. Atkins has never legally used her husband's surname." I smiled my most feminist smile.

Watson gave an impatient gesture. Braidwood scribbled on a legal pad.

"Well, Miss Atkins?" Watson exaggerated the "miss."

"A few weeks back. He called me up from the truck stop on Route 11, we met, had dinner, and spent the night together. He was gone the next morning."

"Was this normally how you met your husband? He didn't cohabit with you?"

"Look, I can answer this part more quickly without playing twenty questions. Ms. Atkins and Mr. Henshaw had been separated for the past two years. She never divorced him because of the problems with getting service on him while he was stationed in Germany and the expense of doing so. She thought he was still in Germany when he called her up and asked to meet her at the truck stop." I wanted to cut this interview as short as possible.

Rambling, long explanations would only lead to more questions, and I knew June. She'd rumble like Vesuvius if Watson or Braidwood got too personal about her private life.

Watson looked annoyed, Braidwood seemed lost. Until, that is, he opened his mouth and spoke.

"Were you aware your husband had received a less than honorable discharge from the Marines, Ms. Atkins, approximately three weeks before he was killed?"

June looked stunned. "That couldn't be. The Marines were Darryl's life."

"Were you aware of any illegal activities in which your husband was involved?" Braidwood was speaking now as if he wanted June's answers on the record. "Did he discuss them with you at your last meeting?"

"No, certainly not!" June's temper was already frayed and I could see it starting to unravel.

"Did he give you any expensive gifts when you met on Route 11?" Watson looked at June as if she'd crawled out from under a rock.

I was wondering how Watson knew so much.

"Yes," June admitted slowly. "A ring, a diamond dinner ring."

"And have you had the ring appraised?" Watson was looking at his notes.

"You know darned well I did. My insurance company

wouldn't insure it until I did." June was hopping mad. I wanted to know why and how they had so much information.

"What was its value? For insurance purposes?"

"Fifty-five grand," June admitted reluctantly.

I was impressed. I'd figured the rocks were good stuff, but I had no idea how good.

"And did you receive said ring in payment for services rendered?" Watson practically sneered the question.

I was beginning to dislike him immensely. Men like him padded their jock straps.

"There's no need to insult Ms. Atkins. Keep it civil, Mr. Watson. We're here voluntarily, in case you forgot." My icy facade hid my growing temper.

"Of course not!" June was close to erupting. I pinched her leg under the table.

"Ouch!" she burst out, giving me her "you're dead meat" look.

"What Ms. Atkins means is, the gift was one from a husband to a wife. Nothing more, nothing less. I wasn't aware it was against the law for a husband to give a wife gifts? If so, a lot of men in Wynnton are in deep cow pies." I gave a little laugh that set me up for the answer I was expecting. I needed, however, to goad them into giving it to me.

"The ring was stolen property, Ms. Atkins. I'll have to demand its return immediately." Braidwood took my bait.

"In a pig's eye, you will." June had that stubborn look I'd learned to fear.

"June, if Mr. Braidwood has proof the ring is stolen, you have to turn it over. Of course, we'll have to see the proof before it's returned as evidence." I wanted to know how and where the ring was stolen.

"I'll have it faxed to your office this morning." Braidwood sounded bored. "The jeweler who appraised it recognized its cut and the quality of the stones from a report that's been circulating for about a year now. The owners had had the stones detailed when they insured the ring. For a hundred grand, for the record."

That floored me. "Why so much?"

"Because," Watson couldn't help interrupting, "the ring's an antique. Belonged to some Russian family, some famous czar or something."

That explained it. "A Czar Nicholas gift to Alexandra, I assume."

Braidwood smiled a tiny, tight flick at the corners of his mouth. "You assume correctly."

I whistled slowly. "No wonder it's a beauty."

"Now, Ms. Atkins," Braidwood continued without missing a beat, "we'd like to know what your husband said about where he's been, what he's been doing, and what he wanted you to do for him. Did he by any chance mention selling the ring for him?"

I thought that an odd question. Once it was on June's finger, she'd have sold it as soon as she'd have sold her body. I knew June, and that wasn't going to happen.

June looked strangely uncomfortable. I wondered if her panty hose was pinching. Mine was.

"So what if he did?" June looked pissed.

"Wait a sec. I need to confer with my client before we continue this line of questioning." I didn't give Braidwood a chance to object. Jerking June from her chair, I hauled her into the corridor.

Checking the hallway for any big ears, I whispered quickly, "Tell me the whole story, and make it fast."

She didn't look like she wanted to, but she started talking, matching my whisper. "He said if I could get a good price for it, I could keep half the money. So I took it to a Greensville jeweler, you know the one who advertises they buy stuff? That guy's a crook, he'll give you about half a cent on the dollar. When he said it was worth twenty grand, I knew it had to be a lot more than that. So I got in my car and drove to Columbia. Found out there what it was really worth. Well, close to what it's worth. I had no idea it was some Russian ring."

"When did you have the time to do all this running around?" I thought June camped out at my house to keep me on a tight rein.

"What I do after work is none of your business, Tal," she retorted like a disgruntled employee.

I wouldn't have minded the tone, except June and I were more than boss and secretary. I'd promised to help get her into law school and through the bar exam. This little blip on the radar screen could blast that dream of hers right out of the water. Now, however, was not the time to tell her she'd better start praying we could get her out of this with her name, not to mention her criminal record, spotless.

"Didn't you have the slightest suspicion that your almost ex-husband, the one drawing an enlisted man's pay from Uncle Sam, didn't come by that ring honestly?" I'd have bet my life June wouldn't get involved in anything illegal, but money like that was a powerful incentive to cross that line.

"He said he'd bought it off some Russian Jews in Germany, ones who were trying to raise money to get to Israel. Said they had a bunch of old stuff they were selling. He gave them a thousand bucks in American dollars, said he had no idea how much the ring was really worth. For all he knew, they could have been crystals. You know men. They throw money away on a whim."

I guessed June was speaking from her own marital experience. "So he had no idea."

"I'd bet my life on it. He liked the way the ring looked, thought maybe he could sell it for double what he paid for it if it was the real thing. If it was fake, he said he'd palm it off on someone else. Get his money back, if he could."

"Did you tell him what it was really worth?"

She shook her head. "Like I said, he was gone the next morning. I expected him to call me later, ask what I'd found out, but I guess he never got a chance."

Her tale was making sense to me. But Dr. Watson in there wasn't about to believe her. I knew those ex-CID types. They thought all civilians were lying scum. Braidwood was the unknown.

"Okay, this is what we do. I'll lay it out for them, you keep your mouth shut and run, do not walk, to wherever you stashed that ring as soon as we get out of here, and produce it in Braidwood's office before I get out of court."

If June was lying to me, she was dead in the water. If Braidwood didn't string her up, I would. And it wouldn't be by the thumbs. I have this rule about friends—they never lie to me. June was my friend. She might not have considered the ramifications, but she would soon if one word she'd told me in the hallway didn't check out.

June clattered in a tight circle, her high heels trying to hurt the poor floor. Grabbing her hand to haul her with me, I breezed back into the interview room. She barely inched through the doorway.

Remaining standing, I made a point of studying my watch. "I've got to go. This is the whole story," I began, giving Braidwood the bare bones. "I've instructed Ms. Atkins to retrieve the ring as soon as she leaves here and hand it to you, Mr. Braidwood, personally. We'll expect a receipt, of course. That'll be all for now, gentlemen."

Gathering up my briefcase, I herded June in front of me.

"Mr. Watson will accompany her," Braidwood barked.

I didn't know he had that much testosterone in his make-up to sound so authoritative. "That'll be fine. Mr. Watson, you are not to ask my client any questions while she's retrieving the ring. If you so much as ask her middle name, I'll have Mr. Braidwood before the ethics panel for interrogating a witness without the presence of her attorney. Am I clear enough?"

Watson didn't like it, but Braidwood was giving me that semi–Cheshire cat smile again. I was beginning to dislike it immensely.

"No problem, Ms. Jefferson. I'll fax the proof of the ring's stolen status immediately."

I wondered why Braidwood was being so nice. Most prosecutors would have bluffed and blustered some more, if only to try to intimidate me. Maybe, I decided as I hurried to the courthouse across the lawn from the government building, the return of the ring was the first objective. I imagined that getting something like that back would be a real coup for a new prosecutor.

I wanted to think carefully and slowly about Darryl Henshaw and that ring, but I didn't have time. My usual motley morning clients, all DUIs, were waiting for me in anxious clusters in the hallway outside the courtroom.

I had their driving records and the results of their breathalyzers. The best I could do was statutory, but that didn't mean they had to like it. I gave them my sympathetic smile, promised them an impassioned plea for a permit to drive back and forth to work, and made sure they'd all paid me up front.

The money part was most important—I needed a new roof on the family manse. One guy was going down for the last time—he was losing his license forever and ever, amen. Thank God, I thought as I saw his blood alcohol content. I'd probably been as looped more than once since coming back to Wynnton, but at least I'd hidden the keys to the Mustang so I couldn't drive.

Shooing my clients into the courtroom, I took my seat behind counsel's table, rubbing elbows with the good ole boys. Harlan Zimmerman wore the same tie to court every single time. I counted three new grease spots. Joe McGlone pulled a chair up beside mine and tried to dazzle me with his shiny white teeth, but I knew his wife Deveron too well to take the bait. I was half-listening to the cases called before mine, wondering why we were all there, when our clients would have gotten the same deal with or without us. Impatience and self-disgust began to creep upon me until I saw Birdie from the clerk's record room in the basement, waving her hankie at me from the door that led into the chamber behind the judge.

Birdie Mills, along with Nellie Hanscomb and Cilla Coffey, ran the heart of the courthouse, that musty, antiquated room where copies of all legal documents were kept for generations to come to lose their eyesight over. The three had been friends of my grandmother, though not of her generation. They'd collectively taken me under their rather wide wings in the past few months.

Excusing myself to Joe, I tripped over his feet, gesturing to Birdie that I'd meet her in the corridor. Janice, who kept the docket moving, noted I was leaving, and I waved to her to hold off calling my clients for a minute. She nodded back.

Birdie could hardly contain herself. Small and birdlike, her white hair was tinted a subtle shade of blue. The chintz dress that covered her spare frame had been cut out of a pattern from the 1950s. She and the other two, the three witches, I called them, had been protegés of Miss Ena. When they'd lost their loves in the Korean War, Miss Ena had made sure they at least had jobs with which they could support themselves. They'd been in the basement of the courthouse so long, I assumed they'd been forgotten. If one of them had left, her paycheck would have been mailed automatically anyway. Like women who've been around forever in the same job, they knew where the bones were stacked and who stashed them there.

"I've got three clients on this docket, Birdie. What's up? How are you?" I added belatedly.

"Fine thanks, and do I have a surprise for you! I'm so glad I caught you. Come on downstairs when you're finished, the girls and I just happen to have brought him to work this morning."

I had visions of a man trussed and gagged, hidden in the vault in the record room, awaiting my kiss to free him. The three witches had fanciful imaginations, and a lot of it seemed focused recently on my single state. Like women of their generation, they found the unmarried condition untenable, and were determined I should avoid its shame.

"I'm afraid to ask . . ." I started, when Joe stuck his head through the doorway and gestured for me to move my ass.

I knew he was referring to my anatomy, because his eyes never left my backside. Heaven knows why—I don't have enough to hold up my jeans.

"Just come on down when you're done." Giggling like a schoolgirl, Birdie glided to the staircase, waving a delicate hand at me.

If I didn't go, they'd track me down. I just prayed they wouldn't be charged with kidnapping or false imprisonment. If the guy had a sense of humor about being shanghaied by three old ladies, maybe I'd give him the time of day.

My three clients whizzed through the system, with Braidwood's subordinate, a young prosecutor fresh out of law school, flushing in triumph. I put up enough of a fight to give his ego a pumping up and my clients their money's worth. The cop and I knew the outcome was foregone. One of Frank's old timers, gray-haired and sun-creased from all the time he spent in his cruiser clocking speeders, winked at me when he left the witness stand.

"Wanna have lunch?" Joe McGlone whispered in my ear as he passed me on his way up to stand before the bench.

"No," I mouthed. "Busy."

He shrugged as if I were missing the chance of a lifetime. *Tell that to Deveron,* I thought as I skipped down the stairs to the record room. Men like Joe were everywhere, but they'd only started hitting on me recently. I blamed June and her revitalization of my wardrobe.

Stopping on the landing of the stairs, I pulled out the cell phone June had insisted I carry and dialed the office. The machine picked up. She just wasn't back from retrieving the diamond ring, I told myself. No need to worry. She'd have called me and left a voice mail if things had gotten sticky over the ring exchange.

Promising myself not to worry, I peeked my head through the record room door. Nellie and Cilla were behind the tall oak counter, busily writing away in large red ledgers.

A quick glance around the room at the machines that pulled up the microfiche showed me we were alone. *Good,* I thought, *at least there won't be any witnesses to the release of their hostage.*

"Let him go," I warned before stepping into the room.

Cilla and Nellie looked up from their books, harried, frightened expressions on their faces.

"Whoever you've got hidden back there, let him go." Teasing, I wiggled my eyebrows at them.

"Oh, Tal, it's you. Thank God." Nellie, one of her big pins sparkling off the shoulder of her dress, opened the gate that would admit me to their hallowed ground. "We've got him in the break room."

"Him?" I squeaked. "What do you mean, him? I thought Birdie was joking."

"Heavens no. He's just what you need, dear, loyal, brave, gentle, all those lovely qualities so few men have nowadays. We know you're still pining over that Jack Bland . . ." Nellie grabbed me by the elbow, pulling me with her.

"Wait a sec. If I wanted a boy scout, he'd be underage, don't you think? Please tell me you don't have a troop leader tied up by the coffee pot." I knew they were slightly daft, but I didn't think all three would go off the deep end at the same time.

"Tal, will you be quiet? Honestly, a girl can't get a word in edgewise." This came from Cilla, who was at least seventy and lying about her age since I knew the truth. Girlhood had been in her distant past.

Birdie shoved open the door, giving the record room one last, furtive peek. "Hurry up, Tal."

Afraid of what I'd find, I hesitated in the doorway. A deep "woof" boomed from the corner, and the ugliest dog

I'd ever seen strained at a leash wrapped around the table leg. The table jerked, teetering the coffee maker and sprawling stacked napkins.

"We told you he's protective." Cilla beamed. "Robert E., down. This is the lady we were telling you about."

This had not been a good morning, and it was rapidly going downhill.

"Robert E.? What on earth? If you think . . ." I didn't get a chance to finish my shunning of the mangy-hided beast. As big as the table, he looked part Irish Wolfhound, part German Shepherd, part raccoon, part Dalmatian, and incredibly ugly. His steel-gray fur was mottled with dark splotches like liver spots, his tail beat at a broken angle, and there were definite patches of raw skin where he had some sort of rash. His eyes were set crookedly in his head.

"We named him after a Southern hero, of course. No one would ever dare call Robert E. Lee a coward, well, not anyone with any breeding, of course. Those Yankee historians who call him a man of no courage are only showing why the South should have won the War. Anyway, Robert E. is just brimful of courage and as charming as any gent we've been pleased to welcome into our home, so that's how we named him." Nellie was definitely pleased with the dog and herself.

"He saved us, you see." Cilla was the only one who noticed my anxious, dazed expression. "We were going home late one night, and we thought we'd been followed by some boys, you know the kind. We were out back, going to the parking lot, and it was dark as all get-out." She sniffed delicately. "We were planning on how to get out of their trap, when Robert E. came galloping out of the shrubs by the back door—you know the ones, those big boxwoods—and chased those silly boys away. You should have heard them howl!" She laughed so hard she had to reach for the hanky she kept in the cuff of her sleeve.

"We know a faithful friend when we see one. So we thought of you!" Birdie's frail hands waved at Robert E. as if sprinkling him with fairy dust.

"I don't want him." I tried to be emphatic, but it was hard to sound sincere when Robert E. was forcing his nose up my skirt. "Stop that, you cur. No gentleman behaves that way!" I shoved at his snout firmly, getting a wet hand for my efforts.

"But you have to take him," Nellie admonished. "If you don't, he'll end up at the pound. And you know what kind of place *that* is. I wouldn't wish it on my worst enemy. Well, maybe on those North Koreans who shot down James's plane . . ."

I stopped her from digressing into memory territory. "Maybe he belongs to someone. Did you look for a collar? Maybe he dropped it in the bushes."

"Certainly we did. He was just skin and bones, and if anyone ever owned him, they certainly don't deserve to get him back. No, you need Robert E., Tal. He'll be company for you at night when June goes home, and protection, too. He has the instincts of a lion," Cilla announced firmly. "We know. He's been taking care of us for days."

I didn't want to know how he'd taken care of them. The image of the beast sleeping on one of their beds was too much.

"No. He's not coming home with me." Robert E. saw an opportunity when it knocked, and throwing his paws on my shoulders, licked off my lipstick. I guess I should be grateful he didn't try to stick his tongue down my throat.

"Oooohh, gross," I spit, shoving the dog to the floor. He left wiry hair all over my suit. "He's worse than a high school boy on his first date."

"But he loves you already! See, I told you, Robert E., it's a match made in heaven." Cilla looked awfully pleased with herself. "I just knew you two would hit it off."

The matchmakers of Wynnton had lost their ever-loving minds and were determined to take mine with them.

"Ladies, I appreciate the thought, but I've got to get back to the office." Maybe if I ran, I'd escape.

"We know," Birdie frowned, looking distressed. "That's why we thought you should have Robert E. We're terribly fond of him, but with the trouble June's in, and her husband being murdered like that, we knew you needed protection over there at Miss Ena's." My grandmother's house would always bear her name. Never in my lifetime would it be known as Miss Tal's house.

"What kind of trouble?" I couldn't believe that court-house gossip had descended to the bowels of the place in such a short time.

"We know all about that antique ring he gave her. Mr. Braidwood thinks June was in on a fencing operation, an-tiques and the like, that her husband was running. Says Mr. Henshaw brought June into the business when she went to work for you, 'cause you wouldn't know a criminal if she up and bit you on the, um, behind, and June would have the perfect cover to run around and get things done for her hus-band, seeing as you leave her to her own devices and all." Nellie took a deep breath.

I was stunned by the extent of their knowledge.

"We, of course, disagree. You and Henry were never fools, and I just don't believe Grace's cousin can be tarred and feathered just because of who she married." Cilla jumped into June's defense.

I didn't follow this line of reasoning, but Birdie did. I was too busy trying to keep Robert E. from chewing my brief-case and figure out how the three witches knew so much.

"Henry would never marry into a family with any crimi-nal or insane blood. He's a doctor, he knows better than that." Nellie was firm in her belief in Henry's adherence to the Southern stricture against marrying into a family that might have a hereditary problem that could cause problems with the law or incarceration of any sort. Like in a loony bin. "So June must be just a fine girl, seeing as how she's related to Grace."

Now I saw what they were getting at. "How'd you hear all this?" I wasn't sure I wanted to know, not really.

"Goodness gracious, you don't think we'd tell on a friend, do you, Tal?" Cilla was properly indignant, puffing her ample chest like a bird about to sing.

"No, ma'am, of course not." I knew better than to ask again. When a lady said she wouldn't say who told, she meant it.

"So you see why you need Robert E. Good, that's set-tled." Birdie slipped the leash free from the table leg and thrust it into my hand.

I envisioned this beast from hell eating me out of house and home. I'd have to hock Miss Ena's sterling to keep him in puppy chow. However, being a lawyer had its advantages. I knew when to bargain and when to fold and take my losses.

"That's very kind of you, ladies." I doubted if Robert E. would fit in the back seat of my Mustang. "I'd better get going."

No kidding I'd better get going. If Braidwood was going to drag June into her husband's death, not to mention what-ever illegalities Darryl had been involved in, I had to get my tailfeathers in gear. Acting as if the truth would keep June free was the worst thing I could do. Now, I had to convince June of the folly of that course of action.

Wrapping Robert E.'s leash around my wrist, I let the three witches escort me to their private entrance on the lower level. The English basement opened to a stairwell leading to an alley, which separated the back of the courthouse from the parking lot, reserved for judges and courthouse personnel. Pretending I walked the beast from hell every day out of the courthouse, I sauntered down the alley as Robert E. took advantage of every bit of trash and every dandelion in every crack in the blacktop to empty his bladder. He was built like a camel. I'd have to hire a kid in the neighborhood to walk him every half hour.

"Miss Jefferson. A minute, please."

I didn't want to hear that voice. Judge DeShazo was subbing in the Circuit Court until the General Assembly saw fit to replace Linwood Jordan. Judge Jordan was engrossed in his appearances before the Joint Legislative Audit and Review Commission, as well as the district committee of the Bar Association. I knew how busy he was; I was representing him. As he said, it takes one to know one.

How could I turn down a client with that kind of charm? I didn't have to wonder what he meant by "one." I knew. We'd both walked that fine line between ethics and outlaw, and he'd slipped. Very publically.

"Yes, Your Honor?" I pretended Robert E. didn't exist. "What can I do for you?"

I didn't like Harold DeShazo. He was a native of Wynnton, but he'd grown up in the country, a man who believed life was hard and judgment should be harder. His guilty scale was easily tipped, and I'd never seen him give the benefit of the doubt to a single African-American defendant. If, however, an accused was white, wearing a suit and tie, and properly obsequious, even if guilty as sin, he might not get more than a tap on the wrist.

That alone made me hate Judge Harold DeShazo. The only thing that kept me from raising a ruckus was the knowledge, gleaned from the three witches, that he was due to retire in a couple of months. He'd already retired once, but had been reappointed when Judge Jordan took a moral and legal fall. This time, however, he'd hit the mandatory retirement age from which there was no appeal.

I was holding my breath until he took his racism and left the bench.

"I was wondering if I might offer you some advice."

I must have looked startled, because Robert E. began to growl through clenched fangs.

"Robert E.," I admonished, reeling in the leash. "Don't mind him, he's just overly protective."

"Interesting animal. Never seen anything like that outside the Westminster Dog Show."

"Oh?" I was too surprised by his speaking to me outside the courtroom to ask him how he knew about the Westminster Dog Show.

"Yes, I believe he's a rough-coat Wolfhound, isn't he?" De-Shazo took off his glasses to kneel down closer to Robert E.

"Please don't get too close, sir. I don't know this dog well enough to . . ."

I needn't have worried. Robert E. cleaned the judge's face with his big tongue. *Traitor,* I thought.

"Yes, most unusual breed. Bred to hunt in the hills of Scotland . . . his fur's waterproof. Massive jaws to bring down the wolf, of course. Fiercely loyal, immensely gentle with his family." DeShazo was staring at me with new-found respect.

"Don't ask where I got him. He's on loan." I needed to protect the three witches. If Robert E. was a valuable dog, I didn't want them to be accused of stealing him.

Resettling his glasses on his saturnine face, he carefully wiped doggy spit off his cheeks. "Yes, well, um."

"Your advice, Your Honor?" I wanted to get out of that alley with that dog so badly it hurt.

"Yes. Just wanted to tell you, well, you know I was a friend of your grandmother's."

Everyone thought he was my grandmother's friend. She let the illusion exist as long as it suited her. Why she never saw fit to take Harold DeShazo down a peg was beyond me.

"I didn't know that."

"Yes, she was very kind to my mother after my father died."

That sounded like Miss Ena. She did her charity work in private, saying that the do-gooders who flaunted it were the publicans of Wynnton.

Tugging on the leash, I tried to keep Robert E. from jerking me off my feet.

"You're good, Miss Jefferson. I don't know why you stick to the losers of clients you habitually represent in my court, but I can assure you, you have it in you to make a very good trial lawyer."

I was flabbergasted. Harold DeShazo must have been secluded in his country house when I returned to Wynnton. I had to give the man credit—he didn't listen to gossip. All of Wynnton had speculated on the nature of my disgrace in my law firm that had driven me away from a lucrative partnership and the big city.

For a second, I almost told him I'd lost a death penalty case I shouldn't have lost, and I'd stick to my loser traffic clients where no one went to the needle in the death house, thank you very much. But I'd rather have ripped open my blouse and exposed myself to him than tell him about Parnell Moses.

"Thank you very much, Your Honor," I answered stiffly. "I'll remember your kind words."

Miss Ena may not have taught me much—well, actually she taught me a hell of a lot. Manners had been at the top of her list, and I knew when to trot them out even if I didn't wanna.

"If you like, I'll see if I can get you appointed to some of the circuit court cases that'll give you more exposure. Nothing breeds success in the law business like being high profile." He seemed pleased with himself for his statement of the obvious.

I wondered if he dyed his hair that shade of black, or if he'd inherited it from some Native American ancestor. The tribes had intermarried through the centuries, but now and then, the Indian blood showed. He was waiting for my answer.

Just what I didn't want. "Thank you anyway, Judge, but I'm busier than I want to be at the moment." I turned to go.

"I heard about your secretary. Such a shame. But you never can tell what'll happen when you hire a black girl."

I stopped in my tracks so fast Robert E. had to sit on his haunches. "Sorry, what did you say?"

DeShazo was eyeing Robert E. over the top of his black-rimmed glasses. "You heard me. Be careful who you bring into the fold, Ms. Jefferson. Our kind are a dying breed, we must do what we can to ensure the purity of the legal system. Its integrity. Justice will be served."

I tried to keep my mouth shut, but it was hard. What had I ever done to deserve such an insult?

I spoke slowly and carefully. This man still had two more months of judging my clients to go. If I kicked him in the nuts now, my clients may as well all bring their toothbrushes when they came to court, or give up and skip out on their bonds.

"I'll remember what you said," I managed to choke out of the anger strangling my throat.

Twirling so fast I caught Robert E. off guard, I hauled him behind me down the alley and around the corner to the Mustang parked in front of the courthouse. I didn't see anyone else, anything around me, just pure, blood-red anger.

"Get in," I snapped at Robert E. Obediently, he leaped into the front seat and sat, staring out the windshield.

Great, just great, I muttered, backing out of the space. I knew what was coming as clearly as if I had a special lens that showed me the future.

June would be indicted and we'd pull Judge DeShazo.

I almost longed for Linwood Jordan and his corrupt ways.

Chapter 6

I hadn't eaten breakfast, nothing new for me. Food before conflict always gave me indigestion. By the time I drove Robert E. home and stashed him in the back yard with a bowl of water and a stern lecture on not eating the rhododendrons, I was starving. No sign of June. I assumed she was meeting Watson at the bank to open her box and get the ring. I'd never thought to ask her where she'd put it since I'd seen her wearing it just yesterday.

Becky's Cafe was easier than trying to make something edible out of the contents of my fridge. The health food June stocked in there was enough to drive me back to drink, but she hadn't added anything in a while. I guessed she was preoccupied.

A hamburger, fries, and milk shake at Becky's sounded altogether the better option. I headed over there, my stomach anticipating the good stuff. With its vinyl cushions, rotating stools, and formica tops, Becky's was a holdover from the days when there was no such thing as restaurant decor, just good, plain food.

Frank Bonnet was perched on a stool at the counter. The odd thing was, he'd chosen the far end of the room away from most of its patrons. Frank wasn't known for hiding from the good folk of Wynnton, just the opposite. His badge seemed to give him an entree he'd never have had in the normal course of events, and he knew it. He also exploited it.

Since he'd saved my life, I had decided to cut Frank a lot of slack. Not an easy thing for me to do, but I could be forgiving of his more annoying habits, like how he always looked at a woman's chest before he checked out her face. I perched my butt on the stool beside him, most oddly vacant.

"What's up, Frank?" I snatched a menu from between the ketchup and mustard bottles and pretended to study it. I knew it by heart, but it was a barrier between my nonexistent breasts and his eyes.

Wiping his chin with one of those tiny, useless paper napkins, Frank didn't even give me a leer. I was startled.

"Not much," he answered sourly. "See you been picking up some clients."

"That's what happens when I hang around the courthouse too much." I ordered my burger, adding onion rings to the side order of fries. Without June's disapproving glare, I was going to load up on all the cholesterol and saturated fats I could stand.

"Doing good, are you?"

For a second, I thought I heard undercurrents of real interest in my legal career. Frank and I had never formed a mutual admiration society, but at least I knew he'd done his job, and done it in time, when it came to saving my behind.

"Not great. But it pays my car insurance." I'd seen Frank eyeing my Mustang on the street a few times, heard him extol the virtues of its 289 engine. I'd had my homeowner's insurance cancelled after Owen Amos burned down the shed in my back yard. So far, I hadn't been able to replace it. But I'd pay anything to keep that Mustang insured.

Frank fiddled with another napkin, shredding it with his thick fingers. His coffee sat undrunk. A quick glance over his shoulder, and he shifted until he was closer to me than I liked.

He fidgeted some more. What, I wondered, could be his problem? I wasn't about to ask, but I had to admit, I was curious.

"Something wrong with the coffee today? Tell Becky, she'll get another pot going." I sipped from the water glass in front of me.

Lowering his voice, Frank leaned over closer and whispered at me, "Watch your back, Tal. This thing with June Atkins is gonna get ugly. You don't exactly have the backing of the Bar Association in Wynnton, and a lawyer or two have been known to sleep with dogs to catch the coon."

I had no idea what he was talking about. Why would I want a racoon? "Frank, if you've got something to say to me, spit it out."

Grabbing me by the elbow, he pulled me off my stool and through the kitchen door at the end of the lunch counter. Amid the racket of the cook shouting out completed orders, he stood very still and looked very worried. More worried than I thought he was capable of feeling. I'd never seen Frank as more than muscles with a minuscule brain. Now, however, he seemed almost human.

"I got taken off that stolen ring case. Why, you ask?" He

snorted most unattractively. A waitress, Mary Jo I thought it was, shoved past us, snapping out a command for us to get our asses off the firing line.

"Seems I'm considered too close to you. Remember that little thing with Owen Amos? Unfortunately, the feds duly noted that you were in the middle of that pile of shit, and as the officer first on the scene, I've picked up some of your fleas." His face, florid at the best of times, was now a deep purple.

I worried about his cholesterol level and what it had done to his arteries. I'd bet nothing good. Maybe I wouldn't eat the onion rings.

"You were doing your job, Frank. I'm probably being thicker than mud in January here, but you're going to have to speak plain English." I sidled closer to the wall, out of Darcy Langston's way as she balanced a tray piled high with edible delectables. My mouth watered.

"For the love of God, you're not exactly clean as the driven snow, Tal. Not as a lawyer. Don't know 'bout your personal life either, but that's none of my business." Frank was getting annoyed with me.

"I've done nothing illegal." Suddenly, I was as cold as winter in the middle of Lake Michigan.

"The feds are asking all sorts of questions about you. Where you get your money, since you sure as shit don't work for it. Why you decided to chuck it all and move back here. Things like that, Tal. Questions that I got a feeling you don't want asked, not by some FBI son of a bitch with promotion driving his tail through the valleys of your personal life." Frank wasn't keeping his voice down any more. I wanted to reach out and clap my hand over his mouth.

"They think June and I had something to do with whatever crap her husband was into."

"Bingo. I knew you were a smart girl once, thought maybe you'd killed those brain cells with all that liquor. Glad to see I was mistaken." Pulling his sunglasses from his shirt pocket, Frank polished them on the end of the his khaki tie. They reflected the overhead lights of the kitchen like mosquito eyes.

"They'll find out we chatted. Do me a favor, tell 'em I was settling an old debt. 'Cause that's the truth. It's settled, as of this moment."

"You don't owe me anything, Frank. Way I see it, I owe you big time. Both for what you did with Owen Amos, and today." I didn't like being beholden to Frank Bonnet, but a Jefferson always acknowledged her debts—and paid them.

"Maybe you do." He slid the glasses onto his face. I couldn't see through the lenses to his eyes. "But I owed Miss Ena more, and way I see it, I'm clear on that one."

I wanted him to explain what Miss Ena had done for him, but he'd slipped out the back door of the kitchen before I could even imagine Miss Ena doing anything for Frank Bonnet. I seemed destined to reap payment on what she was owed for quite a few more years. The coin of the realm here was good will I'd never managed to accumulate. Maybe my dead grandmother had been wiser and kinder than I'd ever allowed myself to believe.

I ate my solitary lunch, thinking more about what Frank had said than about June's stolen ring and ne'er-do-well husband. A thorough dislike of FBI types ran through my veins. I'd do anything to stay out of their way, and if that failed, I'd make a mess of their investigation.

My hamburger and fries tasted like sawdust after Frank left.

June met me at the office, her lips drawn into a thin line, her eyes tight at the corners. Ignoring me as she stacked the mail on my desk, she was clearly too angry to talk.

That had never stopped me before. I pretended a nonchalance I didn't feel. Sooner or later she'd tell me about the ring exchange, but I'd rather it was sooner, after what Frank had said.

"Did they give a receipt for the ring?" I slit open a letter that looked like it might have a check. Checks are good.

"Yes, and everything else I had."

"Like what?" I was right, but it was for twenty-five dollars, about two hundred less than the deadbeat owed me for getting him a quick divorce.

"Stuff I keep in my closet safe."

Now I knew why she was so pissed. She'd had to let Watson into her house and closet, no less. I'd have given my eye teeth to see where June stored her elegant wardrobe. I'd bet it was climate-controlled and arranged by season and color.

"Let me see it." Holding out my hand, I read the chicken scratch of a note from my divorce client in the other. Seemed he didn't think he owed me any more money, since he'd ended up having to pay off the car note on his wife's Blazer.

I expected a short note signed by Watson. When June returned with a two-page document, I knew why she'd been gone so long this morning.

Dropping the divorce diatribe, I studied the list. The safe must be as big as the Taj Mahal, I decided. Studying the precise list of contents, I realized Watson had cleaned it out.

"Did they take everything but your kitchen sink?"

Arms on her hips, June nodded fiercely. "They even took my damned will."

June believed in security for her personal possessions, that much was clear. From a pair of pearl earrings to her high school diploma, she kept it all safely tucked in a Sears model floor safe in her bedroom closet. I could see why Watson took the jewelry in her safe, to check it against the list of stolen antiques, but the rest of the list looked like the usual contents of a safe hiding place. Insurance policies, her will, birth certificate, marriage certificate, original social security card, a packet of letters. God, I hoped they weren't from Darryl saying anything incriminating.

The last item on the list caught my eye.

"I didn't know you had a gun."

"I don't. It's some old thing. A friend of Darryl's brought it by after he left, said Darryl had forgotten it. I said I'd keep it for him." June shrugged.

"So you locked it up?"

"It looked old, you know, like something Darryl would be selling at the Weapons Fair. Figured he'd come back to get it, then I'd get him to talk to me, tell me why he left so suddenly that morning." Her eyes misted, but only for a second. "Should have known the son of a bitch wasn't ever coming back."

"Maybe it was stolen, too." Tapping the phone, I contemplated calling Braidwood and asking if the investigation extended into weapons. In the end, I decided I didn't need to. I already knew the answer.

"I wish you'd told me about the gun," I complained. "If it's on the same list with the ring, and you didn't tell Braidwood about it this morning, he'll think you've got more to hide."

The gun was described as an 1851 Colt. Watson knew his guns.

Pacing in front of my desk with a barely suppressed fury, June began to rail at her dead husband. "I should have known. He was being too nice. Too damned nice. God, you'd think I'd have learned my lesson with him. Nothing Darryl did was for anyone but himself. Least of all for me. I should have taken that ring and thrown it in the river."

"Not a bad idea in hindsight." But I wasn't worried, not yet. They'd have to come up with a lot more than the ring to tie June to Darryl's murder.

"Let's see what we can come up with. You're his widow. Check on his military records. Say you're trying to find out if you're entitled to any widow's benefits."

June glared at me as if I'd lost my mind.

"He was discharged dishonorably. You'll think of something. Let's see why he was given a dishonorable." I had a feeling this was going to get stickier than taffy on a humid afternoon.

"I'll tell you why, he was a son of a bitch of the first degree. . . ." June muttered all the way out of my office.

I was glad to see her riled and angry with her dead husband. Sure beat mourning for him. Because no matter which way I sliced it, Darryl Henshaw was going to cause June more grief she didn't deserve. She didn't know it yet, but the ride was bound to get as bumpy as a backwoods dirt road.

The front door opened, the little bell June'd hung on it tinkling merrily. A glance at the phone showed me she was on one of the lines. Rising, I slid open my pocket doors to greet what I hoped would be a very rich client. June's defense was going to cost us money. I needed someone with a lucrative case to carry us while we got her off the hook.

"Is June busy?" His face lined, Henry was having another bad day. I almost felt sorry for him, but not quite.

"Yep. We're trying to find out why Darryl got a dishonorable discharge. Wanna take a seat in my office?"

"I started to call. But it seemed like the decent thing to tell her in person. She being a relation and all." Henry's dark face was frowning so hard, I was afraid the lines would slice through his skin. This must be bad, really bad.

"Darryl?" I whispered the name, as if by doing so I could stave off the bad news.

"His body's been found. On an old firing range over at the post."

I envisioned Darryl's head sitting in Henry's car. "You think it's him?"

"Who else could it be? The cut marks in the flesh probably won't match exactly, not after the time the head was in the river, but it sounds as if the body lost its head with the same sort of instrument that I found severed Darryl's vertebrae. My guess is a chain saw."

"I don't want to hear this."

"It gets worse."

Sinking my head onto my arms, I listened with my eyes closed.

"He was shot. Through the heart. Bullet's still in there. Because the body was found on federal property, they take jurisdiction. I get to watch the autopsy."

"Goodie gumdrops for you." The gun Watson had taken from June's safe was going to be a perfect match. They'd be able to match the bullet in Darryl in their sleep. I knew it with a clarity that frightened me. When I get sober and stay that way, I see and hear too much I don't like, and what's worse, I can understand it.

"Let me know about the caliber of the bullet, soon as you find out, okay?" I had to think, and fast.

By the end of the day, they'd have fired a test shot from the handgun taken from June, gone for a warrant before five o'clock tomorrow. I'd have to pull together bail money by then. June wouldn't have the cash, that much was evident from what she spent to put clothes on her back.

"See," I muttered viciously. "If you wore jeans from the thrift store . . ."

"What're you talking about?" Henry was frowning the way he did when he caught me with a bottle in the house.

"Nothing. Just call when you find out, will you? Let me know, so I can have time to prepare her?"

Henry knew what I was saying. That's why he'd come over in person.

"June won't be able to cut it in jail," he warned me needlessly.

"Tell me about it. She'd tell 'em to stick their cute little orange suits where the sun don't shine." I had to make some calls. "Get out of here, Henry. I've got to get to work."

No offense taken, Henry slipped out before June could see him. I sat staring at the plaster walls of my office, once the front parlor of Miss Ena's house. One of my first renovation efforts had been to have the walls replastered. They'd crumbled when I steamed off years of old, yellowed wallpaper, and despite advice to put up wallboard, I'd insisted on replastering.

I couldn't tell you why, except I'd wanted to keep Miss Ena's house as it'd been during her lifetime. Painting the outside shutters purple had been my minor form of rebellion, but a harmless one. The heart of this house lay in the walls, walls that had heard family secrets for generations. Leaning my forehead against the plaster, I felt its cool seep into my skin. Even on a hot afternoon, these walls stayed cool.

Which is what I needed to do. First, I had to raise some cash. I hated like heck to take out an equity line on the house, and besides, it wouldn't be fast enough. I could dip into the money Miss Ena had left me, but that was getting dicey. I'd used more of it up in the past year than I'd planned, and I'd have to invade principal if I was right about the amount of bail they'd require for June.

Which left me with one alternative. Listening to make sure June was busy on the phone, I slipped off my shoes and tiptoed upstairs.

June had her closet safe, I had a box under the sink in the old-fashioned porcelain-tiled bathroom. Pulling back the curtain that hid it, I pulled out the shoe box that safe-guarded the Jefferson family jewels.

The women in my family had had good taste for their generations, and the men they married and raised had known exactly what to shower upon them when the occasion called for it. Some of it gaudier than others, the brooches and rings, bracelets and pendants, earrings and lorgnettes were cushioned in yellowed cotton. Miss Ena had refused to wear some of the more colorful pieces, but she'd preserved them all to hand down to me.

She'd always said a good piece of jewelry was a woman's dowry, to be used in emergency situations. Thinking of June in a prison outfit, I knew the moment had arrived. Shoving pieces aside with one finger, I remembered the times I'd seen Miss Ena wear one or two of them, glittering against the black silk of her normal attire. I'd never been a jewelry fan myself, but even I knew these pieces were good, very good.

Selecting a ruby and diamond bracelet, I guessed it was one of Miss Ena's sister's, the flapper who'd gone to New York in the twenties. One thing about Jefferson women, they kept the valuables in the family. Slipping it in my pocket, I closed the box and replaced it. I'd have to take some time to get the best price for it, but it'd be faster than dealing with a bank.

"I can't get anything!" June was yelling at me from the bottom of the stairs. "Nothing!"

Unusual for June. Showed how rattled she was. I reappeared at the top of the stairs.

"I have something to tell you." Descending the stairs, I kept my eyes on the treads and not June. "Henry was just here."

"That who came in? Why didn't he stick his head in my office?"

"Told him you were busy. Besides, I thought you should hear it from me." I was eye level with her now. Her lipstick was eaten off, a most unusual event in June's normal day. I'd never seen her makeup less than perfect.

"Henry said they found a body on the post. He thinks it's Darryl's."

She was as stiff as the newel post I rested against.

I continued. "He was shot. They'll be running tests on the gun they got from your safe."

"So I'm screwed." Smart girl, that June.

"Maybe not. Can you describe the guy who brought you the gun? Give them a complete description when they come ask you about it?"

She paused, thinking. "It was dark. No porch light, because he'd come after ten and I'd already turned it off for the night. Wore a hat, one of those big western things. Had a little beard, one of those stupid kind that looks like a dagger in the middle of a chin. White. Maybe Spanish, I can't be sure. About as tall as you."

"Not bad." I was tall for a woman. Most eyewitnesses were notoriously bad, but June I trusted. "Eyes?"

"No way. The hat was pulled low."

"Big man? Skinny?"

"Hard to tell. Had on a puffy jacket, one of those nylon things. Thought it was strange, it being hot as blue blazes even at night. But not a big man, no."

"Okay, here's what we're going to do." Leading her to my office, I sat her down in the client chair. "First, you're going to sign a formal representation agreement, so if anyone says our conversations aren't attorney-client privilege, we flash it in front of their noses." I pulled a contract out of my desk drawer. "Then I want you to type up everything you just told me. Think hard, add any details that might help identify this guy."

She stared at me. "You think they'll arrest me, don't you."

I couldn't lie to her. "I'd bet my life on it. And according to what Frank Bonnet says, they're after me, too."

"Why?"

"Think about it. Two women working together. One of them has a husband running stolen jewelry. God knows about the guns. One of the women happens to have in her possession a particularly expensive bauble. Gift, quote, unquote, from said shady husband. The other woman is a lawyer who doesn't appear to work too hard for a living. Bit of a loose screw, thumbs her rather long nose at the local establishment. A pain in the butt type. She and the woman with the ring are tight as ticks in a dog's ear. Now what conclusions would you draw, Ms. Prosecutor?"

For the second time since she'd heard about her husband's murder, June's eyes filled with the beginning of tears. But this time she choked them back.

"Well, the bastards aren't going to take me down, or you, either."

"Atta girl. We've got to be a step ahead of them, or we don't have a chance in hell of kicking ass. So get to work."

She worked until eight, revising her narrative over and over. By the time I sent her home, I was exhausted. But my work was just beginning. I needed to raise some cash.

Chapter 7

❧

I wasn't sure where Travis Whitlock was living, but I'd guessed on his old homeplace. Out Route 11, the house had been built after the War by his great-grandfather, and all the Whitlocks I knew came from the same stock. I vaguely remembered that Travis's younger sister died in a tragic accident with her mother. But I'd been in college then, and not much interested in what happened to home folk. In fact, I hadn't been interested in much except my own misery in Jack Bland's marriage the summer after we graduated from high school, to Alma, a girl he'd never even looked at in the years we'd gone together.

Travis's father had planted tobacco and soy beans, but with his death, Travis had come home to fallow fields. I guessed he could pay the taxes and support the place on his income, but still, it seemed strange not to smell the thick, sweetly cloying scent of tobacco as I passed the smoke houses at the edge of the weed-choked fields.

I hadn't been out this way in ages, and with darkness beginning to settle, I slowed down and checked mailboxes on the road. I needn't have bothered—the Whitlocks' white Victorian, classic in its farmhouse simplicity, caught the rays of the sinking sun. With roofed peaks over its second-floor windows and a tin roof painted green to match the shutters, the house was as pristine as I remembered it from long ago. Travis had taken better care of his heritage than I had. I'd wanted to change mine. Clearly, his was acceptable as it came to him.

The road to the house was gravel and lined with tall cedars, some of them weak with age. Parking the Mustang beside Travis's truck, I got out and tucked in my shirt. I was hot, grimy, and dying to get out of the panty hose I'd put on this morning in deference to my appearance in court. Glancing around, I quickly hiked up my skirt and jerked the damned things off, leaving my shoes in the car.

"Always did have good-lookin' legs, Tal." Laughing at me from the front porch, Travis held open the front door. "You could have done that in here, you know."

"No, I couldn't." I threw them on the car seat. "If I'd worn them one more second, I'd have killed someone."

He laughed. "Hope you don't feel like strangling me."

"No," I smiled, patting my pocket to make sure the bracelet was still there. "I need you."

"Words a man always likes to hear. Come on in. I was dying of curiosity when I saw headlights coming down the road." He propped the door open a little wider.

Accepting his invitation, I stepped through the front

door. Travis stood behind me, waiting for me to walk on in. I couldn't move an inch.

The walls as far as I could see down the hallway were covered with framed canvases, bright colors splashed on the pale painted backdrop of the farmhouse plaster. Caught by the images, I stared. I was surprised when he started up the stairs. Not hearing me behind him, he turned.

"Come on, I'm in the middle of something. Can't quit now. Got to get it shipped out tomorrow."

"Okay," I answered reluctantly. I wanted to give the house a good looking over, if the foyer was any indication of the plethora of riches it held.

The walls up the stairs were lined with even more framed canvases. Some were simple still lifes, apples and oranges in bowls, and others were small scenes of countrysides I'd never seen before, jumping from their frames. All of them carried the spark of life within them, and I was mesmerized.

"These yours?" I nodded at the paintings, one foot on the bottom step.

Looking down at me, Travis frowned. "Unfortunately. My juvenilia. Not very good, in fact, I should burn the lot. Just haven't gotten around to it."

"No," I cried. "Don't do that. What about when you're dead and hung in the great museums? These are part of your history."

I smiled. "Besides, I like them. But I seem to remember you were always sketching people in school."

"I was," he answered tersely. "It was the only way I could stand school. Looking at all of you. Knowing you wanted me looking at you as I drew you." He sounded bitter.

His pale skin shone in the overhead light emanating

from the stairwell ceiling. For a second, I saw utter unhappiness. He must not have been as content as a teenager as I remembered.

"Did you do these in art school?"

"Yes. They taught me what I really should be doing was portraits, so I suppose they served their purpose."

"I like them." I touched the frame of one hanging on the wall beside the stairs. "They're innocent, fresh, as if the artist is discovering color for the first time in his life. When did you paint them, your freshman year?"

"Later." Turning back, he trotted up the last flight of stairs, leaving me to follow if I dared.

I did. Travis had gutted part of the upstairs, knocking out bedroom walls to create a studio across the entire front of the house. Stretched canvases, easels, and packing crates lined the walls. The pine floors were coated with paint spatters, the windows curtainless. I felt as if I'd entered another world, a loft in Soho, an artist's lair. A work table in the center of the room was covered with brushes resting in glass jars, tubes of paint, soiled rags for cleaning. Track lights ran across the ceiling, some aimed at the work table, some at half-finished canvases on easels.

"You must have set this up a while ago. Do a lot of work at night?"

Grabbing a hammer, Travis filled his mouth with nails. "Ummum," he mumbled. He was building a frame around a large canvas swathed in sheets of bubble wrap.

"This the Epps portrait you said you were finishing?"

He barely nodded, hammering the frame of the case around it. I guessed the portrait was somewhere around four feet by five. A big one, for sure.

"Wish I'd seen it."

Another hammer blow. "You wouldn't have liked it. Too much society, too much self-importance. That's what he paid for, and paid for most handsomely." Travis pulled another nail from a back pocket.

"I still don't understand why you want to paint me." I was tired, probably fishing for a compliment. I hadn't had any in a long, long time.

"Sit."

"What?" I was stunned. I didn't intend on staying long, just doing my business and getting home to bed. I stayed on my feet.

"You eaten yet?" Studying me like the witch at the enchanted cottage appraising the thickness of Hansel's finger for the stew pot, Travis reached into a minirefrigerator on the floor. "I didn't think so."

"I forget to eat. But at least I had lunch."

"I do, too. Get going on a piece, don't notice anything else." Pulling out some apples and oranges, a hunk of cheese, and some plastic water bottles, he rummaged around again and came up with some hard rolls.

"Plowman's supper," he announced proudly. "Would you clear the table, madam?"

Shoving the paint brushes to one side, I pulled up two rickety wooden chairs from against the wall, setting them so they faced each other across the table. "Sounds good to me."

Travis arranged the repast as if it were a still life, carefully juxtaposing the red apples with the pale saffron of the cheese, the browns of the rolls. I hated to disturb it.

Giving his handiwork one final stare, Travis chomped into an apple. "So eat, already. Then tell me why you're here."

"It's your good looks and good food." I laughed.

"I wish." He didn't sound amused.

My mouth was filled with a piece of cheese he'd handed me. I swallowed fast. "I always thought you were one of the more interesting guys, back in high school. You didn't give a damn about the crap the rest of us thought sent the earth in its orbit. Back then you knew exactly what you wanted to do with your life, didn't you?"

Chewing more slowly, Travis nodded slightly. "But I wished the whole time I'd been more like you. Or like Jack. Being an outsider in the town where you're raised is hard on the teenage psyche."

I thought about that a second. "I never saw you as an outsider. Well, maybe a little bit. It's just that, well, you were always looking around you. You saw things. Things the rest of us had no idea were going on."

Whistling softly, he crunched open a roll, handing me half. "You must be one hell of a lawyer."

"Maybe once upon a time, I thought I was hot shit. Not now." I liked the ways his ears wiggled as he chewed. "But if my instincts are right, I've got one hell of a fight coming down the pike."

I thought of all those rich people Travis must know. Pulling the diamond and ruby bracelet from my pocket, I spread it on the work table and spoke before I lost my nerve.

"I need your help. I can pawn this somewhere in Columbia, but I'd never get what it's worth. It's Cartier. I had to have it appraised when Miss Ena died, for tax purposes, and it was valued at one hundred grand. I need to get at least half that by late tomorrow. Know anyone interested in jewelry?"

I envisioned his wealthy clients posing in zillions of dollars of baubles, the current royalty of our age with their un-earned wealth.

Swallowing hard, he leaned over to take a look at the bracelet. "Planning on skipping town, Tal?"

"Hardly. I'm guessing June's going to be arrested tomorrow for killing her husband, and I need cash to post the ten percent bond. That head you hauled out of the river? Belonged to the man she'd left but didn't divorce. Classic love/hate thing, makes her the best suspect." I cleared my throat. "I don't think the bond will be set over five hundred thousand, but if it is, I'll have to sell the matching earrings and brooch."

"Wow, you're a regular jewelry shop." Travis twisted the bracelet so one of the track lights honed in on it, spattering the walls of the studio with rainbow brilliance. "You'd do this for your secretary?" He didn't sound surprised.

"She's more than that." I wasn't going to go into details. "Can you help?"

Giving me a strange look, he noted, "Never thought you were gay."

"I'm not, June's not, okay? Give me the damned bracelet. I thought you'd know someone with that kind of cash lying around who'd be only too happy to get an heirloom piece like this cheaply." Snatching it from his hand, I clutched it as I started to run from the studio. He moved more quickly than I.

Barring the door with his body, he murmured, "Just teasing, Tal, really. Yeah, I know someone. Rich, very very rich, woman in Hilton Head. Let me find her number. If she's interested, I'll run it down there tomorrow for her to have a look."

"I'll need the cash by the end of the day. I don't want her spending a night in jail." Reluctantly, I handed him the bracelet. "And thanks," I added as an afterthought.

"This was one of Miss Ena's, was it?" Focused on the bracelet, he studied it closely. Its beauty was undeniable. The cabochon rubies, surrounded by German-cut diamonds, numbered ten.

"She inherited it when one of her sisters died. The eldest, Rosemary. Miss Ena wore it one Christmas that I can remember. Never again."

"Still, it's a lovely piece to let go." He looked at me as if he were reassessing everything he knew about me.

"I'm not the jewelry type," I muttered. "People matter more."

Cocking his head like a dog checking out squirrel chatter, he studied me. "Not a very lawyerly statement. Don't lawyers go for the bucks above all?"

"I'm not all lawyers." I was getting tired of this analysis. "So, I've done what I came for. Talk to you tomorrow." I tried to shoulder my way past.

"Not so fast. Don't you want something from me saying you gave me the bracelet?" He was still frowning, as if trying to figure out how to piece me together into a discernable pattern.

"No. I trust you to paint me honestly. I trust you with the bracelet."

"Don't remember you being quite so . . ." He paused. "Free with your trust."

I thought about what he meant. The kid I'd been was no longer around. "You've changed, too. Never thought much about you when we were in school. Sure, I knew you were talented. Everyone knew that. But I'd say I don't have a choice here. If anything, I'm a pragmatist."

"Anything to get you in my clutches, little lady." His long hair was tied at the nape of his neck with a piece of twine which shook as he nodded. "I'll take pragmatism if nothing else is available." He chuckled, pocketing the bracelet.

"Like what?" Instantly, I was feeling edgy. The day had been long and hard. I wasn't in shape for this kind of verbal marathon.

"Nothing." Grabbing an orange, he took my shoulder in his other hand and steered me back to the chair. "Since I have you in my den of iniquity, and I *am* doing you a favor, you owe me."

I wished I'd left my panty hose on. I could have used them to strangle him. My patience had run thinner than turpentine. "What kind of favor?"

"Hold this." Plopping the orange in my hand, he rested it on the table. "I need a bit more on the sketch I started the other day, then I'll be able to get going on the canvas. It'll cut down on your posing time, promise."

Relieved that he wasn't asking for what most men wanted when they had the advantage over a woman, I acquiesced less than gracefully, better than I normally would have. "Okay. But I've got to get home pretty soon here. Got a dog today, and he hasn't been fed."

"A dog? My, you're just a bundle of surprises." Ignoring my mutinous look, he tilted my head. His fingers were strong and scented with fresh wood. "There, I think that's it. Let me get my sketch pad. Hold still."

I stared at that orange until my eyes began to swim. Sitting once more to my left, Travis's hand flew over the paper, working it as if it were sand he erased with his fingers. I wondered how the paper withstood his feverish pace. The back of my neck began to cramp. The sun had long since sunk, and I needed a bath in the world's worst way. Robert

E. had probably eaten the grass, the azaleas, and the rhodo-dendrons in the back yard. I wouldn't have blamed him.

"I've really got to go," I protested, flexing my fingers so the orange rolled across the table. Shoving back the chair, I retrieved my car keys from my pocket. "Thanks for supper."

I don't think he even heard me. Absorbed in the sketch, he never said a word as I tiptoed out the studio door and down the stairs.

I hoped I'd guessed right in entrusting him with Miss Ena's bracelet. I hoped Robert E. hadn't destroyed my back yard.

I hoped I could keep June out of jail.

Me, I probably deserved to be there. But that was another issue altogether.

Chapter 8

ROBERT E. adapted to my lifestyle, or rather, I to his. Chewing my shoes, left in the middle of the kitchen floor while I fixed him a bowl of leftover chili and Cheerios for dinner, he let me know what he thought of my neglect of him. He was right, I had to admit it. But when he jumped on my bed in the middle of the night, I was forced to hold the line at his putting his head on the pillow next to mine. Banished to the foot of the bed, he ran in his dreams with little jerking movements that hauled me awake faster than a bucket of cold water. I wasn't a good sleeper at the best of times. Robert E. and I would have to come to an understanding if we were going to cohabit.

Bleary-eyed, I coerced my early morning client, the one who was paying off a fine for running his GTO through the iron fence around the confederate cemetery, to carry June's statement to the courthouse. He was going that direction anyway, and I figured it would look like I was a lot less worried than I was if I had a guy off the street delivering the narrative. I'd read it through at five in the morning when I couldn't stay in bed a second longer, and June had done a good job. The woman was going to make a great lawyer if she could avoid a felony conviction. Braidwood would probably read it and laugh, but what the hell. Everyone deserved a chuckle a day.

I'd just sent Robert E. to the back yard to figure out if he could destroy the ancient boxwoods lining the house, when June arrived at nine on the dot. Looking as cool as a honeydew in a lime green tunic top and flowing pants, she tossed her purse on her desk. At least she looked calm and collected to the untrained eye. I could tell she hadn't slept.

"Rough night?" I was dressed for comfort today, which meant the jeans I'd worn through the knees and an old knit shirt.

I knew we were in trouble when June didn't bother to chastise me for my attire. "Yes, you could say that," she muttered, looking distracted.

"Don't let the bastards get you down," I tried to joke with her. "It'll all be over with before you get your nails done again."

June took meticulous care of her false nails, having them shaped and relacquered at a phenomenal pace. Mine, on the other hand, were broken and chipped by the restoration work I did every weekend and whenever there was a slow moment at the office. There'd been lots of slow moments.

"I was planning on tomorrow."

Shrugging, I didn't know how to prepare her for the worse. So I gave up before I started. "We can hope."

The phone rang, sending my heart into a weird little dance. My gut said to run away, let it ring, but June was more professional than I. Answering it swiftly with "Law office of Talbot Jefferson," she listened for a minute, her face blank.

"Who?" I said as soon as she'd said "thank you" and hung up.

"Henry. They did the autopsy late last night, sent off the bullet they got out of Darryl to D.C. along with the gun from my safe."

"Well, well. Guy Braidwood and the FBI aren't putting this one on the back burner." I thought fast. Sending everything to D.C. meant the FBI lab. That would take a while. The lab in Columbia wasn't as busy, they'd probably have done the analysis while Watson waited. But the federal addition to the scene bought us some time.

"Didn't Darryl say he was heading for the gun show in Richmond?"

June nodded.

"How good an artist are you?" I wished I had Travis in my office right this minute.

"Not good. I can draw a lollipop."

"Damn. I need something that looks at least a little bit like the guy who gave you the Colt. How he looked that night."

"I could do a stick figure, that's about it."

"Golly Moses, June, I thought you could do anything. You've got me worried, girl." I was teasing, but she'd lost her sense of humor, if she'd ever had one. She gave me a look that told me I could shove it.

"No problem. Travis Whitlock, look him up in the

phone book. Phone's probably still under his father's name. Gray Whitlock. Tell him I'll wear the damned costume next time if he'll help you sketch a pic of the guy with the Colt. Oh, and tell him I want to go away for the weekend with him."

June didn't approve of my current celibate, almost monastic existence, but I think I crossed the line with that one. "I hope you aren't planning on a cheerleader costume?" Arched eyebrows. "And if you're running off for a weekend of hanky panky, tell him yourself."

She had a point. "Okay, I'll do it. But you've got to find me a gun expert. Someone who used to work for the FBI would be best, former state crime lab, better. Antique guns. We're going to need to double check whatever comes down about that Colt."

She whistled. "This could get expensive. I don't have that kind of money."

"We haven't spent it yet. Besides, I've got a few spare nickels this month. Got it covered. I just want a name, a curriculum vitae. Just in case. It may never come to this."

"And pigs can fly." June disappeared into her office, mumbling about men and how she was staying as far away from any and all for as long as she lived. And when she found Darryl Henshaw in the afterlife, what she'd do to him. I don't think June was earning any brownie points with the Big Guy.

As soon as I rang Travis's number, I remembered he'd said he had to ship off the portrait, then he'd run over to Hilton Head with the bracelet. I left him the message on his answering machine, hoping he'd see the humor in it. A guy with ears like that and enough freckles to play connect-the-dots just had to have a sense of humor.

The rest of the day I tried to catch up with all the piddly little cases I had hanging around. Henry called to make sure June wasn't going through the roof, I remembered to eat lunch, and then I thought about tackling the bannister. What I needed more than anything was a chance to think, and working with my hands made me do just that. I don't know why my mind has to be stimulated by manual activity, it just does.

Barricading her door with a bang when she saw me hauling in the varnish remover and rags from the rebuilt shed out back, June let me know what she thought of my work ethic. But no clients were scheduled for the afternoon, and I really needed the strong smell of chemicals to give my gray matter a jump start. For once I used my rubber gloves and mask, and then set about happily mixing toxic chemicals to smear on the crackled varnish. My putty knife, ready to scrape, was stuck in my back pocket.

As the solution I'd mixed did its work eating away years of aged varnish and dark stain, I sucked in the potent odor through the paper mask. This was as high as I was going to be able to get. My mind started chewing on the entire picture of Darryl Henshaw's murder, mentally masticating it into a wad I could eventually spit out. If I could just make the leap from knowing June so well to how she must appear to Braidwood and Watson, I'd have a starting point.

She was an outsider, not one of us, just a resident of Wynnton. That gave her somewhat of an advantage. No ancient history, no slights from grade school to color her in anyone's memories. I had no idea what she did for friends, who she went to the movies with, or even if she planned on making Wynnton her permanent home. Getting a view of June through the reverse lens of a mental telescope wasn't too hard, once I started to work on it.

Like me, she was a loner. If she'd had friends, they'd have called her at work sometime. The only people she heard from were Grace, Henry, and her mother. I knew her mother lived in Atlanta, because when she'd called she informed me she was paying daytime long distance charges, and to get my butt in gear and put her daughter on the phone. I put my butt in gear.

I'd had the feeling from the start that Henry and Grace had called in a favor of some memorable magnitude to get June to babysit me in the days when I was living more in my stash of Kentucky's finest than real life. Whatever the favor owed, June had more than repaid it. She stayed with me, I hoped, because she liked me and the deal we'd cut to help get her her law license by preparing for law school. I trusted her. Maybe I'd been able to give Travis my trust more easily because I'd already taken my first steps down that dangerous path with June.

In many ways, June and I were alike. She'd carried a torch for an unrepentant husband, I'd done it for the faithless Jack Bland. Maybe we were both hiding in Miss Ena's lovely, grand old house on Woolfolk Avenue. If we were, the accusations Braidwood, and probably the feds as well, were about to make would blast us out of our boring little lives. The problem was, I liked my boring life very well, thank you. While June harped at me and gave me grief on a daily basis, it was never malicious. Sometimes I felt as if she were the older sister I'd never had.

While we found a way to convince the people who could make our lives miserable that we had nothing to do with

Darryl Henshaw's shady activities, we had to survive. I wasn't sure how smart the guys were who were working with Darryl, but I'd have bet my firstborn child they weren't the boy scout types. If, as I suspected, the Colt was the murder weapon, someone had gone to the bother of framing June with it. The muscle-bound, Harley-tatooed crowd I associated with gun dealers didn't have the brains for something that twisted.

Unless, of course, they'd found out that Darryl had ripped off the diamond ring and given it to June. Then they'd be only too happy to take her out of the picture in a most civilized manner—they'd let the law take her down.

Oh goody. I was giving myself a headache and throwing in a bout of depression along with it. When the bad guys got smarter than the good guys, it was time for me to get smart, smarter, smartest. I didn't think my Phi Beta Kappa key would impress the goons pulling this scam, but I'd find something that would.

No word came from the sheriff's office calling to say they had a warrant for June's arrest. Grace dropped by at five to pick June up and take her over to Rollins for a movie. Wynnton's only theater had closed in the 1960s, leaving a marquee that looked like the grille of an old Cadillac jutting over the sidewalk on Main Street.

I gave Grace a wave of gratitude as she pulled June out the door, protesting the entire way that she had work to do. Letting Robert E. into the house, I fed him scrambled eggs. I was going to have to drive to the Feed-n-Seed and buy some real dog food before he began to think I was going to cook for him every night. He was looking like a man who expects that kind of thing, and I had to nip that puppy in the bud.

Around seven I'd inhaled enough toxic fumes to shave a few more years off my life. The bannister was going to take a couple more coats, but it was getting there. I had a gut feeling that I needed to find the upstanding members of society Darryl had been associated with before he died. Everything I'd ever known about criminal law told me he'd been killed by them over whatever they were dealing. The decapitation was a macabre twist, perhaps the outcome of a sick sense of humor, maybe a warning to others. I made a note to discuss it with Henry, who knew more about murder than I ever wanted to learn.

Changing into semiclean shorts and a new T-shirt, I gathered up a peanut butter sandwich, Robert E., and a can of soda. When I die, I want to be filled with all the artificial coloring, sugar, starch, and fats that I can stand. My dinner was going to further my goal in that direction.

The swing on the front porch, shaded from the setting sun, hung on metal hooks someone had put in the ceiling so long ago that no one remembered who did the job of getting it up there. If I'd ever needed to get that swing down for repairs, I'd have to take the ceiling down. Plunking my bottom on its seat, I held the soda between my thighs as I contemplated scraping down the porch and repainting it. My mind, when tied into knots, has a tendency to focus on what doesn't matter. Somehow, the solution oozes out of the distraction.

Swinging and chewing, tapping my bare feet on the floor to get a good push, I wasn't paying attention too much. Robert E. tolerated my foot resting on his haunch every time I slowed the swing down, content to poke his nose in the direction of the sidewalk and sniff the night air. His fur felt springy and soft at the same time. I could smell warm earth on him and knew he'd found something else to dig up. I'd have to buy him something to chew beside shrubbery when I went for dog food.

Wednesday nights, everyone heads for church suppers and the midweek socials. Woolfolk Avenue was quiet, only the cicadas and fireflies to keep me company. The houses around me, vintage Wynnton, are in a state of flux at the moment. Many of the original owners, like Miss Ena, have passed on to the great Wednesday night supper banquet, leaving their large, old homes to be subdivided into tacky apartments or inhabited by ne'er-do-well relations. Once the historic preservationists realize what's going on, it'll be too late. A lot of them will end up razed to make way for a convenience store or a car parts shop. Downtown has been dying for years, and the urban sprawl, such as it is in a small town like Wynnton, sees Woolfolk Avenue as the suburbs.

I was thinking how I'd die, like Miss Ena, in this house, and leave what's left of Miss Ena's money, if there was any after June's trial, to someone who'd take care of Robert E. as long as he lived in this house.

"Hear that, boy? You'd make a great heir." I ruffled his fur with my toes.

"Talking to the animals? Didn't know you were so talented." Stepping up to the porch, Travis surprised me so much I almost dropped my soda can on Robert E.'s head.

"Lord have mercy, where'd you come from?"

"No good and beyond." Taking a seat beside me on the swing, he leaned back and gave it a hard push. The chain creaked as we pumped back and forth.

"Been there, done that," I answered. He looked different

this evening, somehow less abstract and more solid. His clothes, I thought, must have made the difference.

Attired in a crisp blue gingham shirt that brought out his deep sea-colored eyes, pressed khaki pants, and topsiders with no socks, he looked like a wealthy preppie out slumming. The long hair was tied neatly at the back of his neck, his fingers almost clean of paint, and he smelled faintly of aftershave. A very expensive, very light aftershave that reminded me of sunshine and champagne. I sucked it in.

"Damn, you smell good," I noted wryly. "Hate it when a man's better looking, better smelling than me."

Wrinkling his nose, he shook his head at me, a knowing smile on his face. "I could name the chemical compounds of whatever you've been soaking in, but I'm afraid you'd die just from shock after hearing what they can do to the human body."

"Oh, I know," I answered blithely. "I'm just praying I'll get this house finished before they kill me."

"I wouldn't bet on it," he smiled.

He hadn't said if he'd been successful in Hilton Head. I was too antsy to wait, too impolite to avoid the topic.

"How much did you get for it?" I figured he wouldn't have been so relaxed it he'd failed to sell the bracelet.

"Not enough to feed this moose." He toed Robert E., who gave a loud snort in his sleep. "But ten grand more than you wanted."

I whistled. "I owe you."

"That you do. I heard the message you left at the house. You paying for the weekend, and do I get to pick the place?" He looked far too pleased with himself. A nasty twinkle had developed in his blue eyes.

"I'm paying, no you don't get to choose, and that costume had better leave a lot to the imagination." I tickled Robert E. with a toe. I was enjoying this immensely. I'd forgotten what it was like to flirt with someone I'd known a long time ago, and not feel guilty about it.

"Oh, and I forgot. I need you to draw a picture of someone. Only I'm not sure what he looks like."

Travis frowned. "Not asking a lot, are you?"

He was close beside me, smelling of the aftershave, warm cotton, clean skin. I could get used to this, and I shouldn't. I leaned forward so our shoulders no longer touched, and glanced at him over my shoulder.

"June didn't get a solid look at the man who brought her a gun, the one I'm betting killed her husband. I was hoping you could take her description and come up with a sketch, something we can use in Richmond this weekend."

"So that's where we're going? Long drive, isn't it?"

"We are. To a gun show. Can you do it, draw something we can show around to the dealers, see if anyone recognizes him?"

Frowning, Travis leaned over to give Robert E. a scratch. "It'll be something, but probably not accurate. I paint from life, Tal, not by words."

"I know. But you're the only man who can do it."

"I'm the only portrait painter in Wynnton." He snorted.

"No, I mean it. You're the only man I trust to go with me to Richmond and do this. I just want a name—I need something to back up June's story."

If we didn't succeed, I'd have to scrounge around for another tack. I didn't have to be clairvoyant to know that June's would be the only fingerprints on the Colt.

"Tell me the whole story," Travis insisted. "Square one.

Last I heard, you expected her to be arrested today, which is why I drove like a bat outta hell through every speed trap between here and Hilton Head."

I patted his knee. "Thanks. I mean that. But they've sent the bullet they pulled out of her husband to D.C., the FBI labs." I filled him on the rest of what had happened. "I'm guessing they'll finish up the forensic stuff by Monday now. Maybe later. If I can get a jump on this, find a solid lead to the men her husband was cheating, maybe I won't need to pay a bondsman. Where is it, by the way, the money?"

"I didn't stash it in the truck, if that's what you're thinking." He smiled like a co-conspirator, enjoying his role in thwarting the grinding wheels of justice. "Stuck it in the freezer at home."

I hooted. "Where'd you get that idea?"

"Nowhere. Just came to me. My, um, client, gave me sixty bills, in thousands, a big enough roll to look funny in my pocket. Went right home, pulled out some frozen hamburgers, arranged the money, put the hamburgers back on top."

"Hope you don't get knocked off before tomorrow morning."

"There's one way to make sure." Travis leaned back, locking his hands behind his head as he turned to stare at me. "Spend the night."

"Woowee," I whistled. "You get right to the point."

"Always."

I was flattered, I had to admit. But not ready, not tonight. "I don't think Robert E. is ready to share me just yet." The dog thumped the porch with his tail, his eyes still shut. "And he hogs the bed."

Travis, I noted gratefully, took my rejection in stride. "I hope he stays here when we go to Richmond?"

"Golly, I hadn't thought of that. I'll get June to come over and feed him and let him out while we're gone. I'd like to leave tomorrow, if you can get a sketch drawn by then."

"Tomorrow's fine. Want me to deposit your money on my way into town to pick you up?" His hand slipped onto my shoulder and began rubbing tiny circles against my upper arm.

"Gee, what do you do for an encore? Hocking my jewelry, making my bank run, I'll bet I could get you to help me paint this porch if I fixed you a glass of something cold."

The sun hit the tops of the trees across the street. Dark patterns began playing on the porch, leaves rustling in a sudden summer breeze, bats roosting overhead in thick, dark bunches. I was relaxed, too relaxed. Travis lightly scratched my back as he chuckled.

"I take that back. Go home and guard my money. June'll be in at nine tomorrow, can you get back here by then? She can do the bank run. If you come up with a sketch after you talk to her, we'll take off from here."

"You don't do much for a guy's ego, you know that, don't you?"

I could see good humor and the eyes of an artist studying me as he prepared to stand. As he did, he pulled me to my feet beside him.

Before I could stop him, he kissed me. His lips, dry and warm on mine, were at first a merest brush, a teasing promise. A second later he was letting me know he was ready, willing, and very able to stay the night in any capacity I desired. Pushing back, I tried to catch my breath.

"You don't fight fair."

He laughed. "Who does?" Running down the steps, he was still laughing as if he were enjoying himself much too much.

"Admit it, I add fun to your life," I called after him.

"I always knew you would. Just took too damn long to get here, Tal."

I heard him slam the truck door.

I knew what he meant.

Chapter 9

❧

JUNE wasn't in the office by the time I headed to court for the ten o'clock docket, nor was Travis. I didn't care what they did without me so long as they came up with a workable picture I could flash around the gun show. I left huge signs around the office saying things like "TALK TO TRAVIS. DESCRIBE THE GUY WITH THE COLT." And to Travis, I posted notes saying "HUMOR JUNE. BE HELPFUL. DRAW WELL."

I had an easy prelim that morning. I expected to be out of court by eleven, heading home to pack my toothbrush for the long ride to Richmond. I hoped Travis remembered his jammies. Yeah, right, he probably slept like I did, with nothing on. I was anticipating this trip more than I should.

The courtroom was devoid of the usual throngs. The heaviest docket was on Monday, of course, with a weekend full of malfeasers anxious to get out of the pokey on bond.

My client had been sitting a few days, waiting for his court-appointed attorney to get his ass in gear and talk to him in the jail. When the guy didn't show, I assumed the usual jailhouse crowd handed him my card. I'd taken his collect call, listened to his tale of woe, gave him a figure I'd have to have in my hot little hand before I showed up in court.

I'd held off doing anything until I got a check. It came in Thursday's mail, so I could make the prelim on Friday with the assurance that my time was covered through today. After that, I was working gratis, and I knew it. But I really expected to be out of court by 10:30 with a free and grateful client in tow, home by eleven. If his witnesses showed up, we were outta there. But at least the check gave me a bit of cushion in my firm account, a few extra dollars to pay for the hotel room in Richmond. I felt like I was cheating the man for taking money for a case as easy as his.

Judge Harold DeShazo seemed anxious to get his docket cleared and out of the courthouse. I didn't have much time to talk to the arresting officer or the prosecutor, but from what my client told me, this was a clear-cut case of mistaken identity.

Ike Coleman, my client, was no saint. He admitted to me he'd smacked his wife around a few times, gotten in trouble for shoplifting when he was a kid, which meant he had a juvie record, but generally, he'd held a job and paid for his county sticker on his pickup. What he hadn't done was run away after smashing into a Honda Accord, leaving a nice little old lady with a nasty gash on her forehead and a broken arm. The fact that Ike didn't own an '86 Toyota pickup with a license plate the witnesses had all told the officer was gracing the Toyota's back bumper, he didn't know anyone with said Toyota, and he was at work with about ten witnesses who saw him pouring concrete for the retaining wall of the new Seven-Eleven going up on the edge of town, should have done the trick. Two guys in dirty jeans carrying hard-hats under their arms sat in the back of the courtroom. The lady who was hit hadn't shown up.

I snagged the construction workers. "So tell me, is Ike telling the truth, was he at work all day Monday?" I whispered as softly as I could. DeShazo has a shitfit about talking in his courtroom.

"Yes, ma'am," they answered simultaneously.

"Quiet in the court," DeShazo snapped, rapping the bench with his gavel.

The courtroom is so tiny, you could hear the mice chewing dust if you tried. About eight benches in the back accommodated those waiting to have their district court cases heard, while the lawyers all squeeze into the front at the counsel table on the right. The prosecutor du jour sits on the left with whatever police officer has the case, then walks to the front of the bench to present his case before the judge. The defense lawyer, or if the defendant doesn't have one, the defendant, stands beside the prosecutor and the police officer, and talks to the judge as if everyone was having a friendly conversation. The atmosphere is deceptively simple. A lot of folks don't realize they start themselves down a very twisted, torturous legal path when they represent themselves at this level.

At least Ike knew enough to know he needed a lawyer.

Jimmy Hart was the young law school graduate assigned today's docket by Braidwood's office. He went through the motions, asking the clerk to swear in the officer. Hand raised, the officer repeated his oath. Jimmy opened his mouth to take the officer through his report in excruciating detail. I'd heard him use the same technique all morning.

I interrupted. "Your honor, we're willing to admit the officer's description of the '86 Toyota truck which struck the victim's car. Can we get to how this vehicle was traced to my client?"

DeShazo looked pleased. "Thank you, Miss Jefferson. Officer, if you please."

The cop was one of Frank's old timers. Never looking at me, he stared at a point just below the lip of the judge's bench, intoning his recitation like a robot.

"The victim identified the color and model of the truck, as well as the first two letters of the license plate. Also, she identified the driver as a black male. I ran the two letters through the computer, and it returned a possible listing of two hundred plates in Wynnton and the surrounding counties. None were assigned to an older model Toyota truck, leading me to believe the plates had been stolen."

He'd gone far enough for me. "So in other words, the plates you found weren't registered to my client."

"I didn't say that. I said they weren't assigned to a Toyota pickup," Officer Robertson muttered. "I also ran a name check."

Puzzled, I stared at Jimmy. This I hadn't heard.

"The victim identified the name Coleman Construction painted on the side of the truck. Under the name Coleman, I pulled the defendant here as the owner of a pickup truck. A late model Ford Ranger. Also a small truck."

"Did any of the license plate letters match my client's plates?" I was beginning to get steamed.

"No, ma'am." Officer Robertson seemed too smug. "But he did own a pickup, and even though the model and years didn't match exactly, I assumed the victim and her witnesses were fuzzy in their identification. I assumed the plates were stolen, and arrested Mr. Coleman, who matched the victim's description."

"You mean Mr. Coleman was a black male, don't you?" My hands were icy, I was so angry.

"Yes, ma'am." Robertson was enjoying himself too much. "And he worked in construction and he owned a pickup truck."

"But not a Toyota, isn't that correct?"

"Like I said, the victim could have been confused."

"And Mr. Coleman doesn't own a construction company, does he?"

My client cleared his throat by my ear.

"As a matter of fact, the State Corporation Commission lists a Coleman Building Company with a Mr. Uriah Coleman as the owner."

I turned to my client. "What's your real first name?" I whispered.

Unhappiness wiped across his face. "What do you think? Uriah."

I changed tactics. I'd find out about his business on the side later.

"Was the victim afforded an opportunity to view a line-up?" I knew Robertson wouldn't have gone to that much trouble. He had a black guy with a truck, that was all he wanted.

"No, ma'am, the victim is still hospitalized. I took her a photo taken of the defendant, and she identified him."

I couldn't wait to get this little old lady into court. I would have a well-deserved reputation for the meanest bitch in town, but the upside was, I was going to enjoy destroying this identification.

"In other words, you showed her one picture, said 'this is

the guy, isn't he, Mrs. Adams, who struck you and drove off?' and she said 'Oh yes, officer, he is!' Am I correct?"

Jimmy wasn't happy with my snide tone. "Objection, your honor."

"Be quiet," Judge DeShazo snapped. "This is just a pre-lim, Miss Jefferson. No need to get huffy."

I wanted to scream at him that this was the most blatant example of racism I'd seen in at least a week, but I remembered I needed to get to Richmond. Spending the weekend in lockup would foul up my plans but good.

"Your honor, I have witnesses here today who will testify that my client was at his place of employment all day." I spoke very calmly, I thought, for a woman about to blow her top. "Where's Mr. Coleman's truck now, officer?"

I was fishing. If it had been impounded and tested for the Honda's paint, Robertson was avoiding admitting it in open court. Only three reasons for that. One, they didn't have the truck, or they'd tested the truck and it was negative. Or, they'd tested it and were holding the evidence as the coup de grace for the circuit court trial. The latter was what scared me.

"We've been unable to ascertain its whereabouts," Robertson admitted reluctantly. "Mr. Coleman says he lent it to a friend."

"Move to certify, Judge." Jimmy at least knew his job. All he had to do was send it upstairs to the circuit court, and he'd get a pat on the head from Braidwood.

"Sufficient grounds to certify. Make your case in Circuit, Miss Jefferson. Bond is continued at one hundred thousand dollars." Smacking the gavel on the bench, DeShazo shuffled his papers together and rose in a swirl of black robes to disappear.

My client tugged at my sleeve as the bailiffs stepped up to return him to the jail. "What happened here?" he asked in total confusion.

"We were sandbagged. Not to mention, you forgot to tell me you lent your truck to a friend. Where the hell is it?"

"I ain't got that kind of money. How long am I gonna have to stay locked up?" His hand was still on my sleeve as he shrugged off the bailiffs. He clearly wasn't interested in my question about his truck and the elusive friend.

"A minute with my client, guys." I stepped back from the bench, pulling Ike with me. Leaning close, I whispered quickly. "I'll get as early a trial date as I can. Are you insured?"

"What do you mean, early as you can?" He was not a happy camper.

"There'll be a docket call, I'll set it for the first available date. Are you insured?" I repeated.

" 'Course." He named the insurance company.

"What're your liability limits?" I knew Robertson would already have checked this out. State law said a driver had to carry a minimum of fifty grand, which was peanuts.

"Half a mill," Ike muttered. "My wife's a lousy driver. I didn't want to lose our house, everything we've got if she killed someone."

"Killing is cheaper than maiming. Mrs. Adams was probably only too happy to identify you when Robertson told her how much your policy carried. There're two things going on here, and you're the bird in hand. You're heavily insured, you're black, and you've got the right name."

"But I wasn't driving anywhere near where that woman got hit!" His face glistened with sweat. "If I stay in here much longer, I lose my business, I lose my house, I lose my truck, I lose everything. You understand?"

"Give me your wife's phone number." Pulling a pen from my briefcase, I handed him my legal pad. "I'll tell her how to arrange bond."

"She won't do it," he snarled. "The bitch wants me in here so she can run around."

Great, I thought, a happy marriage added to the muddy mix. "Who owns the house? Whose name is on the deed?"

"Both of us," Ike muttered. "And she won't put it up to get me bonded out."

"Then unless you've got generous family or friends, you're stuck in jail." I'd had lots of clients unhappy about the stay at the taxpayer's expense, but none of them had died from it. At least, not in the Talmadge County jail.

"Yeah, right. Think those guys'll lend me bail money? Sure, they get about two-fifty a week at the job, they've got money to burn." Nodding at the back of the courtroom where the other construction workers had disappeared, Ike had a better grasp of the reality of his situation than I'd have credited to him. "They're already lookin' for another job about now. Know I'm going under."

"I'll get their names and addresses from the job site, get them subpoenaed as soon as I have a trial date. Meanwhile, stay calm. I'll see what I can do before we get to trial. We may be able to wiggle you out of this before then, but don't hold your breath."

The wheels of justice turn as slowly as a body dangling on the end of a noose, but I didn't want to depress Mr. Coleman any further. The bailiffs were anxious to get out of the courtroom.

"I'll let you know, as soon as I can, what your wife says."

"Tell her I'll kill her if she doesn't come up with the bail money," Ike snapped, his eyes angry slits, his arms clutched by the two bailiffs.

"Oh good, just what we need. Threats."

Snapping my briefcase shut, I wondered how my simple prelim, my mistaken identity case, had fallen apart so easily. Now I'd actually have to work my butt off to get Mr. Coleman out of jail time, and I had a feeling he wasn't going to be particularly appreciative. Clients who're unjustly held for crimes they didn't commit tended to be a bit on the defensive, and their lawyers were usually the only ones being paid to take abuse.

Not that I could blame him. He had to blow up at someone, and I was a handy target.

"Where's your pickup now? Who's the friend who has it?" I grabbed him for one last question before he was locked up again.

"How the hell should I know? Lent it to a guy I haven't seen in years, called him Cool Dude, in high school. Haven't seen it since. Said he'd leave it at my house when he was through running his errands."

"Why the hell would you lend a truck to some guy you haven't seen in years?" His story was getting more tangled by the minute. Some of that tangle was going to trip him up, I just knew it in my bones.

I got a ghost of a smile from Ike. "Money, man."

"How much?" My client could probably afford the ten percent bond better than I could.

He was reluctant to answer me. Staring at the wall behind my shoulder, he shrugged. The bailiffs were getting antsy to get him into the back.

"How much?" I insisted firmly.

"A couple hundred, that's all."

Oh great, really, really great. My legal antennae were quivering. Renting a car from Avis was cheaper than that. I'd ask Mrs. Coleman the rest of the questions. A hostile wife would know more dirt and be willing to spill it on my lap. My very pissed, noncommunicative Mr. Coleman wasn't talking enough to make me a happy lawyer. Suddenly, I wondered how innocent my client really was. The SODDI defense was my favorite—Some Other Dude Did It. I hadn't seen it coming with Mr. Coleman, but the symptoms were there, big, red, and flashing like a zit on the end of a nose.

Using the cell phone June forced me to keep in my briefcase, I called Mrs. Coleman and asked if I could come right over. Travis could cool his heels at my office a while longer. Mrs. Coleman answered in that breathless way women have when they're expecting someone else to call, someone of the male persuasion and seething with overcharged testosterone.

I introduced myself and explained I needed to see her. She wasn't happy.

"I've got to go to work in an hour," she complained. She sounded like a woman who complained a lot.

"No problem. I'll get over there right now."

"There's no way in hell I'll sign over this house to cover his bond," she warned with a nasty twinge to her voice.

"I'll see you in about fifteen minutes." I ignored her comment. What I wanted was her husband's pickup. I wondered why it hadn't been impounded if it had been abandoned by Cool Dude anywhere in Talmadge County. I loved the name. I was going to have such fun tracking him down.

The Colemans lived in a nice new house in a new subdivision filled with big new sport utility vehicles and barking dogs. The house looked as if it had been recently purchased, and sure enough, I saw the hole in the front yard where the realtor's sign had been stuck. Pink lace curtains hid the living room behind the picture window in the front from the neighbors. A new Expedition was parked in the driveway. The single car garage door was closed.

She answered the door on the first ring. "I can't ask you in, I've got a mess in here," she started out as hospitably as a German shepherd guarding a prisoner.

Mrs. Coleman wore a very attractive beige dress with a large gold necklace filling the neckline. I'd have bet it was real. About my height, she was running to fat and enjoying it. Her bust bulged under the dress, as did the hips. She wore oddly sensible shoes. I wondered where she went to work dressed like that.

"I've got to get to the salon by noon. My first client's then."

"What do you do?" I hoped I sounded chatty and interested.

"I do hair," she answered reluctantly. "Over at the Grande Dame."

"You should make it," I answered. I could see past her shoulder to the living room, which was filled with big, overstuffed chairs and a sofa with a recliner built into one end. The fabric was bright pink and blue flowers, early motel taste and probably as expensive as a good antique.

"Thought you should know, your husband's case was certified to the circuit court this morning. Bond's still at a hundred grand. He'd like you to make arrangements." Yeah, right, sure she would, I thought after seeing her eyes light up when I told her the case had been certified. She hadn't asked me what that meant. She knew.

"No way I'm signing papers on this house. We just

moved here. It's gonna stay just like it is." Hands on her hips, she was keeping me from getting through the door more effectively than a linebacker. "Tell that son of a bitch he's got it coming."

"Mrs. Coleman," I began in my most placating voice, "can you tell me what you're so upset about? And can you give me an idea where your husband's truck can be found?"

"You bet I can. Over at that woman's house, the one he's been screwing for the past six months, that's where."

Exactly what I needed, a pissed-off wife with a good reason to be pissed.

"Did you tell the police this?"

"Hell yes. They can't find it. Figure the bitch musta hidden it, gonna sell it probably, when he don't show up to pay her rent this month. Serves the bitch right. But she knows where it is, all right."

"Where does she live?"

"Over there on Yancy Street, a little gray house with black shutters, big magnolia in the front yard. Thinks she's so cute, her and her little ass. Let me tell you, she's just one of a long line of women my husband's kept through the years. And who gets the new house and the SUV and whatever she wants? You better believe it, honey." Mrs. Coleman wore a triumphant look that said she knew where the bodies were buried, and her husband knew she knew.

"Name?" I'd bet Mrs. Coleman knew her bra size.

"Some month of the year, like April, May, one of those cutesy names." She was bored with me, anxious to get into her new SUV and move me out of her doorway.

"Just a few more questions, please, Mrs. Coleman." I hung my head as if sympathizing with her over her philandering husband. "All this is really nice," I gestured widely, meaning the neighborhood. "And not cheap. How can you and your husband afford it, and not the bond?"

Her eyes narrowed, she looked at me as if I'd crawled out from under a rock. "None of your business, sweetheart, and if I were you, I'd get my fee up front from Ike in cash. 'Cause he isn't on my checking account anymore."

Shit. I hadn't cashed his check, just put it in the deposit envelope for June to take to the bank today. She pushed past me, slinging a purse over her shoulder as she hurried to the SUV as if she were afraid I'd trail her like a bloodhound. The door clicked shut behind her.

"Thanks for your help," I yelled after her as she slammed the driver's door.

I'd bet sound penetrated the behemoth vehicle about as well as bullets did. The thing looked like a tank. She didn't glance at me as she backed out of the driveway and sped away down the street.

I waited until she'd turned onto the next street before trying the front door knob, found it stiff, and then decided I could afford another try at breaking and entering. I trotted to the back of the house. Sure enough, the garage had a single window facing the back yard. Framing my face with my hands, I peered in and hoped no one reported a burglar. But I didn't need to break in. The garage was empty, too small to hold the gigantic SUV she was driving, but the right size for a small pickup. No matter how hard I looked, the truck just wasn't there.

I knew I had to find Yancy Street next. Richmond and Travis would have to wait. Using the cell phone again, I called June to pull out the town map in the office and give me directions. Travis answered the office line on the first ring.

"You shoot 'em, we spring 'em."

"Not funny. I hope you haven't driven June into the insane asylum with stuff like that."

Actually, I thought he was funny, but I wouldn't let him know that too soon in the relationship.

"Oh, it's you, our fearless leader." I could hear him telling June in the background that I was on the line. "I'm sitting here waitin' for you, darlin'. When are we gonna hit the road, you and me, babe?"

"That sounds like an old Sonny and Cher song," I laughed. "How's the picture of the guy with the hat coming along?"

"Well, it's about as revealing as a nun's habit. But I've done as you asked, you wicked woman. So hurry up and rescue me from this dragon guarding your office like the last of her breed."

"Be nice to June, she's had a hard week," I warned.

"I am unfailingly polite to the weaker sex," Travis teased. "I just haven't found any yet."

"Oh God, put June on before I have to keep you in a cage in the office just to amuse me." I was still laughing. With the mess I'd gotten into with Ike Coleman and June's and my problems with Darryl Henshaw, I shouldn't have been feeling so chipper.

June picked up her phone. "Come and get him *now*," June ordered, sounding less amused than I.

"Give me another thirty minutes. Tell him to fix me some lunch. What I need right this sec are directions to Yancy Street."

"Yancy? That's easy, I live on Yancy."

Although I'd often been a guest of Henry and Grace, I'd never been invited to June's house. I knew how private a woman she was and never took it personally. "Okay, let me have it. I'm looking for a gray house with black shutters and a big magnolia in the front yard."

Silence filled the line between us.

"June?" Then I remembered, the "other" woman's name was one of the months of the year. "Is that your house, June?"

"Yes," she answered tentatively, as if expecting me to fire her. "Why do you want to find my house?"

"Because my client, Ike Coleman, is, according to his wife, your lover, and you have his truck." I waited.

She didn't laugh. She didn't scream at me. She didn't say a word for a few seconds. A few seconds too long.

"And what if he is? What did he do? Why would it matter if I had his truck, which I don't?"

Oh God, I thought in horror. This was getting worse by the minute.

"He's been certified. I need to know where you put his pickup, the Ford Ranger that says Coleman Construction Company on the side." Please, please don't know anything about it, I prayed.

She hadn't looked into the deposit envelope for today. I hadn't told her about Mr. Coleman hiring me, because I hadn't opened the mail with his check until she'd gone yesterday.

"That sign comes off it. It's magnetic. And I didn't do anything with it. Haven't seen it in over a week. Told you, he didn't leave his truck at my place." She paused. "Why this interrogation, Tal?"

"Well, Mr. Coleman's accused of a serious offense, and I'm his lawyer. Hit and run, in fact, in that truck you don't have." I couldn't help it, I was pissed at her. How dare she get into more of a mess with that no-count Coleman?

"I don't know anything about it, truly, Tal. Haven't seen

him since Darryl showed up. Figured he saw Darryl's van outside my house, knew better than to come knocking on my door. No one's asked me about his truck. No police. I swear, I didn't know he was in trouble."

I wondered why Mrs. Coleman had lied about June having the pickup. She'd used it to get me out of her hair, however. Everyone knew a lot more about what was going on than I did, that much was as clear as a baby's conscience.

"I think we need to talk. Not over this cell phone." I had to see her face when she explained how she'd gotten into this mess. "I'll be right back."

Why did all roads lead to June, I wondered on the drive back to Woolfolk Avenue. The day was getting hotter than I could stand with the top down on the Mustang, but I never noticed the sunburn I was picking up. All I knew was, June wasn't the woman I thought she was, to be involved with Uriah, a.k.a. Ike, Coleman.

Maybe I'd been mistaken about her and Darryl's murder also. I hated to think this way, but all the tangled paths got straighter as they led to June Atkins.

Shit. Ike Coleman hadn't gotten my name from the jail-house lawyers. He'd heard of me through June.

Chapter 10

"I T' S white, kinda beat up." June and I were locked in my office while Travis did his domestic act and made sandwiches. He'd stared at my tense expression with professional curiosity when I'd slammed into the office and ordered him to make himself scarce.

"And you're sure you saw it last a week ago?" I must have asked her five times.

"If you don't stop this, I'll, I'll . . ." June hesitated, "quit. How many times do I have to tell you the same thing? What does it matter, anyway?"

"I'll tell you, my future lawyer friend, what it matters. If you've hidden Coleman's truck, and it was involved in the accident, you're an accessory after the fact. Same crime as committing it in person. Now, do you get it?"

"Oh." June's voice was suddenly very tiny. "I still don't know where it is."

"It better not turn up anywhere with your name on it." I whistled out the back door for Robert E. Travis wisely kept his head in the refrigerator, rummaging around in its minuscule wasteland.

"I don't even want to know how you met this character. Don't tell me anything about him unless it can help his case." I'd filled her in on the details as I'd learned them in court.

"I can't help. I mean, we had this thing going on, but it wasn't all that hot and heavy. A girl can get lonely, Tal. Maybe not you, but real women have needs." June was beyond feeling guilty and into sarcastic. This was the June I knew best.

"Low blow and unworthy of you." I sighed. "There's nothing else I can do for Ike Coleman right this second. If he calls from the jail, don't accept the charges. I've got to get out of here, or we'll never get to Richmond."

June was looking more worried than I'd ever seen her. "Think I should go see him in jail? Ike?"

"Lord have mercy, you've lost your mind. No, I don't think so and if you do, I wash my hands of you. We've got enough trouble with your dead husband, we don't need to add your jailed lover to the docket."

She hung close to my shoulder as I tried to gather stuff to throw in the car for the ride to Richmond. I clattered downstairs, and she echoed my descent. June never clattered. She tip-tapped, she marched, but loud and raucous was never her style.

I herded Robert E. into the front room and grabbed her by the arms to still her random pacing. Looking her in the eyes, I had the feeling she wasn't at home. Somewhere in her very smart brain she was all too aware of how bad things were looking, and she wasn't sure she could work her way out of them.

"I'm leaving Robert E. here, so keep an eye on the office over the weekend, will you? Cilla said she'll come feed him in the evening and make sure he's inside. I need you to let him out in the morning."

"Yeah, sure." She wasn't thrilled. "Now I'm the doggie sitter, too." Worried and pissed warred in her eyes.

"What does that mean?" I'd about had it. Between the wait for the forensics on the gun and Ike's mess, I wasn't in the best of moods.

"Nothing," she sniffed sullenly. "Take that aging hippie and get outta here. I still say you're wasting your time, you'll never find the guy."

"Beats waiting around here for Ike's pickup to turn up along with the arrest warrant for Darryl's murder." I wasn't in the right frame of mind to humor her.

"If you say so." Turning her back on me, she marched to her desk and sat down as if she were going to ignore me until hell froze over.

I was angrier with her because of the way I found out about her affair with Ike than I was the fact that she was sleeping with a guy. Realizing that the woman I trusted more than anyone in my life at this moment was keeping secrets from me wasn't exactly on my top ten list of fun things to do.

Travis appeared in the doorway with a grocery bag in one hand and car keys in the other. "Let's roll, my lady."

"I don't have anything packed yet," I snapped. "Give me a sec." I gestured at the stuff piled on a chair. Luggage had slipped my overly preoccupied mind.

"As you command." One eyebrow flitted up. His blue eyes blinked with amazing perspicacity. I didn't fool him for a second.

"And cut out that stupid language." Running upstairs, I tried to curb my feelings of betrayal. I wasn't angry at Travis, I reminded myself. I was angry with myself. Hauling a duffle bag out of the closet, I tossed in an extra T-shirt as I changed into my jeans and a fairly clean knit shirt. I was as ready as I'd ever be. Clattering down the stairs once more, I scooped up my toothbrush, soap, toothpaste, and God help me, a magnifying mirror and tossed them in after the T-shirt.

Giving Robert E. an extra scratch between the ears, I ordered him to be good while I was gone. Holding a sketch pad under one arm, Travis watched me from just inside the front door as if he were studying me.

"What're you waiting for?" I snapped, shoving past him to slam the screen door open. "Let's hit the road."

I didn't say good-bye to June. The more I thought about it, the more I realized I didn't know her at all.

Still silent, Travis held his truck door open for me.

"I want to take my car."

Shaking his head, he pointed to the passenger side of his truck.

"Cut out the silent treatment. Why the hell do you have to drive? What is it with men, they always feel like they have to be the ones to control the wheel? Is it a domination thing?"

He almost smiled at that. "Hardly. I just thought that these guys might know your car, if they know about June. My truck's a better idea."

"Oh." He had a point.

I had no idea how sharp these guys were who'd run with Darryl, but if they were half as shady as I thought they were, they'd have scoped me out in the process of finding June. It felt good to think about the bad guys, if there were any. June's newly won status as the enigma of the week was throwing me off-kilter. "All right."

I scooted in, vowing to keep my opinions to myself. Travis passed me the sketch pad. I waited until he'd pulled off Woolfolk before I opened it.

The portrait was more one of impressions than actual features. I got the feeling I was looking at someone familiar, I just didn't know who. The funny moustache and goatee could have been fake, but Travis had caught the essence of a full, sensual mouth, a flare of nostril that was, if June had any power of observation at all, probably accurate. I whistled in appreciation.

"Thank you, ma'am. We aim to please."

"Didn't take you long to do this." I was impressed.

"Nope. Not much to draw. This isn't going to get the guy, you know. Most folks won't even give it a second glance." Travis sneaked a look at me as we flew past the outskirts of town. He liked to drive fast, I noted appreciatively.

"It's worth a try, though. Give this to Braidwood, if you don't mind, when we get back. If I don't have a name to go with the face."

"Sure, no problem." He drove casually, one hand on the wheel, one tapping his thigh as if he listened to some internal music.

I liked the feeling of being escorted, having someone to help me do what must be done. I couldn't get too accustomed to it, though. Travis wasn't my type, I reminded myself. He was talented, nice, normal, and a gentleman. All qualities I'd never been known to attract.

Still, not thinking about June was making me feel better. I determined I'd concentrate on Travis and see if my mood improved a whole heck of a lot more. Decided it would.

"So, you going to tell me the plan of attack?"

I'd been so wrapped up in June and Ike Coleman, I hadn't told Travis my plan for the gun show. I did, however, have a good excuse to be there. Reaching for the duffle bag behind the seat, I unzipped it and pulled out the handgun I'd bought and hidden in there a while ago.

Showing Travis the vintage Mauser, I noticed he wasn't thrilled.

"Don't worry, I'm not planning on shooting the guy if we find him. Thought I'd go around, pretending I want to get an appraisal for this. Then I'd whip out the sketch, see if anyone recognizes this charmer." I was rather pleased with my simple but effective plan.

"And if they do? And this guy is as dangerous as you think he is? Then what?" He still sounded dubious.

"Then I call in the troops. Hell, Travis, those gun shows are filled with off-duty cops. If there's trouble, the cavalry will ride to the rescue."

"Just like they did for that guy whose head ended up in the river?"

He was still rattled by Darryl's death. I should have been.

"We don't know what happened to him, except he was shot. I'd bet he was dead before the decapitation."

"Charming image. Thanks so much." Reaching for a pair of sunglasses on the dash, Travis slipped them on.

"You're being a bit cavalier about this, aren't you, Tal? I mean, I guess you've seen things like murder in your practice before, but this guy didn't just die. He was, well," he swallowed hard, "mutilated like someone meant to send a message. You know, like those lynchings back in the bad ole days. Black guys strung up then sliced and diced while they twisted on the town oak tree. That sort of thing."

I hadn't thought of that. "Oh, Lordy. Do you think?"

"Think what?" Travis frowned. "I'm trying *not* to think about it, if you want the truth. I deal in beauty, in the way light hits satin, the arch of a neck. I don't like the ugliness of death. I've hated death for so long, I take it personally."

"Wow, I never knew you felt like that." I was taken aback.

All I could think was that his sister's and mother's deaths had hit him hard, and his father's must have been devastating. Yet he continued to work, producing stellar portraits that would make him immortal one day. Flirting didn't include talk about death in the normal course of events, but I hadn't flirted in a long time anyway. I ran with it.

"I guess I see death as part of life. It's like you have to take the rotten with the wonderful parts. A balancing act of sorts, like a juggler." All except Parnell Moses, who'd met his death before his time because I'd been incompetent.

Travis drove in silence, leaving me to wonder if I dared ask how his sister and mother had died when I was in college. I was a sucker for a challenge.

"What happened to them? Your sister, mom? I don't think I ever heard."

Travis's fingers beat a silent tattoo on the steering wheel.

"Got rear-ended by an eighteen wheeler. Didn't know what hit 'em." His voice was flat.

"You and your dad must have been destroyed."

Travis shrugged. "I was in college. Dad had to handle it without me. Getting the funeral arranged, all that. I flew home for the service, left the next day."

I thought a minute. "I don't remember your sister that well. Your mom, though, she had hair like yours, didn't she?"

Straightening, Travis grasped the wheel tightly and accelerated. I guessed we were doing eighty.

"Yes." His throat squeezed out the word. "My dad lost it, the day we buried her. I was too busy getting my life going, and he was gradually letting go. That's why I owe your grandmother big time."

"Oh?" Another tale of her generosity, I assumed. Miss Ena was generous to a fault with the faults of others. Mine, on the other hand, were always front and center.

"Somehow, she got Dad going again. Had him back on his tractor that spring, plowing like he meant it."

"I'm glad." And I was. Miss Ena had a knack that had been left out of my gene pool for the correct thing to do at the right time.

I thought changing the subject might change the mood.

"Why'd you come back? To Wynnton? Can't be much of a market here for your line of work."

His tone lightened. "Where I keep my studio is irrelevant. I travel to meet my clients, do some preliminary work, take a few photos, get the grunt work done in my studio." He paused. "Got tired of big cities. Noise. Hassles like where to park." He shrugged. "When Dad died, I felt this," he paused, "longing. For home. Like, if I were here, I'd keep their memories alive. All three of them, so I don't feel alone."

Travis didn't have the usual extended family all over Wynnton and its surrounding counties. Nor did I. I knew how he felt.

"The same with me and Miss Ena's house. She'll always be there, not that it's such a good thing to feel like she's looking over my shoulder all the time." I shoved my sunglasses up my nose. I was seldom this honest with anyone, even myself.

"So why'd you come home?" Those blue eyes were giving me a look that should have been fixed on the road.

"Long, long story. Maybe someday." I could go only so far and no further with Travis. "Bottom line, I guess it's home. No matter how much I hate it, hate the way Wynnton never changes, I understand what's going on."

"Know what you mean." He tapped the sketch pad on my legs.

Travis deserved a say in this junket, I decided. "Is there anything you'd like to see, other than the gun show?"

"You, naked. We'd make mad, passionate love in the Jefferson Hotel, have dinner at a five-star restaurant, drink some very good champagne, and make love again." He slipped me a glance from the corner of his eye. At least he was smiling.

I swallowed hard. "Not bad, not bad at all. But I'm not drinking these days."

"Okay, I'll take care of the rest, then." We merged into traffic.

"Very tempting offer." I was more than tempted, I wanted to slide over beside him and run my hand up his thigh, quiet the tapping hand, drape it over my shoulder and slip it down my shirt. "But I think I'll have to take a rain check. Until this is over. I've got to find out if June's telling the truth about that antique gun."

"Damn. And I thought my charms were irresistible." At least he pretended to laugh. "Women all over the world have thrown themselves at my feet, and you decide to say 'no, thank you, maybe later.'" He didn't sound bitter, just lonely.

"Actually I didn't say 'no, thank you,'" I teased him. "But I will if that's what you want."

"I knew I should have gotten you into my studio before I propositioned you. A woman posing gets very, very bored. She's more pliable, more open to, how shall I say it?

Suggestions of a carnal sort?" Flicking on the turn indicator, he accelerated on the ramp onto I-95.

"I didn't say I wasn't open to carnal suggestions. Just that I need to find out about this guy, whoever he is."

"Ah, the other man. Story of my life." He wasn't joking.

I wasn't good at this kind of thing, this sharing of the soul. I guess that's why I was reluctant to pose for Travis, I didn't want my soul exposed for the world to see. He must have sensed my pulling back. His eyes caught mine before they returned to the interstate.

"I was married, briefly. English girl, lovely shoulders, exquisite skin. Looked like pearls in moonlight. Married in haste, repented quickly. At least, she did. Took off one day with an art dealer who'd been buying a lot of my bad landscapes." A self-deprecating laugh followed, hollow and still angry. "I think I was more upset at losing my model than my wife. But that's the extent of the ugliness in my life. How about you?"

For a second, I almost told him about my incompetence in court that had cost a man his life. But I didn't want to share that with him, not now. I cared what Travis thought of me, and I wasn't willing to risk his disdain.

"If you mean have I ever married, the answer's no. Never found the right man." I hadn't found anyone to match my memories of Jack Bland is what I should have said, but Travis knew Jack. I'd finally doused that torch, but not until recently.

"And the right man married the wrong woman?"

So he did remember how I'd been jilted. Such an old-fashioned word, jilted. But apropos. Everyone in Wynnton knew how Jack had married Alma instead of me.

"No, the wrong man married the right woman for him. End of story."

"I'm glad to hear it." This time he smiled as if he meant it. "And the offer still stands. A night of wicked pleasures is yours any time."

"Wicked pleasures. Hmmm, that's more like it," I laughed in return. "Wicked is my middle name."

We rode in quiet for a bit, each of us reluctant to disturb the easy camaraderie we'd achieved. I was feeling flushed and flattered, and I hoped he felt the same. We stopped for lunch at a burger place next to a gas station, sharing a milk shake with the fries. I felt like a teenager again, in the beginning moves of that complicated and intricate mating dance that's so easy to misstep.

Travis pulled onto 295 as we approached the outskirts of the city. "I think, if I remember my misspent youth at the NASCAR races at the fairgrounds, that we take the Laburnum exit."

"That's what the map said that I checked last night. There's probably somewhere to stay near the gun show."

"I can't interest you in the Jefferson? They have great room service."

"I'm not going to ask how you know. Nah, I think the Budget Motel will do me just fine." I waved my plastic card, pulled from my pocket. "And I'm paying."

"I guess I won't object to being a kept man. Not this once." Travis slowed down as we entered an industrial area.

A sign pointed the way to the fairgrounds, while another big billboard advertised the weapons show. My stomach churned, just as it did before a big trial. I was in unknown territory here, and so much depended on the answers I found. I stuffed the Mauser in my purse.

"I hope you have a concealed weapons permit," Travis noted dryly.

"Damn, I don't. What'll I do?"

"Give it to me to carry. I have one."

"You do?" I was never so surprised in my life. "What on earth for?"

"Oh, I travel a lot, places I don't feel very safe. I know how to use a gun, I just don't want to." He slowed down at a stoplight. "See any motels?"

I didn't. "How about we check out the gun show, then find a place to spend the night?" I really didn't want to think of fun with Travis at this moment, although it was a severe temptation.

"Okay." Travis sounded less than enthusiastic. "How about this. We look for the guy while you're flashing the Mauser, show the sketch if we come up empty-handed. Got a story about why we want this dude?"

"Give me a sec." I thought fast. "How about he's my no-count husband and ran off with some piece of poor white trash, and I want to serve him with divorce papers?"

"Naw," Travis countered, "guys stick together. They won't tell you where he is if you put hot matches under their thumbnails, if that's the story you're using. Got a better idea."

"Yeah, right," I snipped. "Let's hear it."

"I'm a gun dealer and I want to find this guy because I hear he has a collection I've been searching for. Friend of mine saw him at another show, one in Manassas, let's say. I flash some cash, say I'm paying anyone who tells me how to find this paragon of virtue."

"Oh, you're good," I admitted. "Very good. Where'd you learn to think like that?"

"I grew up in Wynnton, remember? I'm a guy. You learn stuff like that when you combine the two."

"Ah, the good ole boys' club. I forgot," I snarled sarcastically. "I didn't think you ever played those games."

"I didn't. But I knew how." Travis pulled into the lot in front of the exhibition halls. "We're here. Time to rock and roll."

I handed him the Mauser. "What do I do?"

"You play the little woman. You know, kinda dumb but adoring. Pretend you don't know a damned thing about guns, you're just there to hang onto me and stare at me like I'm God's gift. Meanwhile, keep your eyes open and look around."

I whistled in appreciation. "Adoring, huh?"

"Nothing less." Winking, he opened the door. "By the way, my name's Sammy, and yours is, let me see." He thought a moment. "Brenda Jo."

"God give me strength," I moaned. "I don't think I can do this."

"Sure you can," he encouraged, handing me down from the truck.

The heat rising from the blacktop struck me full force. Reality was this, a hot day at an old fairgrounds where we hoped to find the man June said gave her a vintage revolver, which probably killed her husband.

The fairgrounds had seen better times. Caked with enough layers of paint to keep the framework standing long after the wood underneath had turned to dust, the buildings looked as if they'd been used and used hard. A steady stream of men, dressed in a uniform of shirts from Wal-Mart and jeans, filed into the largest building.

"I guess I can do this after all." Leaning my hip into his, I slid my left hand into his back left pocket. Grinning, I squeezed flesh through the denim. "Whatever you say, sugar. I just can't do a thing without you, you wonderful big hunk of man, you." My accent would have melted ice on a cold day.

"You got that right, baby." Travis matched me drawl for drawl. "Let's find our man."

I think I have, I told myself. The thought was so frightening my hands chilled and I forgot for one second to wiggle my hips as we walked to the booth to buy our entrance tickets.

Then I remembered. I had to find out if June was telling me the truth about this man who gave her the Colt. One thing at a time, I reminded myself.

One step at a time. In everything.

Chapter 11

⚜

ENTRY fees paid, hands stamped, Travis rolling on his heels like a man who regularly wore boots, we sashayed into the weapons show like we knew what we were doing. I'd stuck Travis's sketch, folded carefully, in my purse and slung it over my shoulder. If I'd had any sense at all, I'd have run for the hills hell bent for leather.

Tables jammed the exhibition hall. The smell of old popcorn and corn dogs permeated the air like some redneck perfume, vying with the scent of gun oil and metal and managing to hold its own. I'd never seen so many guns, rifles, and God knows what else, spread in all their wicked glory. The show where I'd bought the Mauser had been half the size of this one. I sensed this was where the big business took place.

Travis and I drifted along the outer aisles, stopping for general looks, smiling when a dealer asked if we were looking for anything special, chatting about the Mauser at the booths with antique guns. Travis spewed the right kind of lingo, the tobacco-stuffed-cheek language of men who believed God in heaven had his finger on a trigger and "lock and load" on His lips. I'd never have guessed he could slip into the role so effortlessly.

I did my job, which was to smile until my teeth ached, keep my mouth shut, and look around. I studied lots of plaid shirts, more beards and moustaches than I could count, about as many goatees, and not a sensual pair of lips that resembled the ones in Travis's sketch.

I snapped to attention when I heard Travis say casually, "I'm looking for a .36 Colt, the 1851 model. The same kind that killed Jesse James."

How the hell did he know that kind of trivia, I wondered. The dealer he was speaking with, whose name tag read "Horace Wimpole," of all things, shrugged.

"Check the Civil War guys in the third aisle. Better luck over there, I'd say."

Travis thanked him, and sliding his arm around my waist, steered us in the right direction.

"I'm not recognizing anyone," I muttered, pretending to whisper sweet nothings in his ear.

"June should have come along. We could have dressed her up like God knows what. Let her find him."

I laughed. "That'd be the day. Besides, I don't want to chance scaring the guy into a rabbit. June's hard to miss, even dressed as plainly as a nun."

Travis was doing a quick study of the third aisle, keeping me close. "This is where we'd find anyone selling antique guns, for sure."

"You want me to run to the washroom, give you free rein?" I'd sensed some of the dealers checking me out while Travis was trying to pump them for information. A desperate lot, if they found me attractive.

"Naw, I may need you. What'll we be now, Civil War reinactors? Know enough to carry it off?"

"Not on your life. But I'm game. How 'bout we're just starting out, we need everything?"

"That'll do the trick. Bring any of that cash from the bracelet with you?"

I nodded. "Thought we might need to pay for information."

"Buying a gun or two might get a few more mouths going. The Mauser hasn't worked."

He was right. The Mauser had invoked mild interest, nothing more.

"Let 'er rip. Think we can keep it under a grand?"

"I have no idea. Wish we had Isham Epps with us."

"Who's he?" I whispered as we hesitated before choosing a dealer.

"My last client. The portrait I just sent off. Has a great collection of stuff like this."

"Damnation. You mean you know an expert on antique guns, and I haven't talked to him?"

"Keep it down," Travis hissed. "There's time. Let's see if we can find your man first." Travis picked a table and aimed for it, me in tow.

We touched the objects on the table sparingly. A face, young and angular, collar too tight in a pale uniform, stared back at me from a daguerreotype. Bullet molds, display racks, extra cylinders for Colt revolvers, rifles arranged by date of production, filled the booth. Patch kits, skin cartridges, and pepper boxes lined the side. I was in awe of the history of man's ability to destroy.

"Looking for a Navy Colt, .36 caliber," Travis drawled after we'd stared at the goods enough. "Friend of mine said it's what I need to get going with my reenacting."

The dealer, a large man with full beard, perked up immediately. "You know it was manufactured here in the States until 1873, don't you? Lots of variations on the theme. Colt tinkered with it through the years, not to mention the ones finished up in England. How good a model you looking for and what year specifically?"

I tensed. We didn't know enough about what we were doing.

"I'd say I'm looking for one of the first models."

"Ah, the 747? Where the barrel wedge passes through the open slot on the basepin and there's a retaining screw set underneath it?"

This guy didn't care what we knew. If he wanted to flash his knowledge to a pair of country bumpkins, I'd play along.

"Yeah, that's it, I think," Travis murmured in awe.

"Honey, now you buy the best," I batted at him.

"Those are hard to find." The dealer looked at us shrewdly. "I'd kill to get one of the first ones with that engraving on the cylinder with the Mexican and U.S. Navy fighting."

Travis chuckled. "Bet they're scarcer than hens' teeth."

"You betcha." The dealer scrutinized his stock intently. "Don't have anything like the 1851 model, but I've got a Dragoon. It's a few years earlier than the Navy model, and, 'course, it weighs two pounds more. That a factor for you?"

Frowning, Travis pretended to study his options. "Figure

I'd better stick with the Navy Colt. Know anyone selling one?"

Horace shrugged. I wondered how he came by his very British name when his accent was pure Carolina. "There's a guy I don't know much about, down at the end of this row, on the right. He's just started the circuit. Seems like he's got a lot of stock, though."

I fingered the daguerreotype of the soldier. "How much?"

He grinned. "For you little lady, a hundred."

I didn't dicker. "Wrap it up." I pulled a hundred dollar bill from my wallet and his eyes lit up even more.

"You need anything else, give me a call at my shop any time." Handing Travis his business card with one hand, he took my money with the other.

Taking the wrapped daguerreotype, I stuck it in my purse against the folded sketch. I told myself I was paying Horace for being a good guy and not trying to sell us a fake revolver, and that we owed him for steering us to another dealer. But the truth was, the bottom half of the face in the daguerreotype looked like Travis's sketch. At least it did to me.

I didn't tell Travis any of this as we fought our way through the crowd to the dealer Horace had pointed out. We found out why he was so popular when we finally elbowed our way to the front.

This guy had great stuff and a lot of it. Even I, in my ignorance, was in awe of the engraving on the rifles, the inlaid stocks, the perfect quality of his merchandise. He not only sold first-rate weapons, they'd been well cared for before today. The cleaning oil beside the dealer's chair testified to his care.

He had that lean, hungry look of a man who never got enough to eat, but probably ate a barn and a half every day.

Not young, maybe in his early thirties, his eyes studied every shopper with a shrewdness that lacked camaraderie. Brown hair cropped short, tan showing through the stubbly edges at the base of his neck, he was nothing like the sketch of the man June described.

Travis went into his spiel. The dealer wore his identification tag so his collar covered the top half. But his name was readable—Fitch Canuette.

"Got an 1860 model," he drawled in a strangely flat voice, reminding me of the hill people in the Carolinas. "Close as I can get ya."

"Thanks anyway," Travis smiled. "Got a card? I'll give you a call if I change my mind."

"Nope." Canuette didn't return Travis's smile. "You want me, come on back here."

"Okay." Travis's smile faded. "Well, thanks anyway."

"Wait," I interrupted. "Can I see that case, please?" Its gaudy colors caught my eye from the corner of a locked glass display box. Something about it seemed familiar.

Acting annoyed, Canuette unlocked the padlock and handed the piece to me. Unclasping it, I opened it carefully. The cloisonné work was exquisite, and I'd have bet Miss Ena's house that diamond chips had been worked into the outer border. Inside, it once held pictures in two faded velvet mats. The glass was long gone.

"What is this?" I asked innocently. I had an idea, but I'd need to confirm it with someone who knew.

"Held photos," Canuette answered with an edge to his voice. "It's not old."

"Looks it." I pulled out my daguerreotype. "Oh look, honey, this'll fit right in here, won't it?" I held the picture up to the box. "Can I have it, please, sweetie?"

"It's not for sale." Canuette's fingers snaked it from my hand before I could stop him. But I'd seen enough.

"Then why's it in here?" I gestured at the booth.

"Already sold it, holding it for the man," Canuette snapped. "Now, can I help you?" He turned to glance at another customer.

Canuette stared at me as Travis turned to pull me away into the crowd. I'd never before understood the expression about the hairs on the back of your neck standing on end, but I did now.

"Where next?" Jostled by the thickening crowd, I grabbed Travis's arm.

"He hadn't sold that cloisonné piece," I muttered.

Travis looked puzzled. "Why'd he say he had then?"

"Don't know, but my guess is it's a Russian piece. You know, like those Fabergé eggs the czar's family gave each other all the time? I'd bet that case is worth you and me put together."

"Speak for yourself." Travis looked unimpressed. "So what does it matter if it's Russian?"

"June's husband gave her a diamond ring that happened to be czarist. Most of its value is from its history. I'd say the same thing about that picture case."

Travis smiled brightly at me as if I'd just suggested we head to a motel and make wild, passionate love. "Gonna be hard to link the two, isn't it? Besides, I thought we were looking for someone who knows about the .36."

"We are. But they're connected, bet my bottom dollar on it." When a hare-brained idea hops into my head, I can't ignore it. Craziness was becoming my forte.

"If they are, there's no way he'll tell us that. So what do we do next?"

"Guess we try everyone, give 'em the same line. Word'll work its way down the rows that we're buying. End of the day, we'll end up back here." Travis thought I'd lost it.

In fact, I was hot and tired and we hadn't been at this for an hour. But we plugged on, doing our act, spinning our tale. I had to credit Travis with more stick-to-it-ness than I'd credit many a man. But by the end of the last dealer, we were nowhere and I had a splitting headache. I'd been ogled, ignored, and had my toes trod upon so often I was aching to kick the next assailant in the shins.

"Time to quit," I announced, dragging Travis toward the exit. "I need caffeine and something to hit."

"As long as it isn't me." He looked as tired as I felt.

The snack bar was still open. I'd noticed, as the day turned into night and closing time drew near, more uniformed Henrico County police around the perimeters and the two exits. Business had been brisk inside the exhibition hall. I'd bet they were keeping a close eye on the folks who'd bought a small arsenal. But most of the crowd consisted of ordinary folks who enjoyed looking more than buying. Travis and I weren't conspicuous in our lack of purchases of anything with a firing pin.

"Two hamburger specials," I requested when our turn came to order. "Everything on both burgers."

Balancing the paper plates loaded with fries and huge hamburgers reeking of onions, as well as large red paper cups filled with still-bubbling sodas, we searched in vain for an empty plastic table.

"Looks like we'll have to go outside," Travis sighed. "I'm used to standing for hours while I paint, but I bet you'd like to sit down."

"We can sit in the truck, watch when they close the place

up." I checked my watch. "Should clear out in thirty minutes. I wanna see where that Canuette guy goes."

I was ready to bet it all on Canuette. The luscious smell of cholesterol and junk food made me hungrier still. "If I don't eat something soon, you're going to have to find a bar and ply me with liquor."

"This is better for you. All that vitamin C in those onions." Travis shoved the main door open with his shoulder.

I slipped a fry into his mouth. "Keep your strength up, boy, you're going to need it."

The huge parking lot was lit with eerily glowing fluorescent lights, giving the sea of cars an odd, other-worldly tinge. We cut left, dodged between the portable barriers set up to keep folks from parking right by the front door, aiming for the truck. A few people drifted out behind us, but I didn't take much notice. The hamburger was smelling better than good by the minute. Taking a nibble, I felt some energy surging back.

"I think I'll live after all," I started to tell Travis when something knocked me on my face.

My first thought was that I'd tripped and looked like an idiot who couldn't keep her feet under her. I'd smacked chest first in a subconscious attempt to keep my food from spilling, and I tried to catch my breath without much success for what seemed like an awfully long time.

I was just starting to panic when I hauled some air into my lungs. My second thought was what the hell happened to Travis. The lack of oxygen had roared in my ears, but now I could hear a few grunts, some thuds, and what sounded like a laugh.

What's he doing kicking the truck tires? I wondered. "Travis?" Struggling to my hands and knees, I tried to see what was going on. The fall must have gashed my forehead, however, because I had wet, sticky stuff in my eyes. Only as I tried to wipe it away, did I notice it was the soda.

By now I was pissed. What the hell was he doing? My hands gouged by the loose stones on the blacktop, my jeans' knees ripped even more, and not feeling all too sound of ribs, I wanted someone to rescue me and make soothing sounds. *Ah, how quickly the mighty fall when there's a man around,* I noted abstractly.

The bundle that twisted and turned beside the driver's side of the truck looked so strange to me I almost wondered what it was. Then it groaned and rolled, and I realized it was Travis's white shirt covered with dark stains.

"Oh my God, Travis," I cried, hobbling around the front of the truck.

He groaned, writhing on the ground like a slinky toy. "What the hell?" At least he was able to talk.

"Hold on, I don't know, let me get some help."

He grabbed my ankle. "Stay here," he hissed. "Get the Mauser out."

"What?" I couldn't imagine why he wanted my antique pistol.

"We've been mugged, for Christ's sake! Get out the Mauser!"

I'd slipped it into my purse after the last showing of it to a blasé dealer. "Where'd they go? Who did this?"

"Tal! Just do it!" He was suddenly very still.

I fumbled for my purse, running my hands over the blacktop where I'd tumbled. I found the hamburger and plate, the remains of my drink. But no purse. I limped back to Travis.

"It's gone. My purse and everything in it."

"Damn. Now they'll know your name and where you live."

"Why on earth would anyone want the Mauser?" It was a collectible, at least I thought so, and a nice gun for a woman, but not that valuable compared to three-fourths of the stuff we'd seen inside.

"They didn't. God in heaven, I think they broke my ribs." He moaned more than convincingly.

"It's not loaded anyway, and it's a little late now to shove it in their faces." Sitting on the ground beside him, I pulled his head in my lap and tried to make soothing noises. "You want me to get a cop? Ambulance? I really should." I wasn't too sure of my Florence Nightingale abilities.

"No, give me a sec. I think they whacked me with a baseball bat. If I can't get up, you'll have to get help." His face was so pale, I could see the pain etched on it in the dark.

I touched his shirt front. Sticky and cold. Just soda, thank God. "How's it going?" I asked after a second.

"Not so hot, but I think I'll live." Staring at the sky, he blinked several times. "At least they didn't mess up my pretty face."

I had to laugh, but pain jerked me up short. "Damn, that hurts." I held my hands to my sides. Nothing broken.

"God Tal, why didn't you say so?" Struggling onto his side, Travis tried to sit up and failed.

"Hey, I'm not the one they kicked in addition to the baseball bat. I think they just wanted to snatch my purse, but you they wanted to immobilize. I musta played the little woman like a pro, if they thought you'd come running to my rescue." Pressing my hand to his forehead, I forced him to lie down again.

"I would have," he said softly. "If I didn't hurt so damned much right now, I'd kiss every boo-boo."

"Save your breath. The boo-boos are fine, mostly scraped knees and the palms of my hands." I held them up to the ambient light from the parking lot overheads. "What we need is a cop and a hot bath."

"The cop'll take too long, they'll haul us to a hospital first, and we'll never get out of there. I don't know about you, but I don't want to spend this weekend filling out forms and answering questions. I don't think they'd give us coed rooms, either."

I had to chuckle. A man with a sense of humor and common sense, albeit misguided, was a rarity.

"Look in my back pocket. Got a clean handkerchief. You could use it on your face."

I touched the scrapes, bleeding freely. "Okay," I mumbled, reaching around him to pull out the cloth. I didn't use it, just held it in my fist to keep my fingernails from cutting my palms as I tried to soothe the frightened beast within.

"Well, they got about fifty dollars in my purse. Most of the cash was in the truck, thank God. Think they were after money?"

"Nope." Struggling upward, Travis gestured for me to help him lean against the truck's front tire. "Well, maybe. We can hope."

"I had the rest of the cash for buying info stashed in my bra." I patted the wad resting where I should have had cleavage. "If you'd bought anything really expensive in there, I'd have had to run to the rest room first to get it out." I laughed.

"At least you weren't hurt. To hell with the money." He squeezed my hand.

"Well now, that's not too sensible. We'd have to sleep in the back of the pickup without it. They got my credit cards with my wallet."

He patted his hip. "They got mine, too. Guess that's what all that knocking me from here to Sunday was about." He coughed and groaned. "I suppose I'll have to be a kept man, living off your cash."

"Suits me just fine." I felt something sharp under my bottom, wiggled aside and pulled it out. "Here're the truck keys. We'd better see about getting a place to stay tonight. We can call from the motel about the credit cards."

Bending his knees gingerly, Travis let me slide my arms under him and help him rise, very slowly, to a full stand.

"That was worse than I thought," he gritted out between clenched teeth. "God, I hope I don't look as awful as you."

"Thanks for the flattery. You do." Opening the truck door, I helped him in. "I'll drive."

"Whatever your little heart desires." He coughed again, this time without the "ouch" accompaniment.

I gave a final thought to the cops at the entrance to the exhibit hall, and then ignored it. Travis was right, we'd never get my purse or his wallet back and all we'd do was waste time. I drove toward the airport and the string of motels. What I really wanted was a hot tub and a jacuzzi, but we settled on a Holiday Inn. The desk clerk wasn't too enthusiastic about our lack of credit cards, but I explained we'd been mugged at the fairgrounds and we needed to report the stolen items. At that he perked up, and said he'd find the numbers immediately and buzz the room when he had them. I guess it had been a slow and boring night so far, and we added some excitement.

Travis was still walking like an old man, and I felt like death warmed over. Shock was setting in, and I began to shiver as soon as we got up to the room. Travis hobbled into the bathroom while I threw our overnight bags on the bed.

At least I had a change of clothes. The sticky soda all over me was getting annoying.

Poking his head out the door, Travis was less pale, his freckles not quite as bright against his pale skin. "Water's hot. Wanna share?"

This wasn't my idea of the beginning of a romance. I debated the intricacies of what we were starting for about half a second.

"Sure," I answered, pulling my shirt over my head and dropping it on the floor. "But I get the soap first."

"Be my guest." His old grin was back, slightly wolfish, definitely devilish. "All I ask is that you take it easy on the ribs."

"Your every wish is my command," I replied as I dropped the jeans on the pile with my shirt.

"That'll be the day." Grinning even wider, he held the shower curtain aside for me and stepped in behind me.

I don't think I even noticed the water stinging my wounds.

We were clean and reasonably decent when the cops knocked at the door of our hotel room. Lying side by side on the king-size bed, holding hands, and staring at each other like teenagers, we considered ignoring the whole thing. We hurt too much to spring to our feet and answer the door.

I was the one who cracked first. Those Henrico police had hard knuckles. "Coming," I shouted, climbing off the bed like a hundred-year-old woman. "Ouch," I complained.

"Double ouch," Travis echoed, swinging his feet to the floor. "One of these days, I'll feel human again, then watch out, Talbot Jefferson. You won't be safe."

"Promises, promises," I teased as I unlocked the door

after checking the peephole. "Come on in," I invited the policeman standing in the hallway, looking annoyed.

We went through our story, the officer made notes, took our names and addresses, and I'm sure considered himself lucky to get such an easy shift.

"There's just about no chance we'll get your wallet and purse back," he offered solemnly.

I leaned back on the bed and shut my eyes. "That's encouraging." My knees and the palms of my hands hurt like hell.

"And I'd recommend you cancel those credit cards as soon as possible. Alert your bank to the check numbers in your purse, ma'am. Get your keys changed. Your address was on your license, whoever got it can find you."

"If they want to drive to South Carolina," I groaned. "Desperate bunch to go that far."

"Well, it's your problem," the officer snapped, annoyed at my lack of concern. "If there's any news, I'll contact you."

"Thank you."

Travis was being the polite one, I noticed. What a suckup. "We'll let you know if we remember anything else."

"You do that," the officer mumbled as he let himself out the door.

I slid the chain on it after him.

"Alone at last," Travis grinned, then winced. "And too tired and banged up to do anything about it."

"Well, at least I can dream." I pulled the sheet up and fluffed a cheap pillow.

Travis flicked off the lights. The darkness hummed with the air-conditioning. His weight on the other side of the bed was like a tantalizing promise. I began to count the years since I'd actually slept beside a man, and not just used a bed for a playground, which I abandoned as soon as I'd gotten my jollies. I quit when the number was disgraceful.

"Tal?" He sounded sleepy.

"Hmm?" I didn't want to break up my self-flagellation with chitchat.

"I should paint you nude. To hell with any clothes at all."

"Dream on," I laughed, rolling carefully on my side and patting his arm. "I like a man with imagination."

He was asleep so fast, for a second I felt bereft. I'd always envied people who could drop off no matter how awful the day had been, how much horror had invaded their lives. *He must,* I thought, *be sleeping the sleep of the innocent.* How I wished.

I lay awake, thinking about the man stretched beside me, snoring lightly. No sense in wishing I'd met him earlier, I'd known him for half my life. I liked him. An odd admission for me, who seldom found anyone to like and only a few to tolerate. If he hung in there much longer, I might even cross over that line I'd drawn a long time ago. I might trust him. The thought gave me the willies, and I reached down to pull up the rubbery blanket.

Travis rolled over and draped an arm across my hip, snoring even more deeply. I scooted closer to him and absorbed his warmth, the way he smelled of hotel soap and wet hair. No, he wasn't a handsome man by current standards, but he was interesting. I'd take interesting any day.

Chapter 12

⚛

THE drive back to Wynnton was less hopeful. We both hurt more than the night before, and without any sex to salve our wounds, we wisely kept our mouths shut and drove in silence. Promising Travis I'd sit for his painting soon, I waved him off and took the Mustang to the bank. Henry left so many messages on my machine, I knew immediately what had happened. Robert E. wasn't home either, which meant Henry must have taken him when June was arrested. Making arrangements with the bank manager to wire the bracelet money to the court account on my verbal authorization, I headed next for Braidwood's office.

My bruises were nice and purple. I tried to hide the ones on my legs by wearing the one pair of tailored slacks I owned. My face, however, looked as if I'd been in a car wreck. Good thing I wasn't terribly vain. I didn't own any makeup to cover them with.

"Is Guy available?" I breezed through the pebbled glass door of the prosecutor's office. The young thang who'd held the secretary's position under Owen Amos was gone, replaced by a woman who looked vaguely familiar.

Graying hair the color of gun metal, skin that had seen too much sun in her younger years, she wore the flowered polyester dress that middle-aged women favor because it has an elastic waist and a belt to hide the fact.

"Do you have an appointment?" she asked with a stress and intonation pattern long accustomed to superiority.

"Tell Guy I want a bail hearing for June Atkins, and I want it now." I'd take odds he'd waited until he knew I was out of town to arrest her. His office door cracked open.

"No need." Guy's face was all innocence and amiability. "Magistrate set it at a hundred grand. Too low for murder, but Henry Rolfe was there rooting for her." A flicker of distaste crossed his face.

"Whoopee. I assume it's a federal murder charge?"

"No, ma'am." He looked too pleased with himself. "The head was found in Talmadge County. We took precedence."

My mouth tasted like I'd drunk Dr. Pepper gone bad. "I'll bet the feds aren't too happy with you."

"Oh, we'll share."

I knew what that meant. There'd be federal weapons charges, all sorts of things tacked onto the counts in the land of Uncle Sam to make sure she went from Wynnton's courtroom directly to the one on base where she'd be prosecuted again.

Reaching for the battle axe's phone, I picked it up without asking, hit "9," and dialed my bank. "Mrs. Conway, will you please wire those funds as we discussed? Yes, a hundred grand. Directly to the court. Thanks, this is Tal Jefferson, of course." Gently, I settled the phone in the cradle.

Guy looked stunned. "Where'd you get money like that?" he blurted before he could stop himself.

Half the town thought I was impoverished, the way I slaved on restoring Miss Ena's house all by myself. The other half just thought I was nuts and sitting on her money. Braidwood believed I'd fenced the stolen goods for the cash. The truth was all over him like mud on a hog.

"See you later," I tossed over my shoulder as I breezed out of the office, ignoring his question.

I'd give the wire transfer a while to settle into the court's account, then I'd spring June. She was probably as mad as a hornet, but I couldn't get her out without the proper paperwork wending its way to the jail, and that'd take a few hours.

Before I got her out, I had to talk to Mrs. Coleman again. Her lies about June and Coleman's truck didn't make sense. Why would she help her husband by pointing to June as the person with possession of the construction company truck? Dislike was too tame a word for Mrs. Coleman's feelings for her philandering spouse. Why people who felt that way about each other stayed married, I'd never understand. Divorce was cheaper than hate. I just couldn't put it together in my head, and I was bewildered by the feeling.

Driving my Mustang helped clear the fuzzies out of my brain. Travis had a great deal to do with my unclear thoughts, I feared. That 289 small eight would work its magic. Putting the pedal to the metal, I flew out of Wynnton proper into the new suburbs where pines and tobacco fields had been scraped clear to throw up vinyl siding and modern taste.

Mrs. Coleman wasn't at home. Her SUV was gone, and as I thought about what to do next, I remembered she said she did hair at the Grande Dame. June, I'd bet, spent a bundle there getting her nails done. I wondered if Mrs. Coleman knew my June was the woman her husband was sneaking out to at night. Mrs. Coleman knew the house, vaguely remembered a clue to June's first name, but maybe not her face. Not much got past that woman, was my bet.

I drove some more, still not thinking clearly. I thought I saw Travis passing me going the other direction on 17, and almost turned around to follow him. Another glance showed the truck was the wrong year, wrong model. Not his. Damnation, I wanted to see him again so badly I could taste his kisses. *Focus on driving. Pay attention to the speed limit, Tal,* I warned myself. Think about June. Ike Coleman. Why now? There are no coincidences. Miss Ena had taught me that.

Sure enough, the Grande Dame was doing a raging business. Set in a strip mall with a defunct bookstore, a discount women's clothing chain, and a sub sandwich shop, it was by far the biggest establishment in the strip. I paused outside, gazing through the glass front at the bevy of women getting hair and nails done. Opening the door, I hesitated. I hated places like this. The level of noise from the blow dryers and female chatter would drive me to deafness in a week.

"Can I help you?" The receptionist stared at me as if I'd crossed the border into a foreign country and didn't have my passport. I guessed my hair showed off its home-styling.

"I'm looking for Mrs. Coleman." Quickly glancing around, I didn't see her anywhere.

"She's not scheduled to come in until noon. Can I make an appointment for another day? I'm afraid she's booked solidly through the end of the week." When hell froze over, her expression said. The receptionist didn't like me at first glance.

"No, thanks." There was no way I'd catch Mrs. Coleman this morning. "Just tell her Tal Jefferson wants to talk to her. I'm her husband's lawyer, in case she doesn't recognize the name."

There, I thought, that would give me a little credibility, I hoped. The receptionist just blinked at me, and said, "Sure," like she believed me as much as she believed in the tooth fairy.

Back in the Mustang, I checked my watch. I figured I had another thirty minutes before I had to pick up June and start trying to calm her down. Thinking about it, I didn't have much ammo in that gun. The weekend, except for the delightful discovery about Travis, had been pretty much of a dead end. My instincts said the dealer, Fitch Canuette, knew something about the Russian stuff that had been ripped off, but that and a dollar and a quarter would get me a cup of coffee. And not the fancy kind. Just a plain ole cup at Becky's.

I needed to think. Feeling good about Travis had put me off my game, and I had to find that groove again, that hard and lonely place that led me to the truth. I didn't much like it down there, but I had to drop back into it.

The Mustang must have steered itself to the spot where I usually parked when I wanted to river-watch. Strangely, I didn't remember much about how I got there, except my thinking about Darryl Henshaw's death. Once I was pulled into the little turnoff that held the car without revealing it to the road, I sat and wondered why I was there.

Back where it all started, I guessed. I wanted a bottle in

my hand to help my thoughts wander where they would, but I settled for slamming the car door and hiking up the incline to the promontory where I could see the bend in the river to my left, the rise of Wynnton's semicivilization to my right.

We're all fools, I thought. *Such fools*. June looking for love with a married man with a piranha of a wife, me mooning over Travis Whitlock like some fifth-grader with a crush, Guy Braidwood trying to pull a fast one on me just to prove he's the *man,* all the good folk of Wynnton fooling around with their lives as if no one would ever know the worst about them if they went to Wednesday night supper and church every Sunday morning.

I didn't want to sit on the ground and ruin the slacks. Red clay stains never came out, they were stronger than blood once they got ground into fabric. I wondered about the clothing Darryl Henshaw's body was found wearing, and whether or not it carried the red clay of Wynnton soaked into its seams.

I stopped longing for a drink and another life the minute I realized Henry hadn't reported anything on Darryl's clothing. Henry hadn't done the report, of course, but he'd have told me if there'd been physical evidence to tell where Darryl had been killed.

Jerking the cell phone from my purse, I dialed Henry's medical office. His receptionist said he was at the morgue, she'd put me through. Whose body did he have now, I wondered.

"Tal." Henry sounded distracted. "This isn't a good time."

"What's up?" I could pry anything out of Henry. "Grace is pissed at me for letting June get locked up while I was out of town? Don't worry, I've got the wheels turning to get her sprung. I'll be by to get my dog later."

"It's not that. I've got another body. A woman named Coleman. She was shot in her husband's truck sometime last night."

My first thought was to pray that June had been incarcerated already whenever Henry determined Mrs. Coleman had died. Next, my hands turned icy. No coincidences. None. They never happened. Miss Ena had never been wrong.

"Did the truck have a sign on the side? One of those magnetic ones. Coleman Construction?"

"That's what I hear. How'd you know?"

I ignored his question. "Where was she found?" I tried to sound casual, but Henry knew differently.

"What's it matter?" I could imagine Henry shoving his glasses up higher on his nose.

I hesitated. "I just wasted time today trying to find the woman."

"Does this have something to do with June?" Smart man, Henry. Smarter than most.

"Yes."

"I don't want to know, do I?"

"No, but you will. Just not from me, and not right now."

"Okay. That dirt road that's out near the Whitlock place. The one that goes around their east field, winds back to the old water tower, that one that's been out of use for twenty years."

"Tell me, was June still free when she died? Can you tell me that much?" I held my breath.

"Hard to say right now. I'm still working on narrowing the time of death. Been pretty warm the past few nights."

Henry wasn't being coy, I knew that. He was a careful pathologist, an even more careful doctor.

"This won't be easy for you, Henry. June's family, after all." I owed him a warning.

He didn't even hesitate. "I've got a job to do, Tal, you know that. I speak for the dead, not the living." His voice was hard. I'd been reprimanded.

"I know," I sighed. "I'm getting June out in a few minutes, but before I do, I'd like to see the truck. Where is it?"

"Far as I know, it's impounded downtown. I don't think they had it hauled to the state lab yet."

"Thanks. I'll see you later." I started to click off. "Henry, what size bullet killed her?"

"That I can tell you. I just removed a .44 lead bullet from her brain." He paused. "Close range. Went through her brain stem. She died instantly."

I thought of the plethora of guns filling the fairgrounds exhibition hall in Richmond. "Not easy to trace, huh?"

"I'd bet not, not without more to go on." He hesitated. "Tal, June didn't have any more old guns that Darryl gave her, did she?"

"God, I hope not." I sucked in my breath. "And if she did and she didn't tell me, she can rot in jail until her trial."

"I knew she was there, of course. But she said she'd wait it out, when Grace and I said we'd put up our house to bail her out. She wouldn't hear of it."

"That's odd, about the bail." I answered slowly, wondering why she wasn't willing to have Grace and Henry put their house at risk on her bond. "I really called to find out if there was any physical evidence on Henshaw's clothes to give a clue as to where Darryl Henshaw was murdered. You know, plant seeds, dirt, that kind of thing."

Henry was silent a bit. "Guess you'll find this out when you get the government's evidence. Nothing but some trace evidence, a few hairs, probably his. No plants, no pollen, no good old-fashioned dirt that didn't come from the spot where the body was found. It was like they killed him in some sterile room, then dressed his body in these immaculate clothes that had just come from the cleaners. The basic evidence recovered showed the body had been dumped on the post. He wasn't killed standing in a tobacco field or anything that simple, if that's what you want to know."

My mind stuck on the hairs on Darryl's clothing. They'd get a subpoena to get some from June's head, as sure as I wasn't a virgin.

"Tal?"

I'd been thinking, holding onto the phone without saying anything for too long. "Sorry, Henry, just trying to think it through. I'll catch up with you later." I punched the power-off button.

What the hell was Mrs. Coleman doing in her husband's truck? Had she been planning on hiding it so no one would ever find it? Or was she bringing it in, in a belated attempt to either screw her husband or June with the law, or to do him a good deed? The possibility of her behaving like an upstanding citizen and helping her husband at the same time didn't mesh.

I got my tail down to Frank's headquarters. Through the chain-link fence that held impounded cars, I could see the white pickup. The magnetic sign was still there.

The truck looked abnormally clean. Not many white pickups, especially those used in construction work, didn't have an impenetrable layer of clay caking the wheel wells at the very least. Turning, I searched for Frank and saw him coming toward me across the parking lot. I was already hot and cranky, and his expression didn't help any. He looked as pleased with himself as a man who's been offered a fresh pecan pie with whipped cream topping. All to himself.

"Counselor, you saved me the trouble of tracking you down."

I ignored the officious attitude. "At least you can't say my client killed her. He's still in your jail."

"Which one of your many?" He smiled, showing teeth that had soaked in too many sodas. "Not why I wanted a chat with you. Why don't you step inside my office, where we can be cool and comfortable?"

I owed Frank for saving my life. I'd be nice. "I already know where the truck was found. You wouldn't, by any slight chance, already have someone in custody, would you? Someone not already represented by me?" I was asking for a lot, but what the heck, a girl has to hope.

"Not hardly." Frank lost his good-ole-boy expression but not the accent. "All right, we can do it here. Mr. Braidwood says you posted a hundred grand in cash to get your secretary out of my fine facilities."

"Yeah, so what?" Why did I feel like a kid getting called on the carpet by the school principal?

"We need to talk." Turning, he seemed to expect me to follow him.

"Not unless you're going to tell me the bond was dropped and I get some of my money back."

Facing me again, Frank hooked his thick thumbs in the black leather holster that cinched his gut. "Well now, I guess you'd better tell me where you got that kind of money, Tal. 'Cause your secretary ain't gettin' out until I know. Got to investigate, Mr. Braidwood's expectin' some answers."

Frank was always dropping the last syllable of his words when he wanted to play his role to the hilt. It annoyed the hell out of me.

"None of your f'ing business. I didn't knock off a bank, if that's what you're trying, rather clumsily, to find out."

"Now, Tal, no need to get on your high horse. Your bank says you deposited the hundred grand in cash last Friday. Filled out all the federal forms to report it, just like you should. No record of any transfers from other accounts in your name. June Atkins was already found to possess a very expensive piece of stolen jewelry. You see where I'm headin', Tal?" He squinted at me in the bright sunlight, then seemed to realize I could read his beady little eyes.

Jerking his sunglasses from the front of his uniform, he slipped them quickly on his nose. Mosquito eyes stared back at me. Just like an annoying insect, Frank Bonnet. Most folks underestimated him. I no longer did.

"How'd you get a subpoena to examine my bank records?" I was furious. My business was already gone from SCB&T.

"Now you know we don't do business like that. Just a simple question, a simple answer will do. No need for a subpoena. Hell, I've known Andy Farmer all my life. Like I know you. Any time, Tal, I'd be right interested in hearing where you got that kind of cash." The sun caught the metallic studs on the gun belt.

I'd strangle Andy Farmer with my bare hands. I knew what was coming. Braidwood already thought June and I were fencing stuff for Darryl. He'd found out that I hadn't had any big cash withdrawals from my trust account. Hell, he probably knew how much I'd paid to gas up the Mustang that morning.

"I sold some jewelry, you son of a bitch. Tell Braidwood I'll have him in front of the state bar for an ethics complaint if he keeps this game going." Turning on my heel, I tried to march calmly for the Mustang. "Forget that, I'll tell him myself."

The pipsqueak was getting on my nerves. I wasn't thinking of what I'd do to Frank, just Braidwood when I got him in my very irritated clutches. So I was startled when Frank was beside the Mustang, his meaty hands leaning on my door, his bug eyes running the length of my classic Ford that needed some body work, but what the hell, that 289 engine was pure gold.

"Why don't you give me a description and then tell me where you sold it."

"Go to hell." I floored the Mustang, leaving Frank hopping aside to avoid losing his toes to my back wheels.

Fuming, I hauled ass for the jail. Time to tell Coleman the bad news if he didn't know already, then take June home. I started with Coleman. Braidwood could wait until I got my clients straight, then after I finished with him, I could go home and get a good night's sleep.

The guard looked at me like I was a bomb about to explode when I demanded to see Ike. I tried to settle my temper under its usual sarcasm, but it kept creeping out like goo from the black lagoon. How dare Frank pry into my affairs on the say-so of a nitwit like Braidwood? I paced the interview room, imagining my triumph when I had Braidwood eating grass at my feet, when Coleman sauntered into the room like a man who didn't have a care in the world.

I guessed no one had told him about his wife.

"Have a seat," I gestured to the wooden chair pulled up to a scarred, prison-made oak table. Phone numbers, obscenities, and names had been carved there by pens and fingernails. I ran my finger around a concentric circle deep in the grain.

"Got some bad news." I tried to forget about Frank and concentrate. "I just learned that your wife was found dead in your truck. I hate to tell you, but she'd been shot."

Coleman rocked back. "I heard already." His stocky, muscled arms bulged under the sleeves of the prison jumpsuit.

Surprised, I studied him. The hard-working good guy image had dissipated the minute I found out he'd been balling June and any number of other women. But I expected more tension from him than this relaxed, who-me-be-upset demeanor.

"You don't seem too bereaved." I waited while he thought about his answer.

"Guess I'm not. Got the bitch out of my hair. I'd thank whoever did it, if I knew."

I wished June could see this act. She'd be so turned off, she'd join a convent. "Do you have any ideas? Who did it?"

I was daring him to make up an elaborate story. The guilty usually did.

"Nope. Just hope my truck's okay." He studied his nails. I never noticed before how long he kept them. Cocaine users kept their little finger nail longer to scoop up the powder, but all of Coleman's were longer than fit with the image of a working man.

"I imagine there're some blood stains on the upholstery," I noted sourly. "And of course, the forensics people will do a number on the whole truck. Is it too much to hope they won't find paint from that Honda you hit?"

"Told you, I didn't hit her. Musta been that guy I lent the truck to. That Cool Dude."

Maybe time in jail had unlocked his memory, and he'd be

willing to volunteer more than he had last week. "Cool Dude have another name?"

He shrugged. "Not so's I'd remember."

I didn't believe him. So much for jail time shaking Ike up. I was thinking it was time to have Ike leaf through the mug shots. I'd know by his face if he recognized one of them.

He continued. "His name didn't come with the money or the van he loaned me while he had my truck. Didn't need to."

The smirk was there, thin but there nonetheless.

"What kind of van?" I stared at my notebook, where I'd drawn arrows from the van to Ike to Cool Dude to June, and they all came back to the same face. I wondered why he hadn't mentioned the loaner van the last time.

"One of those European kind. A Volkswagen, I think. Don't see 'em around here. Sure drove nice, and had this fancy alarm system. Gotta get me one of those."

I was going to kill June. She had worse taste in men than I, and that was saying a lot.

"Did June see you driving the van, when you lent Cool Dude your truck?"

"Heck no." He smiled the lazy, sensual smile of a man reliving pleasant memories. "We had better things to do than go running all over the countryside."

I stood abruptly. "I'll let you know what I hear about your wife's murder. I suppose it's too much to hope that you've made no phone calls, except to me, of course, since you've been in here."

Prison calls were easily traced. I was hoping against hope he hadn't called up a buddy and asked for a big favor. A really big favor he'd be able to pay once his uncooperative wife was rigor mortis in the front seat of his truck.

"Now why'd I be doing that? Calling you? Heck, I got business. Sure, I made a boatload of calls from here. No other way to keep my company running."

"Did your wife visit you in here?"

He face was so guileless, I knew I'd been had by a pro. "No, ma'am. She didn't like jails."

"I'll bet she loved them when you were in one." Slamming my legal pad in my briefcase, I rattled the bars of the interview cage to get myself unlocked.

Chapter 13

❧

I don't know why it's my lot in life to cruise in and out of jails. Maybe it's because I belong in one, but nothing's stuck long enough to get me in an ugly uniform with neon initials on the back for a stylish logo. "TCRJ" had a ring to it, but I don't think any designer stores sold the Talmadge County Regional Jail logo.

Fuming at the desk of the women's section of the jail, I demanded to know when June Atkins would be ready for release on her bond.

"Can't rightly say, ma'am." The deputy dripped with sarcasm as he addressed me as "ma'am." "Ain't got the paperwork yet."

"Give me the phone." I was going to call DeShazo if I had to. He was riding both circuits these days, he'd pull Braidwood into line.

"Tal, sorry about this." Frank was standing behind me,

looking strangely uncomfortable. "But I got a warrant for your arrest."

Well, I always knew it'd happen one day. I just didn't think it would be today. Or so fast.

"You're out of your everloving mind." I refused to believe him.

"Sorry, but I just got handed this." He slapped the yellow sheet of paper into my hand.

I studied it quickly. I was accused of felony possession of stolen goods.

"This is a crock, and you know it. Where's Braidwood? Sitting outside in his car, sniggering?"

Those telltale little red edges were creeping into my field of vision. I was about to lose my temper, an event which didn't happen often these days, but which had a reputation that sent those in Wynnton who knew me well cowering for cover in their storm cellars.

"You know the drill." Frank pulled my briefcase out of my hands and flung it on the counter. "Pat her down," he snapped at the desk officer. "Sorry, Tal, but I've got to give you your Mirandas." He proceeded to recite the litany, despite its jeopardy from the Fourth Circuit Court of Appeals, by rote.

I couldn't think who to call. None of my fellow members of the bar in Wynnton would be willing to come down to the jail and spring me. Much as I hated to do it, I had to drag Travis into this mess.

"Give me my phone," I demanded as the deputy finished feeling me up. I was so angry I hardly noticed. "I get a phone call."

"Sure," Frank conceded, handing me my own cell phone.

Quickly, I dialed Travis's number, hoping I'd remembered

it correctly, praying he'd be at home and answering his phone.

God was on my side. He sounded distracted, but he'd picked up.

"Travis, this is Tal. I need you to get down to the county jail right now. They're arresting me for selling my own jewelry."

Travis was silent for a second. "It was yours to sell, wasn't it?"

"God bless, Travis, of course it was." A thought came to me. "Pick up one of the three . . ." I hesitated just in time, "older women in the record room, in the basement of the courthouse. Any one of them will do. Bring her here when you come."

"Do these women have a name?" I could hear Travis scooting back a chair.

I gave him the details, then hung up and handed the phone back to Frank. "I want Braidwood here when Travis shows up."

"Can't do that," Frank was turning away, leaving me to be fingerprinted and photographed.

"You'd damned well better, Frank Bonnet."

I wasn't above using every bullet in my arsenal of small-town blackmail. Not a soul in Wynnton lived above re-proach, except maybe my dead grandmother and Henry and Grace Rolfe. Frank had his secrets from way back when he was a kid. I'd use them if I had to.

"Braidwood. Right where you're standing this very second. Today. With Travis Whitlock." I hated being finger-printed. The last time it'd been done, I'd registered for my law license, and had wondered why they treated me like a criminal. After a few years of practicing law, I understood.

I continued talking, my voice low. "A reputation's easy to kill. No one will know if what I say is true or not, or give a damn either way. It's easy enough to let slip something not so . . . nice."

He knew exactly what I was saying. The smallest rumor could fly through Wynnton on a wing and a prayer and end up as gospel as surely as if it had been written by an apostle himself. Frank was a popular sheriff. He didn't want to lose his job. I felt small blackmailing him, knowing Miss Ena would give me holy heck in my dreams.

His mouth tightened. A pink hue worked its way up his neck that had nothing to do with heat and humidity. I wasn't going to quit now, conscience be damned.

"It'll be a lulu," I whispered in his ear. I had a great imagination, I could come up with something that'd run him and his kin out of town forever.

Frank knew I wasn't bluffing. "All right. I'll try."

"Thank you." I smiled demurely as my fingers were rolled in black dye and then smashed onto a white identification slip. I felt like the law had finally realized what a criminal I'd always been.

Frank showed the great common sense to have me locked up in a holding cell. It was empty now, since all its inhabitants had already been transported across the street to the courthouse, there to await their hearings from the antiquated cells behind the courtroom. Perched on the metal bunk, I wondered if June and I would get to be roomies if I actually got fitted with the orange jumpsuit. I'd bet June would be tickled pink to see me in the same predicament.

I don't do well in confined spaces. I need to know I can pop open a door and split like a busted lip. I was just beginning to get really tired of playing the eentsy-weentsy spider on my fingers and seriously considering screaming, when I heard the door to the corridor creak open.

"That'd better be you, Travis Whitlock," I shouted. My voice echoed in the empty room.

"Hold your horses," Frank snapped at me. "Got Miss Cilla here, she's movin' kinda slow."

Thank God, I sighed, tucking in my blouse and running a few fingers through my hair. I may have called in one too many favors from Travis, who owed me none, but at least I could get on with my job today. I hoped.

"Cilla," I cried.

She clutched onto Travis's arm and gazed around the holding area as if she'd dropped into hell.

"Thanks for coming."

She'd have the memory to know what I needed. The three witches may have been climbing the year ladder, but their minds were as sharp as a quilter's needle.

"What about me?" Travis complained. Then, standing still and staring at me as if I were a stranger, he added, "It's a new look for you, Tal. Maybe I'll incorporate it in your portrait."

"Portrait? You're doing Tal? Goodness, Travis, how lovely." Cilla was on firmer ground talking about something socially acceptable such as portraiture, with Travis, than she was looking at me behind bars.

"Later, Cilla. Frank, is Braidwood here?" Pacing the small cell, I was ready to get out, like, yesterday. Poor June was probably suicidal if she was handling this twice as well as I was.

"He's on his way. Said it'd better be good, or I'd be looking at a hand-picked opponent at the next election." Frank looked about as worried as a cockroach in a dark kitchen. "This is the last time, Tal."

I shrugged.

Cilla fluttered to the front of the cell, clucking her tongue as if I were an unruly child.

"I'm so glad Miss Ena isn't alive to see this," she whispered dramatically.

"I'm sure she expected it," I soothed. "Travis, thanks. Now, tell Cilla about the jewelry I gave you to sell."

Frowning, Travis started to protest. "I don't see how that has anything to do with what's going on here, Tal. What the hell's going on anyway?"

A good Southern boy, he turned to Cilla. "Pardon my French, ma'am." Back to me. "What're you doing in here?"

"Long story made short. That jackass Braidwood thinks I fenced stolen goods to get the bond money to spring June. I need you to describe the bracelet to Cilla. She knows every piece of jewelry Miss Ena left me, heck, she even saw Miss Ena in it at one time or another. Right, Cilla?"

Frank had left us alone to find Braidwood. At least, I hoped he had. If this didn't work, I'd have to drag in Travis's wealthy client with the ready cash who'd acquired my family jewels. I wasn't sure Travis would appreciate it, as it might put a damper on his cordial relations with the super rich who wished to remain anonymous. I could appreciate his position, but I'd do what had to be done to get out of this pickle. I didn't mind stewing in juices I'd cooked up, but this pot wasn't of my own making and I resented the hell out of it.

"I suppose so," Cilla answered slowly. "Which bracelet are you talking about? And why on earth would you sell any of Miss Ena's pieces? Why, Tal, a good piece of jewelry can make even a plain woman more attractive. You should know that. Now if you'd worn Miss Ena's blister pearl earrings with that blouse, you'd . . ."

"Please, Cilla," I begged, interrupting her. "Travis, tell her which one you sold."

Giving me a look that said he'd humor me because I was clearly insane, Travis described the rubies and diamonds as only an artist could. I was regretting giving them up by the time he finished, even though I'd never worn them.

"Of course, dear. I'd know those Cartier pieces any-where." Cilla looked pleased as punch.

"Frank!" I shouted like a mother retrieving a reluctant child from playing in the yard.

"Hold your britches," Frank snapped, shoving the door aside to admit the baby-faced candidate for idiot of the year. "What's your hurry?"

"I'm suing you for false arrest if you don't get me out of here in ten minutes. Tell them, Travis, Cilla." I forced my-self to avoid staring at Braidwood. I could be arrested all over again if my thinking showed as clearly on my face as I knew it did.

"This is ridiculous, Frank. I don't have time for this crap. Do your job, get her over to the jail." Braidwood shoved at the door, but Frank kicked it shut with a thrust of one leg.

"These good folks came all the way over here to tell you something. Now, they're voting citizens of Wynnton, I'd think you'd take a minute of your time to listen to what they have to say."

Go get him, Frank. I wanted to applaud, but my hands were clenched too tightly to keep myself from throwing a sucker punch at Braidwood through the bars.

Braidwood glanced at Travis and Cilla as if they were

lower than dirt. "Friends of yours, I assume, Tal?" He was trying to sound indifferent, but Frank's insistence had gotten through the thick part of his brain to some functioning area.

"Hope so," I muttered. "More than I'd say you'll have by the time you finish Amos's unexpired term of office if you keep on making bonehead mistakes like this."

"I don't have to stand around here and be insulted by the likes of *you,*" Braidwood huffed, turning again to leave.

"Told you, you're going to hear the lady out," Frank snapped, stepping in front of the door and blocking Braidwood's exit with his body. He meant Cilla, not me.

"Travis, just tell him." I was tired of this. Braidwood had forfeited any benefit of the doubt I may have given him in a cooler moment. "Keep it short, I'd like to get out of here before hell freezes over."

Still sounding puzzled, Travis went through his description of the jewelry and what he'd done to sell it, then waited for Cilla to confirm that the pieces he'd sold did, indeed, belong to me as heir to Miss Ena.

"And I should know, I filed the inventory for Miss Ena's estate," Cilla finished proudly. "I can assure you, young man, those Cartier pieces were listed. I never forget heirlooms like that."

Glaring at Braidwood over the end of her nose, she harumphed. "And if you think I'll ever vote for you in any election, you're sadly mistaken. Now get Tal out of that rat's nest!"

I would have reached through the bars to pat her on the shoulders, but she would have hated any public display of affection.

"What's the name of your client, the one you say bought the stuff?" Braidwood sounded openly contemptuous.

Travis hesitated.

"Tell him," I threatened. "Please," I added as an after-thought.

Travis did. "She's at Hilton Head this time of year, usu-ally. But she may not be for long. She has a daughter in En-gland expecting a baby any minute."

I guessed I'd impressed him with how important my freedom was to me, because he suddenly became downright chatty.

"In fact, I have her phone number at my house. I'd be only too glad to give her a ring, have her speak with you. If she's at home, of course."

The name Travis had spoken finally sank into the mush in Braidwood's brain. I whistled softly. He hadn't told me before who bought the jewelry, and I hadn't really cared. As far as I was concerned, it was gone.

"Is she still as beautiful as they say she is?" Cilla asked innocently.

"Yes, ma'am, but not half as lovely as you." Travis was playing the gallant with her. I really liked him for it.

Frank was unlocking the door. "Guess it was all a misun-derstanding, right, Mr. Braidwood? No hard feelings, I'm sure, Tal."

"I don't owe you anything," I hissed as I barreled past him to the corridor.

"Never said you did, darlin'." I could have sworn Frank winked at me.

Travis and Cilla shook hands with me as formally as if we'd just been introduced.

"Thank you." I wanted to hug them both, but I needed to get out of lockup even more.

Ushered by Frank, they escaped in front of me.

"I want June Atkins, and I want her now," I whispered as I edged through the door past Frank."

I was already heading for the desk. I wanted my briefcase, my watch, my belt, and some satisfaction as I wrapped it around Guy Braidwood's skinny neck.

He had the good sense to leave me alone, steaming out the glass doors to the sidewalk as if I didn't exist.

"We'll talk later," I shouted after him.

"Really, Tal, a lady never raises her voice." Cilla clucked at me in a great imitation of Miss Ena.

"A lady never gets locked up either." I hugged her briefly, unable to stop myself. "Cilla, you're a dear, and I thank you from the bottom of my heart. What can I do to make this up to you? Dinner next Friday night? I'll cook."

She frowned. "I think not, dear. You know it's our canasta night, every Friday."

I didn't. "Then Saturday?"

Again, Cilla looked uncomfortable. "We play bridge on Saturdays."

"Then you tell me when." Travis, I noted, was standing to one side, watching this exchange with great interest.

"I really don't know when we'll be free." Cilla plucked at her skirt, for all the world like a child caught telling a lie.

"How about I take everyone to Greenville for dinner on Sunday after church?" Travis looked as if he'd made up his mind and was ready to take over. "There's a great Greek place I know, with fresh baklava."

"Oh." Cilla sighed. "I adore baklava, and it's so hard to get in Wynnton."

"Ask the other ladies if they're free. I have a van, I can carry us all."

I was surprised at his invitation. "You never offered me dinner in Greenville," I complained.

Why, I wondered, did he have a van in addition to his pickup? The truck was big enough to haul huge canvases packed in the sturdiest of crates.

"Later, Tal." He turned back to Cilla, handing her a card. "Here's my number, just let me know when I can pick you all up."

"Why, thank you, Travis." Cilla slipped the card into her purse. "I'll do that."

"Can I escort you back to the record room?" Travis was playing Rhett Butler to beat the band.

"No, but thank you for the offer. I'm fine, really. Though it's getting mighty hot out." Smiling beatifically, Cilla followed Braidwood out the door, moving slowly but with great dignity.

"Bye, Cilla, thanks again," I called after her. "You can tell me what this is all about later," I snarled at Travis, slipping my watch back on my arm.

"Easy," Travis whispered. "She couldn't stand the thought of your cooking. I merely made a civilized gesture to repay your obligation in a socially acceptable manner."

"Did you learn all that fancy talk from your mama, or did you pick it up when you were knocking around the world rubbing shoulders with the fancy rich folk?" I slid my belt into the loops around my waist. "I'm not that bad a cook."

"And how long is your nose by now?" June appeared at the door to the back of the jail, dressed in real clothes. I was infinitely grateful I didn't have to see her in the orange jumpsuit. "Lying like that'll get you locked up."

"Don't give me any guff, I've had a hard day." I was so relieved to see her, I felt like crying.

"You think you've had a hard day? Wait until I tell you about body cavity searches."

I didn't want to think about them. She stared at Travis as she spoke. "You still hanging around? Thought she'd have run you off by now."

"June, be quiet." I had the beginnings of a colossal headache. "Travis, I hate to chat and run, but could we talk about this later?"

Shrugging, Travis turned his freckled face from me to June, watching our expressions like a man who kept them catalogued in his mind for future use.

"Just like a woman, use a man when she wants him, then throw him out." He was laughing softly.

"You betcha." I grabbed June by the elbow. "We have some talking to do."

The deputy behind the desk watched us with eyes like slits as I hauled June out of lockup, hot on Travis's heels. Pent-up energy from being cooped in the cell ate at me like aphids on roses. I was dying to take a big bite out of something, and I'd rather it was June than Travis. I owed Travis a debt I'd try to repay in a private moment, and that meant not letting him see my really nasty side.

I wasn't releasing June until I got the whole story from her about her husband and her lover. But I wasn't sure about letting go of Travis Whitlock, either. I'd never counted on a man before who managed to come through for me and keep his humor intact at the same time.

A man like that was as rare as free liquor in a bar. And I was a thirsty woman.

Chapter 14

JUNE said little to me on the way back to the office, despite my best attempts to get her to open up. Once there, she phoned Henry to pick her up, playing with the files on her desk, ignoring me, as she waited.

"I want to go home and take a bath. A long bath," she explained, eyes averted.

I wasn't amused. "So when are we going to discuss Ike Coleman? And his recently dead wife?"

Her face was as tight as the skin on a face-lift victim. "I didn't know she was dead."

"Well, she is. Shot in her husband's white pickup, the one that was supposedly stolen or whatever." I refused to let her open a file, slamming it shut with my hand.

"I'm sorry about that." She didn't sound it.

"So you gonna go running to Ike, tell him you love him,

get him to marry you? Then you don't have to testify against him, marital privilege being what it is. A nice, easy way out, isn't it, you being a widow and him being a widower." I was going over the line but I had to shock her into talking to me, really talking.

"That's a dreadful thing to say, Tal Jefferson, and you know it." June wasn't nearly as riled up as I thought she should be. Rubbing her hands together, she was doing a good impression of Lady MacBeth.

"Maybe, but it'll play real well with a jury. You may have both been locked up when his wife was murdered, but accessory before the fact carries the same punishment as the trigger man. Oh, my, I guess we haven't gotten that far in your legal studies, have we?"

My temper was frayed as thin as the knees in my jeans, and I was unraveling fast. If she'd ranted and screamed at me, I'd have known what to do, how to handle her. This quiet, cowed creature wasn't June.

"I don't give a damn what a jury thinks," June blurted out, sounding like a petulant adolescent condemning the standards of the cool crowd.

"Well, girl, you'd better." Sighing, I took her desk chair from her and sat in it myself. "Because it's heading that way, and my best hope is to make sure you and Ike are tried separately. Oh, and guess what? Henry says it was an old-style lead .44 that killed her. Ring any bells? Another antique gun just happens to be floating around Wynnton, and gets used on someone else you're linked with?"

Her eyes were as big as a child's at Santa's knee.

I was tired. "Can't you tell me anything about Ike, anything at all that'll help you?"

Shrugging, June gathered up her purse and refused to look at me. "All I did was sleep with him. When Darryl came back, I went with him. Ike understood."

"Wait a sec. What do you mean, Ike understood?" Something was funny if June discussed Darryl with her lover. She didn't strike me as the kind of woman to have civilized relationships with more than one man at a time.

"Ike knew Darryl. I'm not sure how, I think they knew some of the same people from way back when."

"And everyone was friendly with everyone else? Sounds very sixties to me." Much too civilized.

"How the hell do I know if they were friendly? But Darryl lent Ike his van for a little while once, I know that much. Before he called me up from the truck stop. Ike told me later he'd seen Darryl, when I told him I had to stop sleeping with him, I either had to get my divorce or get my act together with my husband."

"I'll bet Ike loved hearing that." Men, I decided, were beyond female comprehension.

"I'm sure he didn't let any grass grow under his feet. Ike has a way with women." She didn't sound upset.

"Boy, I sure missed it. I thought he was just some dumb construction worker caught in a big snafu." My laugh was as bitter as sour mash. "Plus, his check'll bounce. Last thing his wife told me was that she'd taken him off her account."

"Well, if we're both going to get cooked in the same pot, I don't see as how you can be his lawyer anyway." June sniffed self-righteously.

I thought about it for a second. "Got me with that one. Yeah, if there's a conflict, you're right. So what do you want me to do, keep on with Ike and you get other counsel?" This was her call.

"Screw Ike. You're my lawyer." June breathed fiercely. "He can scramble around and find someone else."

Sighing with relief, I acknowledged to myself how important it was to me that June saw me as her savior, her legal knight in somewhat shining armor. Helped a hell of a lot to have a client who believed in you.

"Besides, he can pay for a lawyer, I can't. So I get the freebie." She dodged around me and got as far as the front door.

I should have seen it coming. My smugness dissolved like sugar in tea. "Nothing in life's free, Ms. Atkins. If you haven't figured that out by now, you'd best get your tail in gear."

"Just what I aim to do. I'm going home to take a long, hot bath, then I'm going to sleep for the next twelve hours straight. You have any idea how noisy that hellhole is? I haven't slept over four hours." Shoving me aside, she traipsed through the front door, throwing over her shoulder, "Tell Henry I'll talk to him later."

"You mean you're going to walk all the way over to Yancy?" June didn't like exercise. She considered filing to be aerobic enough.

"I've been cooped up for almost three full days. Hell yes, I'm walking while I've got the chance to stretch my legs."

With all the sass I'd grown to expect, June sashayed down to the sidewalk, head high, tail swishing. "All right," I whispered, "all right girl, you show 'em." If she wasn't back yet, she was on her way.

I was tired as hell myself. The phone rang; I ignored it. Henry showed up, and I gave him the condensed version.

"Is it asking too much for you to find out what you can about Ike Coleman? I'm removing myself from his case tomorrow. So far, I've just been on the hit-and-run, I've never

entered an appearance for anything else. I should avoid
conflict-of-interest over June, don't you think?"

"What on God's green earth do I know about legal
ethics? Shoot, far as I'm concerned, Ike Coleman can rot in
jail. Just do your best to keep June out of it. Grace won't
take kindly to visiting her kin after a body search by some
guard."

Henry had such a neat, tidy way of summing the situation up.

"Yes, sir, do my best, sir." I saluted. "By the way, June
mentioned that Ike knew Darryl from way back when. Ring
any bells with you?"

Henry shook his massive head. "Never met Darryl until
June married him. I'll ask Grace." He rose from the horse-
hair sofa in my office. "I'd better get back to work."

He gave me a long, hard look. "You're looking right fine.
Not what I expected."

"You mean you thought all this fuss and feathers would
have me in the bottom of a liquor bottle because June wasn't
here to haul me out?" I wasn't bitter, just stating it as I
thought he saw it.

"Not what I meant." Henry tugged at his tie, loosening
the top button on his shirt. His neck was still as big as a
fullback's.

"Just that you're not exactly the sort to take well to being
locked up. I thought you'd have at least broken your nose
banging your head on the cell wall." He wasn't joking.

Once, when we were in grade school, some girls from one
street over had asked me to play with them. This had been a
red-letter day in my life, being included in the girlie games
of the Mathis sisters and their pals. They painted their fingernails with pink polish and played dress-up, parading

around the block in old evening gowns and their mother's high heels. I'd grown extremely envious, but I'd never have begged to be admitted to their private club.

That golden summer day when Verdi Mathis knocked on Miss Ena's front door and asked, with her polite manners and proper phrasing, if Miss Ena would permit me to join her and her friends for a few hours, I thought I'd been selected by the gods. The rest of the day had been hell.

I didn't know the rules of girl play, and I kept making colossal mistakes, like wearing the feather boa in the dress-up box that was always reserved for Lucinda Mathis. As I tried my best to learn the rules of their play, Verdi, Lucinda, Catherine, and Georgina whispered behind their hands and giggled as they stared at me.

I finally gave up and hid in a corner of the small room that was a big walk-in closet in the Mathis basement. It also served as the repository for the dress-up finery. I figured I'd stick around until lunch, then go home and tell Miss Ena I was a social failure. The four girls didn't want to include me in their fantasy games, and I'd at least try to be polite and excuse myself at lunchtime to go home. Back then, I still harbored delusions of social graces, drilled into me by Miss Ena.

"Wait here for us, won't you, Tal?" Lucinda Mathis smirked as she drew off her mother's old kid gloves "We're going to serve lunch down here, and as you're our guest, we don't want you to have to come all the way upstairs to get it."

I stood. "I'll go home for lunch, thank you. Miss Ena's expecting me."

"Oh no," Verdi breathed through a smile as false as that on a jack o'lantern. "My mama called her and said you'd be spending the day."

"Oh." I was too young to be rude. That was an art that had to wait for maturity. "Okay then."

They all traipsed away, and before I realized it, they'd locked the door to the closet behind them. At first I couldn't believe it. Then the light went out. Fumbling on the wall, I tried to find a switch, but I remembered it was outside on the wall beside the closet.

The scent of old cedar and musty satins filled my nose. The darkness was so complete I literally couldn't see my hand in front of my face. I remember feeling myself to make sure I was still solid, still a human being in darkness that deep.

With no sense of time, I found a pile of dress-ups in a corner of the closet and burrowed down to wait. Surely, I thought, it had been an accident. They'd come back with peanut butter and jelly sandwiches and be surprised to find they'd abandoned me to the dark and a locked door. They'd be very sorry and become my best friends to make up for their carelessness.

By the time I had to go to the bathroom, I knew it had been no mistake. With no idea of what sins I'd committed to deserve such cruelty, I nonetheless knew I must be a totally stupid girl to be deserted by all four of them. I dozed some, hoping the urge to urinate would go away. But when I awoke, I really had to go.

Swaying in the inky blackness, I screamed until my throat throbbed in pain. Wetting my pants, I kept on yelling, crying for Miss Ena to save me from second grade hell. When my voice gave out, I clawed at the wooden walls until every nail on my hands was broken and bleeding. That's when I used my feet and head as a battering ram on the door.

When it gave way suddenly, I tumbled onto the basement floor, sobbing.

"Goodness, Tal, what're you doing here? The neighborhood's been hunting for you since suppertime." Mrs. Mathis frowned down at me. "I took a chance that you were hiding down here, although the girls said they saw you go home for lunch. Couldn't stand to leave, hm?"

I lifted my head from the concrete floor to stare at her. The blood in my eyes made it hard to focus.

Shrieking as if she'd stepped on a rat, Mrs. Mathis bounded up the wooden basement stairs, leaving me in my stinking heap. I guessed she'd fled from my odor, so I couldn't blame her. Gathering the last of my self-respect, I managed to crawl up the steps after her and wobble home to Miss Ena.

I cut around the back of the Mathis house, wiggled through a broken board in the fence separating their yard from one of Miss Ena's neighbors on Woolfolk Avenue, and from there wended through the intervening yards until I trudged to the back porch of Miss Ena's.

Mrs. Rolfe was in the kitchen, scrubbing the oak table where we ate lunch sometimes, Miss Ena, Henry, Mrs. Rolfe, and me. She looked angry.

"Mrs. Rolfe?" I tried to speak, but it came out like a croak from a dying frog.

She took one look at me, swept me into her arms against her ample bosom, and hollered for Miss Ena. I heard something drop and Miss Ena ran from the front of the house.

"I was just on the phone with Louella Mathis . . ." Miss Ena's words froze in her throat as Mrs. Rolfe turned so she could see me in her arms. Shuddering visibly, upset, I thought, at my filthy appearance, she pulled herself up to her full height. Her blue eyes glittered. "I'll tell her you're safely home. Olivia, would you start Tal's bath water? I'll bring her up in a second."

The two women stared at each other. While I never knew what that look meant, they made sure from that day on that the two Mathis girls and their friends were denied every social entree that Wynnton's meager society offered. None of Mrs. Rolfe's friends would do the Mathis sewing, Mrs. Mathis had to start cleaning her own home, and to add insult to injury, Louella Mathis was never offered a place on the altar guild at the Episcopal church. The social ostracization of the Mathis family extended through black and white Wynnton society for the next twenty years.

"They left the lights on in lockup," I told Henry dryly. The memory of that day had been with me as the door slammed shut behind me, but I wasn't a seven-year-old kid anymore.

"Well, I'm glad you survived it. Next time you need cash, let me know, okay? Especially when you're trying to bail out one of my in-laws." Henry shrugged his shoulders as if his shirt were too tight.

I knew he was right. He'd been my best friend forever, and I'd cut him out of the loop. Quickly, I hugged him, remembering how he and Grace had offered to bail June out with their house as collateral. "You're right. Sorry. But you know how I am. I thought it was easier to sell the jewelry. What the hell do I need it for? Besides, it'd take too long to qualify your house to do the bond. June would have organized a riot in the jail by then."

He laughed. "Okay, you win this time. And Tal, if this happens again? They lock you up?" Peering at me like some elder of the church, Henry turned me to look at him.

"Yes?" I knew what was coming.

"Call me. First."

I hugged him again. "Now get outta here, I hate this mushy stuff. I'll be fine. The worst is over."

"Yeah, right." Throwing his hands in the air, Henry left me alone.

All alone. In the silence of Miss Ena's big house. The roof popped a nail in the heat. A jaybird cawed loudly in the front bushes. I was so alone I didn't know if I could stand it.

I did what I've always done when faced with my solitary seclusion. Retreating to my office, I hauled out all my notes and went to work. The night was going to be long, but that's when I do my best work. Darryl Henshaw's murder, the death of Mrs. Coleman, and the antique guns were knotted like an escape sheet hung from a hotel window with flames licking the panes.

I hoped to high heaven the sheet didn't catch on fire before June and I hit the ground. We were already smoking.

Chapter 15

꙳

THE lab report Henry faxed through the next day was conclusive. The gun in June's house matched the weapon that had fired the bullet that had entered her husband's heart. I wasn't surprised.

She wasn't home when I phoned her at ten to find out where she was and to give her the results of the ballistics test. I was busy wondering where the .44 would be found, the one used to kill Mrs. Coleman.

Working on that basic feeling that I needed to know more, I found a phone number for Emperor Productions, the company that put on the weapons fairs all over the East Coast. I progressed from the receptionist to Mr. Hingham himself. I had no idea who Mr. Hingham was, but I knew how to get information.

"Hi, I'm looking for a dealer who works your gun shows by the name of Fitch Canuette. I wanted to buy something from him when he was in Richmond, didn't have the cash, but I've pulled it together, finally. Then wouldn't you know it, I've lost his business card. Can you give me his address or phone number?"

I tried to sound innocent. Not an easy task.

Mr. Hingham didn't give a rat's ass. "Check with my girl. She'll give you what she's got." Click. I was talking to Cheryl now, who was clearly not a girl, but well into womanhood.

I gave her my spiel, hoping it didn't sound too hokey.

"Sure, honey. Just a sec, let me pull up that screen." I heard tapping on a keyboard.

"Fitch Canuette, yeah, he operates under his own name. Address and phone number are . . ." She rattled them off.

I recognized Fayetteville as next door to Fort Bragg, North Carolina. I thought he'd looked military. One of Darryl's ex-military buddies, I'd bet my bottom dollar.

Before I chickened out, I dialed the phone again using the number Cheryl had given me. Ringing five times, it finally snagged an answering machine.

"Not here. Leave a message." The speaker obviously didn't care who called him or why.

Using my best drawl, I said I'd seen an antique .44 at his last show and wanted to buy it for my husband's birthday. If he'd sold it already, did he have anything similar? I mentioned the words "cash" and "paying the asking price," hoping they'd do the trick. I added my cell phone number and the name Lucinda Mathis for good measure. No sense giving the guy my real name.

Hanging up, I wondered if I'd wasted my nickel calling Fitch Canuette. But even if it led nowhere, I was doing something. What June was up to was anyone's guess. I just hoped she wasn't at the jail chatting with Ike under the guise of being my paralegal or anything else.

Hopping in the Mustang, I headed for Yancy Street. I'd never been inside June's house, but it was time I broke down the barrier. If she was moping about being in jail, I'd drag her back to work by the scruff of the neck. It was the least I could do for her, and she'd thank me later.

The little house on Yancy Street wasn't at all what I'd imagined. Expecting a modern, sleek house with a rock garden in the front yard, I found a brick rancher tiny enough for a play house. Built sometime in the '30s, it had a gabled roof and ancient wisteria climbing up the sides to hang over the eaves. A large magnolia dominated a corner, its rich flowers as sweet as a thousand lilies gracing a grave. Rose bushes lined the property, crowding carefully edged beds and a slate walkway that led to the oak front door.

I knocked, half expecting the gatekeeper of the castle. June answered instead, dressed in black and looking downright somber.

I almost asked her who died, then I remembered.

"I picked up Darryl's ashes this morning. They called and left a message I could, while I was in jail." Turning, she retreated inside, leaving the door ajar.

Assuming she meant for me to follow, I slipped the door shut behind me. June was standing next to a metal urn reposing on the middle of a Chippendale end table beside a rose damask sofa.

"When's the funeral?" I had the most awful feeling I should run home and throw on proper garb.

She was staring at the urn. "Won't be immediately. Can't get him into Arlington, and his family can't decide. I know I should be the one to put him in the ground since I married him, but given the circumstances, I felt his people should pick the spot. They're fighting over the family farm in North Carolina and the Baptist cemetery." She gave a hard-sounding chuckle.

"Darryl'd say to put his ashes in the trash can. But I can't do that to them. It's going to be hard enough when they find out I'm supposed to be the one who killed him." With an awkwardness that was totally unlike her, she flopped on the damask sofa.

Taking my cue, I perched on a fragile looking French provincial number covered in a muted striped satin. I was afraid I'd have dirt on my fanny that would stain the fabric, so I scooted so far forward, my weight was resting mostly on my feet. Where June got this elegant, delicate taste for decorating was a mystery. Someday, when we weren't discussing the disposition of her dead husband's ashes, I'd ask her.

"Won't hurt to let him stay put until they're unanimous." I cleared my throat. "Was he close to them, his family, that is?"

June snorted in a most unladylike way. "Not hardly. I should really try to find his Marine buddies, they're the ones he'd want at any funeral."

I hoped I hadn't tracked any dirt onto the pale Oriental carpet under my feet. I should give June free rein on Wool-folk Avenue, let her have a heyday decorating the place. Miss Ena would do somersaults in her grave, but June's sort of good taste was rare. I liked it.

"Got any names? Maybe we can track them down." I wanted to help June through this, but she wasn't giving me much of a chance.

"Ah, hell, who cares. He's dead. He doesn't give a damn who's at his funeral, and I sure don't." Grabbing the urn,

June slammed it on the mantel over the small fireplace. "I'm already tired of looking at the damned thing."

Tears slid down her cheeks.

"It's been a hard few days. Take a break, go to the beach, do something fun." How I qualified to give stress advice was beyond me. I either shifted into overdrive or cracked up under stress, channeling it into anything relaxing was way beyond my ken.

"Like I'm about to do that," June sniffed, disappearing into another room where I heard her honking into a hanky.

Following her to a bright, tiny kitchen painted lemondrop yellow, white counters gleaming, I was impressed.

"Okay, then let's get back to work." I hesitated, then decided the frontal attack was best. "Does the name Fitch Canuette mean anything to you?"

"Why?" Wadding up the hanky, June frowned. "Should it?"

"Just think." I didn't want to raise false hopes, but of all the gun dealers, he was the only one who was nervous when Travis and I asked questions. That Russian picture frame wasn't standard weapons fare either.

"Wait a minute." June pronounced "Canuette" as "Canyet," unlike my pronunciation of "Can-u-et." "There was a guy Darryl knew by that name. When we were married. White guy, thin. That's about all I remember."

I whistled. "Mind like a steel trap, courage of lions. Yeah, you'll make a hell of a trial lawyer, Ms. Atkins."

She tried to bristle, but a small smile broke through. "So what about him?"

"Well, how do you feel about a road trip? I like the idea of North Carolina myself." I grinned.

"What're you up to?" Arms folded, June was bracing

herself for what she knew was a hare-brained scheme. "Nothing good, right?"

I told her about the Fitch Canuette I'd seen at the weapons fair and his strange reaction to my inspection of the Russian picture frame and Travis's inquiry about the Navy Colt. "That guy was hiding something."

"Maybe you and Travis looked like escapees from the State Pen. Ever thought about that? He probably thought you'd rip him off when he loaded up his car to go home that night."

"Come off it. Everyone in that place looked like they slept in their clothes. Naw, it was like he recognized us. Or me."

"How'd he know you? I'll bet he never set foot in Wynnton in his life."

"What if he was with Darryl when you met him at the truck stop? Darryl was with you in one room, Fitch had another room to himself?"

"Anything's possible, but that doesn't mean it's probable." Ever the skeptic, June was at least focused on what I was saying and not her husband's ashes.

"So cut me some slack. We find this Fitch guy, you say howdy, and by the way, have you seen my husband lately? If he's clueless, you'll know. But if he's doing the backstroke like a water bug running from a bigmouth bass, we push him a little harder." I was pleased with myself.

June was seriously considering having me committed, I could see it in her eyes. "Just because he knew my husband doesn't mean he had anything to do with his death. I can't go up to a stranger and start accusing him of murder!" Flouncing to the ice box, she jerked it open and extracted two cans of soda, which she slammed onto a small table under a window. She sat, popped a top, and shoved the other one at me.

Aha, I had her interested enough to sit at her tiny kitchen table and talk about it. I was making headway here.

"You aren't. Accusing him of murder, that is. What we need to find out is who knew your husband, who was with him just before he died, that kind of thing."

"Won't the FBI do all that?"

"Probably not. Not with the county taking jurisdiction because the head was found on the banks of the river in Talmadge County. Need I mention the charming and inappropriately named Mr. Watson? You really expect a thorough and impartial investigation from him?" I swigged the soda. Still rotten stuff, but getting more bearable.

It was time June had her first ugly lesson in the law.

"Grow up. I learned the hard way, you make your own justice. You're condemned until proven innocent. I don't care what the Constitution says, we've got to find out who killed Darryl before we both get locked up."

"Damn, damn, damn," June swore under her breath. "If I'd known coming to Wynnton would throw me into this much manure, I'd have stayed in Atlanta."

"It wasn't Wynnton that did it," I noted dryly. "You're the one who married Darryl Henshaw and slept with Ike Coleman."

"Thanks for reminding me."

"Speaking of Ike," I wiggled my eyebrows at her, "can you think of anyone he'd get to kill his wife? I'm planning ahead. Something you need to learn to do when you have your license."

"You mean 'if,' don't you?" June looked whipped again.

"No, I mean 'when.' I just want to have some possibilities to throw at Braidwood when he hands you a warrant for Mrs. Coleman's murder."

"Oh, goodie. I'm going to get consecutive sentences, aren't I? Will I ever see the light of day?" June traced a finger through the wet spot left by the soda can, her eyes on it as if it contained the answers to all her problems.

"Don't think like that." I wanted to shake her. "It's just that I thought we'd do some brainstorming. We can do it on the way to North Carolina. Grab your toothbrush. We're shutting up shop and hittin' the road."

Rising, June seemed to make an effort to pull her act together. "Give me a minute. At least I won't have to stare at that damned urn. Maybe I should stop off at Darryl's people. Near Fayetteville. Let me get the address."

I didn't hear anything after "Fayetteville." "Did you say Darryl was from near Fayetteville?"

"Yeah," June shrugged. "So what?"

"That's where we're going to find Fitch Canuette. Small world, huh?"

Her dark eyes brightened with interest for the first time since I'd crashed her pity party. "You don't say."

"Wanna place any bets what we'll find out?"

"Nope. I know better than to take odds that bad. I'll find my bag, throw in a few things. Be with you in a sec."

I listened to June rummage around in the bedroom off the kitchen. Drawers slammed. Closet door clattered. My idea of traveling light didn't match hers, I knew the instant I checked out her suitcase when she reappeared in the bedroom door. The Mustang's trunk would be jammed.

"I'll stop at home and grab some clean undies and a toothbrush. Let's rock and roll."

I quickly called Henry to leave a message on his home answering machine, warning him what June and I were up to. I was afraid to call his office and tell him directly, because

I knew he'd hunt us down and stop us by force, if necessary. For an instant, I considered calling Travis and letting him in on the plan, but something held me back. Call it female pride, call it foolishness, but I didn't want him to insist on going with us. And I knew he would.

The drive to Fayetteville was a straight shot up I-95. I stopped in the first visitor's center in North Carolina and picked up a map with details of Fayetteville. We kept on driving hard. June had been silent for much of the trip, refusing the bait I wiggled in front of her to talk about what was going on. I finally gave up, figuring she'd open up when she was ready.

She was probably sick and tired of me by the time we got to Fayetteville. The sun was going down, I was hungry and cranky, and she looked as if she wanted to kill me. I kept my mouth shut for once, and checked us into a motel near a mall. At least we'd find food at the shopping center.

After splashing our faces with water in the sink, we trudged across the lot and grabbed some pizza in the food court. Not exactly nutritious, but fast and filling. Slurping noisily with the straw pushed against the bottom of the cup, I finished my drink.

"Stop that," June snapped.

Good, she was still among the living. "You want to go find Fitch Canuette now, or wait until morning?" I pretended I didn't care, but in fact, I figured we'd have better luck now than during the daytime hours, especially if Fitch held down a job. He wouldn't see us coming at this hour, so we might have a chance to get inside his house to chat. Some men don't like shutting the door in a lady's face after dark if she looks like a good time. Fitch struck me as that type of man.

"Guess we can figure out where he lives."

I almost jerked her behind me to race into the motel's lot and find my car. I thrust the map into her hands.

"Here, navigate."

"It's too dark to read this," June grumbled. "Besides, what's he going to think when two women show up at his door?"

"There's a flashlight in the glove compartment. If we're lucky, he's not married and he'll think we're a couple of babes on the make. Leave it to me. I took lessons from the best. Spent a year of my life representing hookers once."

"What?" June screeched.

"Hey, they're only doing for money what we do for free," I noted as I turned out of the parking lot. "I know I need to turn on Bragg, then I think it's a right on Oakton. Double-check it, will you?"

"You're going to get us in real trouble, aren't you?"

June was thinking more clearly, I noted with relief. "We're already in real trouble. What else is new?"

"I wish I were Catholic. I feel like I should be praying a rosary about now."

"Ah, don't you worry. We Baptists got an inside track." I turned on Bragg. "Get out the flashlight, I need directions here."

June quit complaining and studied the map. Following her directions, I ended up in a trailer park. Cutting the lights but leaving the engine on, I studied the layout.

Tucked behind a small strip mall, the trailers were generally not new and on the whole, rather crummy. Even in the dark, I could see rust. Foundations consisted of cinder blocks with peeled aluminum siding, and the cars parked alongside had more mileage on them than my Mustang, which was saying a lot.

"Not exactly upscale," June remarked dryly. "But then, Darryl never had much taste in friends."

"I've got his number written on the front of the map." I tapped it.

June sighed. "What're you going to say if he recognizes you from the gun show?"

Leaning over to the back seat, I pulled Miss Ena's sun hat off it and onto my head. Because she'd worn it over a massive French twist, it was bigger than my head with its short hair. Riding low on my forehead, it covered up my eyes and most of my nose on a bright day. On a night like this, I'd be invisible.

"That'll do it," June remarked dryly. "Now you look like a hooker for sure."

We cruised the dirt track running between the rows of trailers, shining the flashlight on twisted and decaying mailboxes to find the right address. If Fitch Canuette was making money on the show circuit, he sure didn't spend it on living well. I cut the engine, letting the 289 tick down as I stared at the trailer that had Fitch's address slapped in paint on the mailbox. An older Toyota van, curtains around all windows but the windshield, was parked in the designated spot. I wondered if he kept any of his merchandise in it.

I took a deep breath. June did the same.

"Hellfire and damnation, let's let 'er rip."

"Wait," June protested. "Shouldn't we plan it, like what you'll say, what I'll say?"

"That takes away all the fun." Climbing out of the car, I unbuttoned the top three buttons on my blouse, just enough to show the edges of my bra. The jeans were scruffy enough. But I didn't smell right.

"Quick, got any perfume?" I hustled over to June's side to haul her out. I wasn't going into this alone.

"Why on earth do you . . ." June almost fell on my feet as I jerked the door open.

"We gotta smell good. It's part of the act."

"Yeah, sure we do." June fumbled in her purse. "See how you like this."

"I don't have to like it, I just have to smell like I bathed in it." I squirted a healthy dose on my arms and behind my ears. Very expensive stuff. Something French was my bet.

"This is too good for a hooker, but it'll have to do."

I hauled a lipstick out of June's shoulder bag and leaning over the side view mirror, slapped some on. "Come on, get in the spirit, girl."

I slid the spaghetti strap on her left shoulder off. "Leave the jacket in the car."

"God help me," June groaned. She did as I asked, I noticed.

A light was on, and I could hear a television. With no preconceived plan, I knocked on the door. No answer.

"Let's go." June tugged at my arm. Handing her her lipstick, I motioned for her to apply more to her own lips.

She looked at me as if I were insane.

I rapped more loudly. My knuckles hurt. "Hey there," I shouted as loudly as I dared. "You home, Fitch Canuette?"

The metal door creaked open slowly. "Who wants to know?"

The man himself stood before us, as thin and mean looking as I remembered.

"Well now, darlin', we're looking to party, if you know what I mean." I cocked a hip and licked my lipsticked lips.

He didn't slam the door in our faces. "Who sent you? Weed? Tell him I ain't takin' what he owes me out in trade."

I almost fell off the stoop when I heard June's voice, soft and sultry as I'd never heard it before, from behind me.

"Now sweetcakes, if you think we're here for somebody else, you got another thing comin'. We're just lookin' to party is all, and we done heard you give a girl a good time."

Frowning, he stared at June, then me. I ducked my head and fiddled with the last button on my blouse between me and harlotry. Miss Ena would have killed me if she'd seen me now.

"Ain't got no good stuff." He sounded cautious.

"Sure you do, honey." I wiggled closer, trickling my hand down his back. I was so good at this, I was scaring myself.

"Well, come on in then." Moving aside, he let me catch the screen door on my hip as he strutted to the mustard yellow Olefin couch with foam pouring out the holes in the back. Such a gentleman, I thought.

"Don't get too comfortable," Fitch warned, flicking the remote and watching the screen jump. "I gotta get me my beauty sleep." He laughed as if he'd made a truly funny joke.

I had to force a chuckle. June ignored it.

"So," I said conversationally as I settled beside him on the couch, "got an extra beer or two?"

June glared at me.

"Nope." He stared at the television as if it contained all the answers to the universe. "Let's get down to business. And I don't do it with black girls. Sorry sugar, didn't see you good out there in the dark. Thought you were a Mex or something." He flicked June a dismissive glance.

June was off the hook. Roaming the interior of the small trailer, she was studying each pile of junk and all the pictures on the walls, hanging at crooked angles.

"Let's do business first."

"Told you, I'm fresh out." He leered at me this time, his teeth crooked and stained. I wondered why the military hadn't done more for his dental hygiene.

I could count the pores in his skin. Short hair on the top matched the short-clipped sides. His ears had blackheads.

"I'm willing to trade for something else." I leaned closer, giving him a good view of my boobs as I squished my arms closer and puckered my bra open. What the heck, there wasn't much to look at.

He noticed though. "Like what?"

"Like information. We, my friend and I, want a gun. Not just any gun. We need one the cops can't trace. Can you help us?"

He froze. "Why you come to me for that kinda shit?"

"Oh, a little birdie told me." I squinched closer. The overdose of perfume was enough to gag a maggot, but he didn't seem bothered by it. At least he didn't move away.

June was casually flipping through some magazines on a formica table. I thought I saw her slip something into her purse.

"I get you for the night. She leaves." His eyes flicked to June but didn't really see her.

My toes turned cold and my stomach flipped. Time to put up or shut up. I hoped I could run fast enough.

"Let's see what you got afore my friend here puts out." June's voice was flat as river bottom mud. "We don't do business leastwise we see the goods."

I wondered where she'd learned to talk like that. Too many movies was my bet.

"Yeah, gotta show us somethin' useful, you know what I

mean." Pulling away, I wiggled to the edge of the sofa and started to stand up. His hand was on my ass like a tick on a dog.

"Sit yourself down, sweetcakes. Let me get you a piece of candy."

I held my breath, staring at June, willing her to get closer to the front door. I didn't want to have to run back for her. Somehow, I didn't think Fitch Canuette was the sort to play keepaway without winning, fair play or not.

Rolling his hips, Fitch disappeared through a narrow door to our right. I heard a drawer squeak open. Quickly, I mouthed at June to move toward the front door. Inching that way, she picked up more papers and folded them into her purse like a professional thief. I was dying to know what she'd found.

"How's this, baby?" Flashing a beauty of an antique pistol, Fitch held it in a piece of flannel cleaner than anything in the trailer.

I don't know much about the antiques game, but this one had an embossed grip and years of care behind it. I whistled.

"Nice. Got any ammo?"

"You want ammo, it'll cost you. I get it any way I want it." He smirked. I wanted to kick him in the nuts.

I reached for the gun. Before I could touch it, he thrust it behind his back with one hand and grabbed me from behind my waist with the other. Jerked against him, my bosom flattened against his chest, I realized just how strong he was and what an idiot I'd been to think I could run.

His mouth came down hard on mine, knocking the hat off. I tried to grab it before I lost it totally, but all I did was make him squeeze me tighter. My back was breaking under his iron arm, and all I could do was gasp for breath as his teeth bit my bottom lip so hard I tasted blood.

With my last bit of common sense, I spit in his face. "Don't you do that again, you backwoods bastard," I snarled, stomping on his instep as hard as I could.

My sneakers weren't very effective weapons, but he got the point and loosened his grip a bit—enough to toss the gun on the couch, clutch me tighter, and smack me across the face.

"That does it, lover boy." June was behind him, the gun in her hand, grip side out. In one fluid motion, she cracked him on the back of the head and grabbed my hand.

"Run," she snapped, "I didn't hit him hard enough to knock him out."

"Why the hell not?" I gasped, racing after her for the door.

I fell down the front steps, scraping my knees on the concrete ledge at the bottom. My purse was still slung bandolier style across my shoulders. Crabbing into the car, I clawed for the Mustang's keys. June was already behind the wheel.

"Get in," she screamed as the screen door slammed behind Fitch. Grabbing the railing, he leapt down the three steps like an athlete. The son of a bitch was in better shape than he looked.

Throwing myself in beside June, I hit the lock with my elbow and dumped my purse in my lap. Snatching the keys, I jammed them in the ignition and turned.

"Floor it," I screamed as Fitch kicked my door. The dent would cost me five hundred dollars to fix, I bet.

June drove like she was a regular on the NASCAR circuit. If Fitch Canuette could read my license plate in the dirt she cut loose with the rear wheels, he had x-ray vision. Ducking down, I realized I'd lost Miss Ena's sun hat in that hellhole of a trailer. I regretted its loss in such an ignominious place.

I kept an eye out behind us in case Canuette decided to follow us. Evidently he knew hopeless when he saw it. By the time we hit Ft. Bragg Boulevard, I was begging June to slow down.

"Wow, you've got a future if you ever want to take to the tracks." I tried to lighten things up. June was looking grim.

"That was stupid. You could have been killed. That guy is crazy."

"Do you think he got a good look at me?" I hoped I'd been moving fast enough when the hat came off to keep my face a secret.

"He wasn't looking at you, honey, in case you didn't notice. All he wanted was your pussy."

I was shocked. I'd never heard June speak like that before. Well, I wasn't really shocked, more like surprised. I was the profane one between us.

"I hope you're right. If he puts me together with the gun show, all he has to do is find the card Travis gave him to call him if he found a Navy Colt. Then it'll really hit the fan."

"Speaking of fans . . ." June lifted her right hand, still clutching the gun. "I think I'm guilty of grand theft, although if it's already stolen, I guess we can plead it down to receiving stolen goods."

"Shit." Taking it from her carefully, I noticed the bits of blood and hair on the grip. "You really smacked him one."

"Not hard enough." She turned on the turn indicators, pulling into the motel. "I think I'll park this around back where there're fewer lights."

Blood. DNA. Evidence. This bit of matter on this gun

might come in handy. If Fitch Canuette had been around when Darryl or Mrs. Coleman were killed, I might have the link right in my lap. Carefully, I scrounged around on the floor for the baggie I kept my jelly beans in. Dumping them in my jeans pocket, I wrapped the plastic around the pistol grip.

"What're you doing that for?" June looked almost ashen in the shadows from the few parking lot lights.

I told her my theory. "It's a long shot, but what the hell. You and I know whose blood's on this gun. It'd be enough for a subpoena to get a blood sample from him."

"But I thought there wasn't any evidence yet about where Darryl was killed."

"Not yet. But we know where Ike's wife took a bullet." I told her about the old water tower.

"You've got no reason to link him with her," June noted with alarming practicality.

"No joke. But it'll all come together. There's a reason for everything. My grandmother taught me that, and she was never wrong." I locked the Mustang's door, hoping I'd find it in one piece in the morning. I loved that car.

"It'd better." June was trembling. "Because I can't do that scene back there again."

"Me, either." Taking a deep breath, I grabbed her elbow and steered her toward our room. "And thanks. You saved my ass in there."

"Won't be the last time," she grumbled.

She was feeling better if she was complaining. Life would go on. We collected our stuff from the room and left the key on the dresser as we closed the door behind us.

Chapter 16

"WHAT'D you pick up in there, at the trailer?" I was driving by now, and feeling on the far side of groggy. Dawn had become a hot morning.

We'd been pushing it for too long, and if June didn't say something to wake me up, we'd have to pull into a rest stop on 95 and hope we didn't get a ticket for sleeping in the car. Our night driving hadn't been restful. I was dozing and drifting, awaking with a start, thinking I heard Fitch Canuette banging on the Mustang's door, screaming obscenities.

"Some papers, one looked like it was an invoice for some guns, or something like that." Leaning over, June hauled her purse from behind the back seat. "I wondered where Darryl got the guns he was selling. How many people deal in that kind of thing and how do they get started? Thought that creep might give us a leg up on how to find out."

That woke me up. "Good for you! Theft is definitely the way to go."

"Well, hell, you know me. I'll steal just any ole thing lyin' around for the fun of it." June jerked the papers from her purse, sounding as if she'd smack me silly if I said a word about her larcenous nature.

I took the hint and ran my finger over my mouth as if closing a zipper. June wasn't amused.

"Well, lookee here, what do you know." Smoothing the papers on her lap, June muttered to herself as she read. "Looks like our clever Mr. Canuette kept track of who he sold stuff to. Like, names and addresses. What do you know."

"So if these guns he's selling are stolen, we can find out who has them?"

"At least these, the ones on the list I lifted from his trailer."

"Wonder why he kept something like that, unless he's legit and declaring the sales on his taxes?"

June snorted. "Not likely. Guy smells like skunk any which way you stand downwind. Wonder if he's planning on ripping them off again?"

My twisted little brain began to think like the lowlife Canuette definitely was. I'm good at that type of thought process, having had a lot of practice.

"Nice and handy to have a name and address, huh? He resells the guns he steals back in a different part of the country, and the poor suckers who paid him cash are out of luck."

June was silent, staring at one of the pieces of paper as if she wanted to rip it into shreds.

"So what'd you find now?"

Staring at me so hard I finally peeled my itchy, tired eyes

off the road and glanced at the paper she held out, June asked quietly, "Is this Travis Whitlock's number?"

I felt my stomach twist like a wet dishrag. The scrawl on the scrap wasn't Travis's, I was almost sure. But the phone number under the name "Whitlock" sure enough was his.

"He gave the guy his card when we hit the gun show in Richmond." I thought furiously back to that day. "Maybe he found a Navy Colt and was going to call him."

"Okay." June hid the paper under the others. She didn't sound convinced.

We drove in silence, me trying to rationalize any reason on earth that made sense for Fitch to be calling Travis. Or maybe Travis had called him, thinking we were headed that way, or Henry had told him we were, and Fitch had taken Travis's name and number off his answering machine. All explanations were extremely plausible, but I wasn't a happy woman anyway. If Travis was talking to Fitch Canuette, why didn't I know about it?

Truth to tell, I was too tired to think. Watching for signs for the next exit, I was ready to crash. My eyes needed to spend some time completely closed. I couldn't drive that way.

But June had more urgent needs. "Gotta go. Pull over the first place you can."

"I'm not stopping illegally beside an interstate highway unless it's an emergency." I sounded like a prig to myself.

"Find me a bathroom!" June demanded angrily. We were both on the far side of ragged.

"Okay." I signaled I was pulling into the turnoff for a rest area. "But make it fast. If I have to sit here much longer, I'm gone, snoozeville, the Queen of Snores."

"Drink some caffeine," June snapped as she wrenched the car door open before I had stopped in the parking space.

"Great advice," I snarled in return. Rummaging around in the glove compartment, I found a dollar's worth of change and headed for the shelter covering the cold drink machines.

Jerking the can from the hole in the machine, I broke what was left of my one semigood nail popping the top open. Cursing the aluminum manufacturers of such an idiotic device as pop tops, I wandered over to the picnic area to sit down and wait for June. The grass was summer-brown, but the pine trees shaded the concrete tables in cheery greenery. I was hot, tired, and gritty under every pore of my skin. I don't mind getting dirty, but I hate not being able to wash off.

Slugging the soda down quickly, I was more thirsty than before. I wasn't paying attention to the other weary travelers stopping at the rest center. But a large woman in a red-striped shirt, with the stripes going the wrong way, blocked my entrance to the ladie's rest room. I needed to splash my face and hold my hands under cold water before I got behind the wheel again.

"Hey, what's the problem?" I almost bounced off her behind in my rush to get to the sinks.

"Place is closed for cleaning," she muttered in annoyance. "Can't you see the yellow cones?"

But June's in the rest room, I thought abstractly. "Can't be. My friend's still in there."

"Well, she's not in this one. Must be another one around back." She stepped on my toes as she pivoted. "Door's locked."

I was too tired for this. "June," I shouted through the locked door. "Where the heck are you?"

I was sure she had to be in there. I hadn't seen her walking around back, and I would have from where I'd bought the drink.

"June?" Now I was getting worried. Following the woman in the awful shirt, I crashed through a bank of azaleas and scattered mulch, running smack dab into the same woman on her way back to where she'd started.

"Nothing back here. You in that much of a hurry, I'll watch the door to the men's room for you." She was amazingly good-tempered about the number of times I'd poked and prodded her.

"I'm looking for my friend. If there's nothing in back . . ." June had to be in the closed rest room.

"Well, I'm gonna hold it until the next one." Shrugging, the woman loaded herself into a minivan that sagged on her side. I could see a man waiting for her in the driver's seat. They pulled out, leaving my Mustang and a nondescript pickup plastered with mud.

Running to the small brick building to the side with a sign saying it was off-limits to the public, I knocked on the dark green door. If the pickup belonged to the custodian, and he wasn't in the office, he had to be in the ladies room. With June. Unless June had decided to hoof it back to Wynnton, something was wrong.

No one answered my knock.

Running to the car, I popped the trunk and dragged out the crate I used to haul peaches. I'd meant to put it away in the shed until next year, but somehow, I hadn't remembered. Praising my laziness, I dragged it to the back of the building and set it carefully on the ground under the small window set high in the back. Dead bugs clung to the metal-braced glass, but it was open.

I'm not big on working out or anything that requires dedication to the body. But I'm wiry, with muscles in my arms like a gymnast from hanging onto a ladder and painting shutters. I had just enough strength in my fingers to pull myself to the edge to get a look inside.

June was backed against the wall opposite from me, a man's body hiding her face from my view. I could hear her ragged breathing and see the man's reflection in the wavy mirror to his left. His hands were wrapped around her throat, and June was almost limp. A dark pony tail ran down his back, reminding me of some Bosch killer cavorting in hell.

"Hey," I screamed before I could think of anything more original. "Let her go, I've called the cops!"

His fingers still latched onto her throat, he turned to stare behind him. I didn't recognize the face, but I knew the expression. I've seen it before on the face of lawyers who smell blood in the courtroom and are circling in for the kill.

"You, I've seen you! Let her go!" I was such an idiot, I had no idea what I'd do if he came after me.

Realizing I really needed to get help and fast, I jumped off the box and sprinted for the pay phone in the middle of the sidewalk by the car park.

Breathless, I dialed 911 and hoped the damned thing worked. I've never been so relieved to hear a human voice in my life. The only problem was, it was recorded and told me the call would be forwarded to the proper jurisdiction and that I needed to stay on the line. My second problem was barreling out the door of the ladies' rest room.

For a second, I was afraid he'd snapped June's neck. The image of June lying crumpled on the yellow tile floor infuriated me. The Mustang was between us, and I bolted for it like a kid racing to jump into the pool on a hot day. He saw my direction and tried to cut me off.

A white man, he was dressed in a black T-shirt and jeans, with a fancy haircut that left the pony tail hanging down his back. I saw him clearly, his face a snarl of anger as he shifted his balance and ran for me. He looked big enough to throw my car and me over the treetops. I gunned the engine, praising Ford for that 289 and its reliability.

Jamming the pedal, I slammed the car into gear and hopped over the curb like a little old lady who forgot to put it into reverse. He must have thought I was going to run, because he wasn't prepared to have my front end flying over the sidewalk in his direction. The surprise in his eyes was worth ruining a perfectly good set of tires.

Hanging onto the wheel, I swerved toward him as he tried to dodge. But he had the advantage over me, and jumped the other direction faster than I could control the Mustang. Taking out some boxwoods, I slammed on the brakes and hit reverse. I was tearing holes in the careful plantings around the rest area, which I hoped my insurance would cover, but I didn't really give a damn. I figured I had the advantage of two thousand pounds over him, and I was going to use it to avenge my friend.

He must have seen blood lust in my eyes, too. Twisting as he hightailed it toward the truck, he reconsidered his plan and decided retreat was the better idea. Stuck in a thickly mulched bed of pansies, I rocked the Mustang from reverse to first gear and back again, trying to free it. I'd run into the killer's truck if I had to, but I was going to stop him.

Before I could free the car, he was in the cab and gunning it. Cursing, I tried to read the plates as he peeled away in a cloud of smoke and burning rubber, but all I could see was the blue and red of North Carolina tags. Falling out of the Mustang, the engine still running, I stumbled to the peach crate. I was almost afraid to look.

Sprawled on the floor, June was inching her way to the door.

"He's gone, can you get the door unlocked?" I knew I was screaming, but I couldn't help myself. "June, can you hear me?"

She waved one hand at me, a faint flutter that said it all. She was going to survive this. No way she'd let some honky take her down.

Flying to the rest room door, I shouted encouragement, words I never even knew I could express out loud. I was afraid she'd pass out before she could open it, that she'd lie there alone and dying on the floor of a public rest room, and I couldn't do anything about it.

"June, June," I chanted, refusing to give up. "Come on, June, you can do it. We'll kick ass from here to Raleigh, we'll get the bastard that did this, just open the door, June."

I heard the sirens in the distance. Weak with relief, I told her help was on the way. I'd never been so happy to see a cop in my life. One of them relayed the information I stuttered about the black pickup while the other one used a weird tool to get the door open. June was inches from it, her face twisted in pain.

Sobbing, I sat on the floor beside her and cradled her in my lap. I was aware the policeman was calling for an ambulance. Squeezing June's hand, I tried to keep my tears from hitting her in the face. My bare arm had to double as a hanky. Miss Ena would have been shocked.

"That's the last time I let you go to the potty alone, little girl," I managed to choke out.

I could have sworn she smiled.

As June was loaded in the ambulance, I gave the police the full story, my address, June's address, and a more complete description. The sun was shining on this new day as if it bore all the promise in the world. When the police finally released me, helping me get the Mustang unstuck, I drove very sedately and calmly to the hospital where June had been taken.

My mind was a jumble of images, my hands like ice. All I could see was June's twisted face, mottled and choked. The doctors at the hospital took one look at me, answered my questions quickly, and sent me to June's room for a few minutes. I guess they could see I would have murdered them all if they'd said I had to wait.

June was propped up, her neck in a brace, her eyes shut. The blue hospital gown looked silly on her.

"That's the most unfashionable thing I've ever seen you wear," I whispered.

"What do you expect? It doesn't even cover my butt," she whispered back.

I was so relieved I began to cry all over again. "The doctor said you'll be okay. I can only stay a few minutes. They gave you something to konk you out. How're you feeling?"

One elegantly plucked eyebrow went up. "Like death warmed over. You take care, Tal. Go home, get Frank to pull out the militia. That guy wasn't there to rob me. He didn't even try for my purse."

I sat hard on the edge of the bed. "Maybe he just didn't have time."

"No," June denied, the sound of her voice hurting me. "He followed me in the second I opened the door. He didn't even look at my purse. He just said I'd be sorry I was sticking my fucking nose where it could get cut off. Then he tried to throttle me."

I chuckled. "Didn't know you're made of steel, huh?"

June's eyes crackled. "Don't make jokes about this, Tal. He was after me. Then he was going to get you. He said so, more or less. He said 'the white bitch is next.' He meant you, I know it. He followed us there."

Her voice was raspy as badly poured concrete.

"Don't worry about it. The cops'll get the guy." I tried to sound more confident than I felt.

"Just be careful." I could barely hear her.

"Hey, caution's my middle name." I wiggled my finger at her. "Now go to sleep. The doctor says you should be sprung tomorrow. I'm staying at a motel tonight, be here bright and early to get you in the morning."

June was already drifting off. The doctor had said she was severely bruised around the neck and that time and pain killers would take care of it.

I wasn't so sure. June had fought for her life, and that's a life-altering experience any way you cut it. I knew from my own sorry example in the shed in my back yard, burning around me like a witch's cauldron. You never forget that moment when you have to decide if you're going to give up and die because living is too hard, or not. She'd been thoroughly rattled, something I never thought I'd live long enough to see.

I found the closest motel to the hospital and checked in. But before I pulled the curtains to stare at the TV with the sound muted, I wedged a chair under the door knob and made sure my windows were locked. I didn't care that they wouldn't open more than three inches, I wasn't taking any chances. Even with the silence in the motel, I listened. And thought.

Thought about Travis's name and phone number in Fitch Canuette's trailer on a scrap of paper. Thought about an escapee from an asylum attacking June in a rest stop ladies' room. Thought about antique guns, June's husband, and Travis.

About his clients, the wealthy ones who collected all things beautiful and unique.

About Ike Coleman's wife, dead on a dirt road bordering the Whitlock farm.

About Ike Coleman and Darryl Henshaw and stolen jewelry and guns.

About Travis, jewelry, and guns.

I wondered if Frank or any of Braidwood's investigators had looked carefully around the Whitlock place for signs that Darryl Henshaw had been killed there before he was decapitated and spread over Talmadge County like so much manure.

I didn't like the way I was thinking, not one bit.

I needed a drink.

Chapter 17

G UY Braidwood and I would never be friends. Funny
how you just know something like that without a lot
of analysis. Some prosecutors hate defense lawyers on general
principles, some grow out of the stage like they would adolescent acne, and some nurture it until it's a king-size zit.

I had to talk to him, however. I'd driven June home and
deposited her in Henry's care. Henry was a pathologist,
true, but he was also a great doctor. I'd called him from the
motel to warn him what had happened. Grace would probably insist June quit working for me after this little escapade.
I wouldn't blame her if she did dump me.

Time to beard the proverbial lion, I told myself. Why I
thought of Guy Braidwood as a lion was beyond me. He'd
never have that hungry, rapacious look that truly stunning
prosecutors wear like a badge of honor. His face would look
babyish at fifty.

I called Frank first. "Meet me at Braidwood's office, will you?" I asked in my most sincere voice.

Frank recognized a favor when he heard one, and knowing I'd have to come through when he needed it, he assented. He would hold every one of my chits. Like Scarlett, I'd worry about it some other day. I only wanted to go through this once.

Part of me needed to write it all down. The other part knew that if I had it in front of me on paper and in ink, the reality of what was going on would sneak through and bite me in the heel. Like a Biblical serpent's poison, the venom would run through me like a raging river and send me to my grave.

I sailed into Braidwood's office like I owned it. "Frank Bonnet'll be here in a minute," I announced as if I ran the joint. "Send him in."

The prune who stared at me from the outer office looked as if she'd like to scream at me but didn't know any appropriately dreadful words.

"Don't bother to buzz him. He knows I'm coming." I knew Frank had called him.

Guy's face was as red as a Santa Claus suit as I made myself at home. I left the door ajar for Frank's grand entrance.

"We need to talk." I tried to sound serious, but it's hard when your throat is clogged with apprehension.

"I don't think so." He didn't rise from his chair.

His hair, slicked down with something shiny, smelled faintly of an old-fashioned drugstore. I wondered where he could buy hair goo for men from the fifties in this day and age.

Tch, tch, his mama didn't teach him proper manners. "Yes, we are going to talk, and I'm going to be very civilized about this, and so are you." That was a threat. I hoped he noticed.

Frank caught my words as he tried to slip into the office unobtrusively. Hard for a guy with a gut like his to be unobtrusive, but I didn't begrudge him a pound. He'd saved my life once and I hoped he'd do it again. And again. If and when . . .

I stopped pacing long enough to stare into Braidwood's eyes. He averted his like a rat terrier going down a hole after a possum.

"I don't know all that's going on, but one thing's clear as Swift Creek used to be, someone's out to kill June and me. Well, the 'me' part I'm not so sure of, but June is."

Resuming my pacing, I switched glances from Guy's face to Frank's. Frank looked interested, Guy as if he'd paid the hit man himself. Much too cool.

I told them about the attack at the rest stop. About my suspicions. I didn't tell them Travis's name was on a piece of paper in Canuette's trailer. I just couldn't, not yet. Not until I talked to Travis.

Braidwood twisted a paper clip open and began to use it to scrape under his nails. Frank's classic cop pose, thumbs in his heavy leather belt, was at least neutral.

"I want protection for June, if not me. Frank, if you can't spare a man, I'll pay for someone off duty. You just send him over." I was semipleading, but not enough to grovel.

Braidwood hadn't said a word.

"But Tal, all that happened in North Carolina. You said the man had Tarheel plates. What makes you think he'll show up here?" Frank, at least, was thinking about what I'd said.

Braidwood harumphed. I half-expected him to spit on

the floor. "Real question is, what makes you think this whole thing isn't a big story?"

He saw me jerk toward him, my hands itching for a smack on that smooth, pink cheek. He shoved the chair back against the wall, realized what he'd done, and propped his feet on the edge of his desk as a cover.

"Way I see it, Ms. Atkins," he stretched out the "miss" like a bee-buzz, "is in trouble with the men she's fenced the goods with. Maybe they didn't like her helping herself to some of the goodies. Maybe they're tired of giving her a cut, and she won't retire gracefully."

His smile didn't fool me. The little twitch in the muscle in the corner of his mouth gave away his real feelings. He was playing blindman's bluff and about to wet his pants, he was so anxious for me to slip up and 'fess all.

"Frank, you know that's not true." I didn't know Braidwood, but I knew Frank.

He may not be much, but he knew me. That may or may not have been a liability. "Help her. Please. I'm worried. This guy was scary."

Frank considered what I'd said, his face firm under the jowls as he concentrated. He was thinking, I realized with surprise.

"Got the report back on the Navy Colt." Frank spoke quickly, as if he didn't want Braidwood to interrupt him.

I thought I knew what he was going to say, that the marks on the bullet found in Darryl Henshaw matched the marks in the gun's barrel.

"Stolen. From a man named Epps. Big gun collector. Has a house in Florida, keeps some of his collection down there, where it was robbed about six months ago. The Colt and a bunch of other nice pieces hit the weapons underground."

Epps. I'd heard the name before. My hands clawed into each other as I tried to still their trembling. Braidwood had noticed.

"Sound familiar, Ms. Jefferson?"

The portrait Travis had been nailing up to ship was of a man named Epps. At least, I thought it was. Travis had told me Epps was a gun collector. I hoped I'd remembered it wrong.

"Nope." I tried to be nonchalant. I was getting nowhere.

I looked to Frank, but he'd clammed up. He'd thrown me a bone of information, and that was all I was going to get. Frank was trying to stay neutral, pleasing no one in the process.

"So what if the gun was stolen. The guy who gave it to June to hold for her husband is in on it, not June."

Braidwood had the gall to snort.

"Won't take up more of your time," I declared sweetly, although lemons were sprouting in my mouth. "But if anything happens to June, I'll sue you personally, the police department, Talmadge County, and the County Board of Supervisors for their incompetence for giving you a job in the first place."

"Then tell her to come on in, tell the truth for once." Braidwood glared.

"She has, you piece of . . ." I barely caught myself. I'd sworn I'd be civil, but I wanted to take him down a whole lotta pegs in the world's worst way. "And so have I. Any more stunts, like hauling me in on some other trumped up charge, and I'll be enjoying a civil practice a hell of a lot. The county won't be too thrilled at the legal fees they're going to have to pay, but it won't cost me a cent beyond the filing fee. Let's see, that's about sixty-five dollars, isn't it?"

I turned to Frank, who was watching my act with more shrewdness than I'd ever credited him. "Do what's right, do what you have to do. Just make sure nothing happens to June. These guys play rough. Her husband's dead, and I don't plan on burying her next to him just because she had the poor taste to marry him."

I could have sworn Frank nodded, a barely perceptible tilting of the head, but nonetheless, an acknowledgment.

"Oh, we wouldn't want to deprive the State of the honor of housing you and Ms. Atkins in the finest we have to offer in correctional facilities for women." Braidwood chuckled, turned it into a bray.

Great, he laughed at his own poor jokes. Trying a case against him was going to be like pulling out my leg hairs with tweezers. I was sure I didn't have that much patience.

"Just remember what I said. Frank here's a witness."

Frank didn't look too pleased. Braidwood almost sneered. Frank's hackles bristled just like Robert E.'s when he went after a squirrel who chattered and teased him from a magnolia in the back yard. He didn't like Guy Braidwood much, either.

"Good day, gents." Sweeping from the office in what I hoped was a regal swirl, I wasn't at all sure I'd done what I wanted to accomplish.

Getting Braidwood to use his investigators to throw a wider circle over June and me was unlikely, if I was any judge of character. And being a pain in the ass myself, I was a pretty good judge. Letting Braidwood know I'd hold him accountable for any harm to June was more a nuisance factor than anything else. He probably figured I'd be locked up by then, if I didn't die of apoplexy first.

The real question was, did I trust Frank to stir his

stumps? The logical part of my brain, left side, right side, I have no idea which, said no. Frank would do whatever kept him sheriff.

I hoped my logic was faulty. Before Owen Amos, Braidwood's predecessor, tried to kill me, I wouldn't have bet an empty soda can on Frank doing the right thing. Now, I wasn't so sure I'd been mistaken, and would be again. I sure hoped so.

I drove home, wondering how I could ask Travis about his Epps client without sounding like the Grand Inquisitor, how to tell June the gun that had killed her husband was definitely stolen, and what I'd do with myself if my life began disintegrating around the edges any more. I could feel the acid sizzling at the corners of the barrier I'd set up to keep those hungry monsters, conscience, caring, compassion, at bay. The Big Three. Coming to get me, me without any neutralizer in the house.

One of the symptoms of the Big Three came bounding through the front screen door as I trudged up the steps of Miss Ena's house.

"Whoa, hoss," I admonished Robert E. as he decided I needed a good tongue-cleaning. Forcing him down, not an easy task since we weighed probably close to the same thing, I corralled him to my side as I perched on the top step.

I'd spent many a wasted hour of my youth in this spot, watching Woolfolk Avenue in hopes of finding a way out, a special bike that would fly me into the heavens to explore the moon, a boy in a blue Thunderbird who'd drive and drive and not stop until I told him to. Not a dream came true, a sad but honest evaluation of my wool-gathering.

Not having parents had made me an oddity in Wynnton, where everyone we knew had at least one living. Miss Ena had explained, when I was old enough to ask questions and expect reasonable answers, that I would have to tolerate my status as someone who was "different" because that's how it was. Nothing would bring back my dead parents, killed in a car accident while driving to New Orleans to have a few days alone after the birth of their baby daughter, Talbot. She'd told me the New Orleans story since I could talk. I imagined New Orleans as a place that held the souls of the newly departed.

How a woman could drive off and leave an infant had always puzzled me, since most mothers I'd seen were glued at the hip to their progeny. Gradually, I'd made up a story that my mother had had a premonition that she'd die on that highway, but had been forced to go by my unfeeling father.

Henry's mother told me the truth one day when I was eight. Henry and I had spent the afternoon knocking worm-eaten wood into a semblance of a tree house, when I decided I'd spend the night. Excited as only eight-year-olds can be with a new adventure, I asked Mrs. Rolfe if I could call Miss Ena to bring over my pillow and teddy bear, because Henry and I were going to christen the new tree palace with an overnighter.

Mrs. Rolfe looked shocked. "Tal, dear, I don't think so."

"Well, maybe she can leave Teddy at home," I relented, thinking she didn't want Henry to know I still slept with my bear.

"No, honey, it's not that." Gently, she pushed me into the kitchen chair at the old oak table that held the family meals in Henry's house. "Your grandmama can't allow you to do that. You're a girl, and a Jefferson at that. Things aren't as bad as they were when your mama was young, but they're not that much different, either."

I had no idea what she was talking about. "So what if I'm a girl. I helped build the tree house. And I'm Henry's best friend."

"That you are, sweetie." Mrs. Rolfe drummed the table-top, her glasses magnifying her eyes like a fish lens. She wasn't looking at me, however. Henry was nailing the last boards onto the tree for a ladder. I could hear his hammer smacking away.

"I'll call her." I moved to the wall phone, ready to tell Miss Ena what I was going to do, not ask her.

Mrs. Rolfe gently pried the phone from my hands. "Honey, there's no way you can spend the night with Henry in that tree house, don't ask your grandmother. You do, she'll get upset, feel like she has to explain it, and that's going to be right uncomfortable for her. Good woman like your grand-mother, you don't want to go making her uncomfortable."

I couldn't imagine Miss Ena fidgeting about anything. If she didn't want to explain something to me, she told me I was too young, and I'd just wait and ask Mrs. Rolfe.

"Why would she get uncomfortable?" I expected noth-ing less than the truth from Henry's mother, who did sewing for Miss Ena and other ladies in town and knew everything there was to know, as far as I was concerned.

Resting her forehead in her hands, Mrs. Rolfe sighed deeply. "Not my place, not my place." She sighed again. "But if I don't tell the child, someone will. Someone who'll make it sound ugly."

She wasn't speaking to me. I could hear Henry calling me to hurry back and bring some peaches when I came. Henry was always hungry.

Her hand on my head, Mrs. Rolfe smoothed my wild hair. "You look like your daddy when he was a youngster.

Bet you'll grow up tall and skinny like he was. Your mama, now, she was tiny, real small and pretty as a picture. A lot younger than your daddy. He loved her lots, but he wasn't home much. Got elected to the state legislature before you came along, had to do a lot of staying overnight, away from home."

None of this made any sense to me. I knew I looked like my daddy. Miss Ena, his mother, had told me that she thanked God every day I had the Jefferson looks. Whatever that meant.

"So what's that got to do with me sleeping in the tree house with Henry?" I was known for my obstinacy and Mrs. Rolfe wouldn't be offended by my bullheadedness.

"Your mama died in a car wreck with another man behind the wheel, honey. A man not your papa. He was a captain over at the fort, and he wasn't a white man. Oh, he probably was close enough, but he was colored as far as Wynnton's concerned."

I had no comprehension of what she was telling me, other than my father hadn't died in a car wreck with my mother, as Miss Ena had always told me.

"Does that mean my daddy's alive?" What that had to do with the tree house was beyond me, but the prospect of pulling a parent out of the hat was astounding. Then I'd be like all my friends and have a real parent, not just a grandmother.

"No, sugar. He died not long after that. Got caught on a railroad track in his car, hit by a train. You were just a tadpole." Squaring her shoulders, Mrs. Rolfe stared down at me as if seeing me for the first time. "That's why you can't sleep over in the tree house. White girls don't do that with boys like Henry, not in Wynnton. Henry and you may be best friends, but you've got to watch the proprieties, Tal. Watch them careful as a hawk, or folks'll say you'll turn out like your mama." She hesitated. "And it won't mean a good thing."

I was wowed by all this grown-up truth-telling. None of it made any sense to me, but I was sharp enough to understand Mrs. Rolfe was explaining something to me I'd need to know and remember for my later life, when I was maybe ten or eleven years old.

"Now, call your grandmother and ask her if you can stay for dinner. Then I want to talk to her."

"Yes, ma'am." I did as I was told. As I grabbed the peaches from the ice box before running back to the tree house, I overheard Mrs. Rolfe speaking in a low, hurried voice to Miss Ena. I distinctly heard her say, "Better she hears it from me or you, than someone who'll make it sound dirty."

Mrs. Rolfe was probably the only black woman in Wynnton, or the only woman for that matter, who could tell Miss Ena off to her face and live to remember it. I never quite understood the import of what she'd told me until I was much older.

I never forgot the day Miss Ena confirmed that my married mother had run off with a black army captain and left my father in despair. To give Miss Ena her due, she never said a word against my mother, except that she'd been very young when she married.

Robert E. shoved a wet nose into the palm of my hand as I sat there like a bump on a log, remembering. I thought of June and Darryl Henshaw, and wondered how old she was when she wed the man in the uniform. Men in full uniform, June had said, made a girl's heart beat faster.

My mother had tripped across all the Southern mores and its rigid code into the arms of a uniform. A black man in a uniform.

I wondered who else had fallen into Darryl Henshaw's arms besides his wife. And what color she was.

Chapter 18

S CUM, it has been said, rises to the top. I should know. But at the moment, I was resting comfortably on the bottom of the barrel, thank you very much. We bottom feeders have a way of getting what we need to survive. May not be much fun, but in the end, it's better than being a floater.

I wasn't looking forward to talking to Ike Coleman again. But as one bottom feeder to another, we should have something to talk about.

I waited for him in the interview room, my sneakers poised to run if he got nasty. I expected nothing less than one pissed-off tirade when I told him I was dumping him as a client, and why.

"Got me another lawyer," Ike announced as soon as the deputy rounded the corner out of sight.

He had me with that one. For a second, I wondered who

would take a case like his with no money up front. Then, I knew. Another bottom feeder, of course.

"Guy in here swears by Richy Ritter. Says the guy'll do what has to be done, if ya get my meanin'."

Yeah, right, I wanted to sneer. "That's nice. So I guess Mr. Ritter asked for a retainer?"

I knew Richard Ritter from the days when I began to be conscious of the law as a career. A beefy, florid-faced man who hired a chauffeur to drive him because he'd lost his license to several drunk driving convictions, he'd played fast and loose with the law so often he was known as the legal whore of South Carolina. He kept a "satellite" office in Talmadge County, but he was never there. The big city swam with more bottom feeders than Wynnton would see in a millennium, and he made his living off them. I couldn't imagine why Ritter would bother to trek down to Wynnton for the likes of Ike Coleman. I always thought he advertised all his satellite "offices" to make it sound on his TV ads as if he had a thriving personal injury practice all over the state.

"Sure. But he says he'll only take one-fourth of my recovery."

Recovery. Personal injury terminology or some plan for recovering alcoholics? The two clicked in my mind so fast, I could hear the hammer hitting.

I grinned. "My malpractice limits are only fifty grand. One-fourth of that's barely enough to pay Mr. Ritter's driver."

Coleman wasn't fazed in the least by my astuteness. "You got more money than that. Ritter says so. And seeing as how it's your fault I'm locked up, and everyone knows you're a lush, it won't be hard to collect from that family money you got stashed."

Such blatant greed was almost admirable. I'd been conned by a con man.

"Sorry, kiddo. Trust can't be invaded by those seeking to enforce judgments."

Miss Ena had had the foresight to keep the money out of any troubles I might tumble into, remembering, perhaps, my errant mother's impetuous actions. Smart woman, Miss Ena.

He had no idea what I was talking about. "I'll explain to Mr. Ritter when he calls with a demand for settlement."

Coleman frowned. "Said we'd sue you in court."

I chuckled. "Lawyers like Ritter don't try cases, they settle them. That's how they make their money with a minimum of effort on their part. Tch, tch, were you looking forward to blaming me in public for your legal woes?" I clucked sympathetically.

"Well," Coleman grumbled, "It'll look bad for you, maybe help me, since your secretary's the one who got me into this mess."

I harumphed. "Hardly. If anything, you dragged June into your cow pie. I don't care if the world knows you were sleeping with her while she was still married to the dear, departed Mr. Henshaw. Gee," I paused, tapping my chin with my finger, "that'll look right suspicious, won't it? Your lady friend's husband gets knocked off? Then there's the guy you knew and lent your truck to? The truck that was found holding your dead wife's body?"

I hummed tunelessly while he processed the big picture. If he had any ability to think at all, he'd know June wasn't going down to protect him. What she knew, I knew.

He tried to bluff. "Won't make me no never mind. They

ain't lookin' to me for a rap for her husband. And who says I loaned my truck to her man?"

I made the leap unconsciously. "Cool Dude by any chance stand for Darryl Henshaw's initials?" I remembered the enscribed metal vase holding his ashes on June's mantel. "I seem to remember his real first name was Charles. Charles Darryl. CD. Cool Dude."

"Damn it, woman." Coleman was growling now. "Don't you go talking like that so someone in here can hear you." He had been lying when he'd said he didn't know his friend's real name.

"A little too close to home, huh, Ike?" I liked this game immensely. "Seems awfully convenient. You blame a dead man for a hit and run in your truck. Same dead man's wife is now a free woman. You're a free man with a wife in the morgue. Oh yes, I'm getting this into focus now. Bet I can do the same for the county prosecutor who pulls your case."

"You can't do that, you're my lawyer," he snarled.

"Not any longer. You fired me, right? And none of this is privileged information. You brought up the name Cool Dude in court at the prelim. The rest was my own rather astute powers of deduction, if I say so myself." I wanted to rub my fingernails against my vest and say "ah" as I blew on them, but I wasn't wearing a vest.

"What do you want?" He was a fast thinker, my Ike Coleman.

"Not much. Just everything you know about Darryl Henshaw." I smiled innocently. "Oh, and I want you to leave June alone. If you ever get out of jail, that is."

"You bitch." He wasn't taking this well at all.

"I've been called worse by scummier men than you." I

shrugged. "And it goes without saying, Ritter leaves me alone."

"What do I get out of this?" He wasn't a happy camper, not by a long shot.

"You get my silence. I don't say a word about you and June. I even manage to keep my mouth shut about you and Darryl being buddies." I was cutting it close to the legal line here, if I wasn't already long over it. But it would be worth it, if I could get to the truth about Darryl Henshaw.

"Deal." Despite the warning sign on the wall to the contrary, he hawked a wad of spit on the floor. "Darryl and me, we knew each other back in my army days. Long while ago."

The common thread here, the military. "And why was he gracing our fair metropolis with his presence?"

"Huh?" Ike stared at me as if I'd just disembarked from a flying saucer.

"What the fuck was he doing in Wynnton, and why'd he take your truck?"

"Oh that." Ike shrugged, rolling his shoulders in the orange jump suit as if it were too small to hold him. "Well, Darryl had to handle some merchandise, you see."

I didn't see. "Tell me all about it," I purred silkily. Damn, but I was good at this.

"His old lady. She was holding some stuff for him. Said he needed a truck, wouldn't fit in his van."

My inner radar blipped, sensing another bottom feeder about to try for the top of the barrel. "I don't believe it."

Studying me as if he'd never seen me before, Ike laced his fingers over the edge of the table and locked on for a bumpy ride. He was cool, but not that cool. I saw the sweat dotting his upper lip. "God's truth. I ain't shittin' you."

"Like hell you aren't." I wasn't going to let him take June down, no matter what she'd done or not done. "I'm going to enjoy giving Guy Braidwood your little ole self on a golden platter. Hell, I'll take the stand against you myself. Upstanding member of the community like me, I'll raise my right hand and tell how you shot Darryl in cold blood using his own gun."

He looked startled, as if it hadn't occurred to him that I'd lie. "Well, he wanted her to get in the business, he said." He must have believed me. "Said he had some other business to take care of, needed my truck to keep himself out of sight. From his friends, you know, those guys he was doing business with." He pronounced "business" like bizzy-ness.

I felt all the worry within me slipping away like a lead blanket. This felt like the truth. "What friends?"

"How the hell do I know?" The whites of his eyes were turning yellow under the constant glare of the fluorescent lighting in the jail. "All I know is, he wanted some cash free and clear. Ran into him at the Gas Mart on the edge of town."

"And?" I knew where he meant, it was near the Whitlock place.

"Recognized me before I saw him. Been a long time, a man changes. But not ole Darryl, not once he opened his jaws and started flappin' 'em." He snorted. "That guy could talk a lady preacher outta her britches."

"I'm assuming he didn't have that problem with you?"

"Naw, I could always use a few extra bucks. Women take money, you know?"

I nodded as if I understood his world, wondering how the hell June could have found him attractive. Maybe he was the proverbial silver-tongued devil with women he wanted.

He wasn't bothering to turn the charm on me, that much was for sure.

"So he says he wants to go see his wife, his little June Bug. I put it together, see, and Darryl's talking about big money and how he needs his goodie-goodie little wife to pull it off, and I just know we're talking the same woman here."

"And you were only too happy to oblige Darryl by backing out of the picture and letting him get back with his wife?" Yeah, right, and I believed that Darryl's head just jumped off his neck and threw itself in the river.

"Darryl wasn't going to stick around. He'd get what he came for, he'd split. I'd be around a while longer." He licked his lips slowly. I wanted to smack him silly.

"So give me the whole picture, like draw it out for me, can you do that, Ike?" I was being so sweet I wanted to suck a lemon.

He gave me a look that said I was dumber than dirt. "Had something he needed her to sell. You know, a fine upstanding woman like June wouldn't cause any unlucky phone calls. She'd sell his shit, give him his half, no one the wiser.

"Who the hell in Wynnton'd know him? He was gonna give her a cut of the take for helpin' him out, he said. She's a woman who likes money." His grin said he knew he had me there.

"Figured his pals would never find him, not in a backwoods dump like Wynnton, and when he caught up with the two of them later, they'd never know about the piece he got rid of before it made it into the pot."

His story felt right. I let it sink in a little longer.

"You two had quite a little chat, didn't you?"

Ike grinned. "Well, we shared a couple of six packs for old times sake. Bought 'em at the Gas Mart."

I'd bet they sat in Darryl's van and tossed the empties in the river. "Seems like he was talking right much for a man with stolen goods."

"Well now," Ike drawled slowly, watching me carefully. "I guess I let slip I might have some, um, influence, shall we say, with June Bug."

I cringed. "So he knew about you two."

Ike nodded. "Man's been gone awhile, he can't expect a woman like June to sleep alone. I knew she was married to Henshaw. He wanted me to make sure she gave him his cut of the full price she got."

"So you were supposed to be his insurance. Go with her when she hocked it." I never said a word about the ring, waiting to see if Ike really knew what he was talking about or if he was making this up as he went along. "Bet you were gonna make more than a couple hundred bucks."

"Maybe." He wasn't about to tell me he could afford to pay me what he owed for the prelim.

"So what happened?"

"You know what happened. Drove with June to get the ring appraised. Called him when we got back, told him how much it was worth. Then the son of a bitch hit that Honda, I got thrown in here. Shoulda figured he'd weasel outta what he owed me."

I had to smile. "You think he did it on purpose, don't you? Got into an accident, made sure your name was on the sign on the side of the truck."

"Darryl never was one to play by the rules." His fingers beat the tabletop to a harder rhythm.

"Doesn't sound like you are, either." I couldn't help

myself, I was feeling like a Sunday School teacher. Odd feeling for me.

"And what about the merchandise?"

"Don't know a damned thing about it. She didn't sell it, not then. Wanted to talk to Darryl 'bout it. Only she never said she got it from Darryl, just that a friend wanted her to sell it. Then next thing I know, June's tellin' me she's thinking about getting back with her husband, I get arrested, and wham, bam, thank you ma'am, I'm taking shit for Darryl, and he's dead."

"Ah, such are the vagaries of life." I pretended a heavy sigh. "Where'd Darryl come by stuff that valuable?"

His eyes glittered. "Got it in a trade, he said. A deal."

I wondered what was worth the ring in trade. Probably something untraceable. Darryl had been dumb enough to believe the diamond ring was free and clear. The guy may have known weapons, but he sure as shootin' didn't know the first thing about stolen gems.

I snapped my briefcase shut. "Okay, we've got a deal. I'll keep my mouth shut, you do the same. Call it a draw."

"This ain't no gunfight, case you're makin' a mistake here."

"That's where you're wrong, Ike. This is one hell of a gunfight, and I plan on being the first one with my gun out of the holster." I stood up.

"What about me?" He sounded like a whiny child.

"What about you?" I shouted for the guard to let me out.

"I still need me a lawyer." Positively petulant, the bottom lip protruding. "Seeing as how Ritter won't take me on, not now. No money in it for him, and you know how lawyers are."

"That you do. I'm sure any member of the bar in Wynnton

will take you on for the hit and run, if you pay cash up front. By the way, I wouldn't admit to knowing Darryl from the military, when you discuss this with your new attorney. Just say you ran into him at the Gas Mart, he offered you cash to borrow the truck for a few hours. Never saw the guy or the truck again."

This was a new one, prepping an ex-client on how to lie to his lawyer. I was surprisingly good at it.

"Will it get me outta here?" Now he was chewing the bottom lip. "Got me a business to run. Women out there who depend on me for a good time." He was serious.

I tried not to gag. "Eventually, if you're lucky enough to get a jury who buys your story. The cop's ID of you with the single photo shown to the victim at the hospital will get it overturned on appeal, if you get stuck in the lower court."

"Get me a good one, you hear?"

"Excuse me?"

"Get me a good lawyer in here, fast. I'm tired of sitting around, doin' nothing. Hell, my dick'll fall off if it don't get some exercise soon."

"My oh my," I clucked, "how sad for Dick. However, I think I know just the lawyer."

Joe McGlone, I thought, would speak the same language as Ike Coleman. Birds of a feather, and all that rot. "This is the last time I'm talking to you, Ike Coleman. If there's anything else you should be tellin' me, spit it out now. 'Cause if I find out you held back on me, I won't talk to you, I'll head straight for the prosecutor's office."

His face impassive, he shook his head. "Just get that fuckin' lawyer in here fast."

I stood on the steps of the jail, soaking in the sunshine, hoping I'd lost my semitriumphant look when I finally got around to telling June what I'd found out. No one likes a smart ass, especially me, but I was feeling so good, I wanted to gloat. Two friends, Ike had said Darryl was hiding from. One was Fitch Canuette, I'd bet my bottom dollar, and the other one had to be the guy who planted the Colt on June.

Darryl had seriously underestimated his colleagues. I didn't plan on doing the same. I had to have more to offer Braidwood. He'd never take a sketchy outline and work it through.

He had June and me, he thought, by the short hairs. I'd have to deliver the goods to Braidwood in an airtight container if I wanted him off my back.

The thought of an airtight container brought back memories of the locked cedar closet that had scared me silly as a child. I didn't like confined spaces, but this was one time I'd have to walk into one willingly.

I wasn't raised to be jail bait, but I'd have to do it.

Someone had to set the trap in the box.

Chapter 19

I was getting ready for bed when I knew I was right about the second man. Lying there on top of the sheet, trying to get cool, my mind floating like jellyfish in the surf, I saw the daguerreotype that had been stolen in my purse in Richmond. The sensual lower lip of the long-dead soldier. Like a transparency, I saw the guy who'd been throttling June, and knew I'd been right. My mind had hidden his face from me until I was ready to handle it.

Throwing myself out of bed, I ran downstairs and dialed June. She picked up on the second ring, sounding frightened.

"Hello?" Tentative, not at all like June.

"Do you remember the face of the man who tried to kill you?" I didn't believe in preliminaries.

"Tal? Have you lost your ever-lovin' mind? Good God, it's almost midnight."

"You weren't asleep. Think."

"I tried. Don't you think I wanted to tell the cops what he looked like? Why didn't you?"

"I only got a good look at the back of his head, then I ran and he ran, remember? At least, that's what I thought. But it just came to me, I saw enough of him when I tried to plow him down to know you were right on target with that picture you got Travis to sketch. At least, I think so."

My hands turned into frozen claws as I realized what I'd said. Maybe June wasn't a great describer. Maybe Travis had seen the guy himself. I didn't want to think about it.

"Where's the picture now?" I had her full attention, and she was sounding more sure of herself.

"In my purse. With the daguerreotype, the one I bought at the gun show because it looked like the picture. The purse that was stolen in Richmond."

"Travis can draw another one." She yawned.

"Maybe." I didn't want to say more. "What I really wanted, needed, to know, is if you've remembered enough that you could say with certainty that this guy who tried to kill you is the one who gave you Darryl's gun."

A long pause. "I'm not sure, Tal, and that's the truth. The doctor said the mind blocks out unpleasant stuff, like a safety mechanism to keep us sane. I'll try. That's the best I can do."

"Okay, just try real hard. It's important."

"You're tellin' me? I'm the one who's got a purple set of handprints on my neck." She was getting sassy again, a good sign.

"Between the two of us, we'll get the bastard."

"If he's anywhere around, I'm running the opposite direction. You can play cop, I'm planning on living a while longer. The guy is, in case you hadn't noticed, not exactly a fun person to be around." She threw in a cynical laugh in case I thought she was spoofing. "Good night, Tal. Go to sleep."

"Right," I muttered, hanging up the phone. Sleep and I were never the best of friends, and I'd lost all hope when the face of the guy at the rest area had popped into my head like some vision from God.

I spent the rest of the night in the back yard with Robert E. Like me, he didn't mind nocturnal games, so while I threw a ball for him to find in the dark, he obliged by finding it. When we tired of that, we hit the kitchen.

A bad time, those hours just before false dawn. I've never been a channel flipper on TV, and it takes a hell of a book to settle my mind when it's racing like the wind. Tonight, nothing was going to calm my thoughts but something smoky and smooth, and all the liquor stores were closed. So I was stuck.

Robert E. and I had a cup of hot cocoa. He liked his better than I did mine. I think the cocoa had been in the pantry since Miss Ena passed on. Robert E. didn't seem to care.

"Just like a man," I crooned, scratching his ears, which perked up at the tone of praise. "Anything in your stomach, as long as a woman fixes it for you."

Why June? Why had they gone after her first? Did they think she knew about them, the guys who'd killed Darryl? Did they assume Darryl had, during his night of passion at the truck stop with his wife, given her all the gory details of whatever operation he was running? All of which meant, Fitch Canuette must have realized who June was after we flew out of his trailer like kids caught stealing candy. When she stole the list with the names, she'd sealed her fate as surely as if she'd licked the envelope and dropped it into the mailbox to hell.

I was avoiding the inevitable, and I knew it. Throwing cold water on my face, I dressed quickly. Stashing the gun wrapped in the baggie in my pocket, I loaded Robert E. into the Mustang. The 289 engine rumbled like a hungry critter as I pulled onto Woolfolk Avenue. I wasn't sure what I was looking for, and whatever it was, I prayed I didn't find it.

The edge of the horizon was gray and pale yellow, just beginning to wake up when I pulled onto the dirt road that bounded the Whitlock fields on the east. Cutting off the headlights, I crept the Mustang into the trees that bordered the unplowed land.

My door creaked as I got out. I left it hanging open. No WD-40 on hand, and sound carried in the early dawn like a rifle crack.

"Come on," I hissed at Robert E. Cocking his head at me, he looked as if he contemplated disobedience. We had a staring contest. I blinked first, but he got out of the car anyway.

I knew there'd be nothing left by now, but I wanted to see where Ike Coleman's truck and dead wife had been found. The road was county property, leading as it did to the old water tower, but I still felt as if I were trespassing. Like Hester Prynne, I should have been wearing a big red letter on my chest, only mine would be a *T*. *T* for "traitor" or maybe *T* for "tease." Definitely *T* for "Terrible Person to be Thinking What She's Thinking about Travis," but there was nothing I could do about it.

I had to find out if Travis was involved in this mess, or start drinking again. The *T* had better stand for "Truth" if nothing else, I decided.

Yellow plastic tape cordoned off a big square around some trees where the truck must have been found. I'd forgotten to ask who'd found her. Ducking under the barrier, I stood beside the tall, ancient cedars and sucked in their cloying aroma. They reminded me of Christmas when I was a child and Miss Ena would have Mr. Rolfe bring in a cedar from the country every year the week before Christmas. Each holiday, the towering tree, prickly enough to make me cry as I hung ornaments, rose to the top of the sixteen-foot ceiling in the front parlor.

I was looking for a gift under these cedars, and I hoped like hell that it would prove that Travis wasn't involved in any of this. I knew I was asking for a lot, but what the hell, a girl can always ask.

Squatting down, I unwrapped the gun and stuck it under Robert E.'s nose.

"Okay, kiddo. DeShazo said you're a huntin' dog. Probably need a good ole-fashioned Carolina yeller dog for this, but you'll have to do."

Robert E. cocked his head, cast a disapproving eye at the antique pistol I held under his nose, and decided to scratch.

"Smell this, you mangy cur. Earn your keep. Prove to me Fitch Canuette was out here." I'd stuffed something else in my other pocket. The handkerchief Travis had given me to wipe the blood off my face in the parking lot in Richmond had been in my jeans pocket when I went to do the laundry. I hadn't washed it. I'd never used it, either.

Flea attack complete, Robert E. stuck a wet nose on the pistol grip and sniffed.

"Good boy. That's it," I encouraged. Stepping away, I waited to see what he'd do.

He did what any smart dog would do, he began to snuffle at the ground. Whether he was after rabbit and frogs, or traces of Fitch Canuette, I had no idea. I'd never done anything like this before, and if Robert E. came up with something, I could be accused of tampering with evidence. But I wasn't about to back out, not this deep into the hole.

Hunkering down to watch, I kept my back to the Whitlock house. The east fields were the small ones, and they lay fallow now. I guessed Travis wasn't going to lease them out to someone else to plant with tobacco, and what he did with his own land was his business.

I wished that they'd been filled with crops flourishing in the summer sun. The presence of plants would have meant a more permanent relationship with the land, a physical setting down of roots that would have given me encouragement. A man with crops in the ground is one who stays around, who chats with other farmers at the Co-op on Saturday mornings, who watches the weather and not other folks.

Travis, I realized, had imposed his big-city life on the farm. Ripping walls out of the house, he'd made a studio that would have fit into a loft in Atlanta, Dallas, San Francisco. He was from Wynnton, but he wasn't one of us. I may have painted Miss Ena's shutters purple, but I was a daughter of Wynnton in every way I'd tried to avoid all my life. I could trade jokes with the guys at Becky's if the spirit moved me. But Travis had settled here like a crane over another bird's nest, a temporary habitat to suit the moment.

Why?

I was eaten alive with questions, as surely as if beetles were feasting on the corpse of my doubts.

I stared at the ground, pacing it off in small squares, kicking dirt and leaves, rocks and trash like a child out to find a lost quarter. Robert E. circled intently, his nose down, tail up, happy at whatever job he imagined I'd given him.

There'd been no rain, and the dusty soil showed everything that had trampled around in there for the past week. The truck tracks had been obliterated by bigger tires belonging, I assumed, to the wrecker that hauled it to the evidence lot. I didn't have much faith in Frank, but enough to know he'd have scoured the area for evidence.

Pulling the handkerchief from my pocket, I was careful to hold it by the edge. It smelled like me, my jeans, I was sure. But even I could catch a wisp of the smell of whatever soap Travis used, a lemony scent that mingled with a faint trace of his aftershave. I guessed that was why I'd deliberately forgotten it was in my pocket. Some part of me wanted to keep him near.

Robert E. was ranging far afield. Whistling softly, I called him back.

I was just about to hold the piece of cloth out to Robert E. when he came prancing up to me, head high, practically grinning.

"What is it, boy?" I reached out to give him a scratch under his chin, his favorite tickle spot, when he darted sideways, head down, all business.

He ran for an area far enough away from the yellow plastic tape that I wondered if he was going to tree something he'd expect me to shoot.

"Woof." He was insistent I get my ass over there, so I did.

Hippity-hopping like the Easter bunny, Robert E. circled a spot in the loamy dirt surrounding a cedar. Crouching, I shoved aside cedar tags, sticky as pins, and rocks kicked back from the gravel road.

The cigarette butt was smoked down to the last drag. Robert E. waited proudly. More than one, I saw when I shoved the first with the tip of my pen.

"I'll be damned."

My first instinct was to pick it up. My second instinct was more professional. I had to get Frank out here to check this out. I didn't trust Watson or the feds. Frank was one of us, a Wynntonite.

I marked the spot with a pile of rocks and a quick slash mark on the tree beside it with my pocket knife. For the first time, I wished I had that darned cell phone June made me carry in my briefcase.

I glanced through the trees at the Whitlock house. The sun was just beginning to strike its windows. Reflecting the rays, they were like the pupils of an eye, dark and depthless, shrinking in upon themselves in the onslaught of full-bore sunlight. I could ask to use Travis's phone to call Frank.

I didn't. Back in the Mustang, I hightailed to town as fast as I could.

Chapter 20

ری

FRANK wasn't in his office yet, and I still had a life to lead. Those cigarette butts weren't going anywhere, I told myself as I paced the front hall, waiting for Frank to return my call. How I was going to explain finding it was another matter. I wasn't real thrilled at the idea of showing Frank the pistol we'd stolen after June bashed Canuette on the head with it.

Retreating to my office, I studied the list of names June had pilfered from Canuette's trailer. Since June had connected us to the Internet, I'd spent more time avoiding it than doing the legal research she'd planned for the account. But I knew enough to find the Internet phone directory and how to start plugging in names from the stolen list.

A few sounded familiar. They didn't show up. Others popped up in small towns all over the country. Canuette moved around a lot, or his customers did, but I couldn't see a pattern. I thought of calling the local constabulary for each town later, and finding out if there were any reports of stolen antique weapons. I really didn't need to. I knew the answer was yes.

Stashing the list, I scribbled down all the reasons I could for Ike's wife to end up dead at the hands of the same scum that had tried to kill June. None of them sounded plausible, which was par for the course. My best reason was that she was married to Ike Coleman, and somehow, she'd gotten in the way. I couldn't see her as a player in any game Darryl Henshaw had been running.

Men like Canuette and the guy who tried to strangle June didn't think like the rest of us, I reminded myself. Early in my legal career, I'd expected to find ordinary logic, a simple symmetry to the cases I defended. My first trials had left me bewildered. What I'd learned, mostly through trial and error, is that all crime boiled down to sex, drugs, money, and temper, the last of which was usually triggered by one or more of the first three. There is no logic to sex, drugs, or money.

I started with sex. Ike Coleman was a ladies man, but his wife hadn't seemed too upset. As she told me, she got the new house and car while he rotted in jail. Darryl, according to June, could charm the pants off a nun. I was back to wondering if there were other women who were more jealous than June. Maybe Darryl wasn't visiting just his wife in Wynnton.

The drug angle hadn't yet reared its ugly head. But where there was a lot of money, there were bound to be drugs. Money, of course, was in the picture. Darryl had wanted June to hock the diamond ring quickly, offering her and Ike a cut, he was so sure it was worth a pretty penny in change. He'd wanted to keep his partners out of the loop, hiding his presence by borrowing Ike's truck.

Good enough reason to kill him if I'd been one of his partners. Bad guys don't like to lose anything, not even spare change. Money from the stolen guns was a given—but what they used the cash on was still hidden from me. I was laying odds on one or both of the other two—sex and/or drugs.

My head was beginning to throb. No sleep and a conundrum were surefire headache makers. Plus I had to be in court that morning.

I made one decision. Phoning Henry, I caught him with a mouth full of something.

"Swallow," I commanded.

"Tal, what the heck? It's just past the crack of dawn, in case you haven't noticed."

"I know. Been up all night. Henry, this is going to get sticky, and I don't want you to do anything that'll get you into trouble."

"My God, that means you're about to do something I'll be sorry for, doesn't it?" I heard a cup hit the table. "Give me a moment, I need to sit down."

I waited, counting seconds. "I can't tell you how I got this, but I have in my briefcase at this moment a pistol with blood and hair from Fitch Canuette, that gun dealer I saw in Richmond, the one I told you I had my suspicions about."

I waited. Henry hadn't hung up yet.

"There's a cigarette butt, more than one in fact, out near where the Coleman truck was found that I think has something to do with Canuette. I've called Frank about it," I hurried on, "but he hasn't called me back yet. Can you go get it now?"

"I'm part of the chain of evidence, not the originator," Henry answered slowly. "Is there a chance this evidence is about to be tampered with?"

"I don't know," I replied honestly. "But I'd feel a hell of a lot better if I showed you where it was. Before I have to get to court this morning."

"Okay," Henry snapped. "I'll be out of here in five minutes."

I told him to meet me at the turnoff for the county road going to the old water tank. Throwing on my court suit, I grabbed the files I'd need and floored the Mustang back to the edge of Whitlock land. Still dark, the windows of the old farm house refused to let me see inside. I didn't have time to wonder if I was making the second-biggest mistake of my life, when Henry pulled up.

I handed him the gun in the baggie and led him to the tree I'd marked.

"I haven't moved or touched them. Robert E. did some sniffing, so there's probably dog snot on it, too. But that's not going to give you a problem with DNA, is it?"

Henry didn't say much, squatting in the leaves beside the cedar, staring at the butts.

"I've got to get to court. I'll call you later." I was being unfair and I knew it, dropping this in Henry's lap.

Henry rose, pulling a large plastic bag from a pocket. As if disposing of dog shit, he dropped the pistol, baggie and all, in it and tied it shut with a little plastic gizmo.

"Tell me you haven't killed someone."

"Lordy, no." I snorted. "Should have. My prints are on it." I hesitated. "June's are, too. She hit the guy with it."

"Damn it to hell." Henry's eyebrows drew together in a straight line. "I should have guessed."

"It's not what you think." I hesitated. "June and I, we're more than boss and employee—she's my friend. But you knew that. That's what you and Grace were hoping for."

His nod answered me.

"I'm doing better, Henry, really I am. I haven't had a drink in months."

Again with the slight nod. His gaze stayed on the water tank in the distance.

"Tell me why June showed up here. In Wynnton. I'm not just curious, honest. Something tells me her reasons have a lot to do with her husband. If I know the why . . ." How could I explain my sex/money/drugs list that I knew led to the worst messes in which good folks became mired?

Henry stared down the road, still focusing on the old water tower. "Not really my place to say. Ask her yourself."

I shook my head. "Not yet. It's just that, well . . ." I hesitated. "I'm risking a lot here, Henry. More than my law license. Hell, that can take a long jump off a short pier. What I mean is, I'm sorta committed." I cleared my throat.

"And you haven't been that in a long time. I know, Tal." Henry threw me a tight smile. "She's a pain in the ass sometimes, but she's good people."

Staring at the antique pistol, Henry wrestled with whatever loyalties he owed June, Grace, and me.

I'd been around longer than the other women in his life. I won.

"She was pretty broken up when that creep left her." Henry's words grumbled in his throat. "Can't imagine why, good riddance to bad trash, to my way of thinkin'."

"May I point out you're a man? We don't think the same way, old pal." I shrugged, stating the obvious. "All kinds of smart women get in trouble with the wrong guy. And vice versa."

"Yes, well, June hit bottom pretty hard. Harder than you did."

"Oh my." I couldn't imagine June as anything but under control. Even weeping over her dead husband had been only a release for her, rather than an act of despair over his death.

"Yeah. Tried to kill herself. Grace found her in time. Those two were tight as sisters when they were kids. We got her help, professionals, that kind of thing. Grace thought, when June got out of the hospital, that a change of scenery would do her a world of good." He winked at me. "That, and a purpose in life. Someone else she'd have to focus on."

"You mean someone worse off than she was?" I wasn't sure how much I liked this.

"Only temporarily. Always knew you were killing time in that bottle, waiting for the right moment to pop up again and be the Talbot Jefferson I know."

"The one who still gets in trouble and does things like drag you into it?" I waved my hand at the trees.

I didn't want to think about, much less bring up, the day when we were nine and both of us almost died down by the river.

"Yeah, that one." He didn't smile. "Now, what do you say, I get this back to the lab, run some quick tests before Frank comes to get it? I'll verify the chain of custody on the whole thing, and if Frank doesn't like it, he can stick it where the sun don't shine."

"Thanks, Henry." I felt as if half the weight in the world had lifted off my shoulders. "I don't think our problem's going to be Frank, though. My bet is Braidwood's going to say you set this up. You and I together," I amended.

"Screw him. I've been around a lot longer. My appointment comes from town council. I'd like to see him try to fire me. Hell, half my relatives are on the council."

I knew that was true. "Okay, then. I just don't want to

see June hurt. I'm scared, honest to God, that the guy who tried to kill June wasn't some random crazed weirdo. He has something to do with all this. I could almost swear he's the guy who framed June with the Colt."

Henry tensed. "You've got to lay it all out for someone who'll listen."

"Not Braidwood. He's made it clear he thinks June's in the middle of this mess, and I'm swimming around in it with her."

"Feds?"

"Why should they listen to me? They work with Braidwood, they get all sorts of goodies on their records. Nah, don't know 'em."

"Call in state investigators?"

"How long do you think that'll take?" I had no illusions.

Henry turned, heading toward his car. Hesitating, I waited for him to say something else. When he didn't, I ran after him, tugging at his arm when I caught up. Turning, he stared at me.

"You know what you have to do. Get yourself a judge to get this show in order."

"Yeah, right. A judge in Wynnton. Am I nuts?"

"Just do it, Tal, and quit bitchin' about how screwed up everything is. I can take this so far, then you're going to need someone on your side with power and authority." Henry slammed the car door.

As he drove off in a rattle of gravel, I knew why I didn't want anyone but Henry in on this. I was scared, scared to my toes, to the tips of my hair, to my fingernails. Scared of what a full-scale investigation would do to Travis Whitlock.

Travis was the man who knew the rich and famous. Travis was the man who'd just finished painting Isham

Epps, gun collector, recently a crime victim whose weapons showed up in the hands of the man who'd killed Darryl Henshaw, if I was any good at guessing.

Travis's name and number were in Canuette's trailer.

Travis had a concealed weapons permit. Why would a portrait painter need a gun? His explanation didn't do it for me.

Travis was hiding out in Wynnton, just as I was.

Only my past was dead, while his was very much alive and still pissed at the folks who'd tried to stop their little game dealing in stolen antiques.

I made up my mind, staring at the dirt and gravel road, driving like a bat out of hell. I avoided looking toward the Whitlock farmhouse as the Mustang fishtailed onto the highway.

Chapter 21

I corralled McGlone in the corridor, a dark corner where I threw him Ike Coleman as if I were tossing jewels.

"You'd get a hell of a lot of publicity out of it," I whispered. "There's a great chance to win on appeal if you lose down here."

"I hate appeals," McGlone muttered. But his eyes sparkled at the idea of publicity. "How does this one make front pages?"

"Think of it. The old South is alive and well. Black man identified by woman given only one photo. License tags don't match, but what the heck, there's an off chance he's the guy because the man driving was black and the door had his name on it. Golly Miss Molly, all you have to do is call the Southern Poverty Law Center, and you're all over the wire services. Southern justice and its blind eye to the truth when it's a black man. Very stylish, don't you think?" I kept my voice low so the cops milling about, waiting for their chances to testify in the traffic cases that morning, couldn't overhear us. "Plus there's his wife's death. He was in jail, but you can bet they'll try to pin it on him.

"And I happen to know he has some cash. You might kill the proverbial birds with this one—fame and fortune. What do ya say?"

"Why are you tossing me this goodie?" McGlone was a quick study, even if he was a sexist of the first order.

"Conflict of interest. I'll probably have to testify. Saw his wife before she was killed. They'll call me for sure." I shrugged, pretending it was no problem.

That made sense to McGlone.

"Okay. I'll talk to him." He checked his watch, his black eyebrows thin lines drawn across his face like slash marks. "Got a couple of free minutes, I'll run over to the jail now."

"Great. I already told him great things about you." I smiled my most charming smile. I was bushed, wrung out, and ready to throw up my hands and run like hell from Wynnton, but I could still bullshit the best of the bullshitters.

McGlone preened under my admiring gaze. "Maybe we can discuss him in more detail over dinner tonight?"

"Sorry." I pretended distress. "Got a late client, coming in at six. I know your wife will worry if you're really late."

He caught that one on the fly. One eyebrow twitched. "Okay, I'll catch you tomorrow then."

"Sure enough."

I heard my case called, gave him a remnant of my sparkling smile, and ran for the front of the courtroom.

My client gave me a panicked grimace as I hurried to his side. We were talking an open and shut DUI, with no prior record. I ran through my litany about chain of evidence for the blood test taken at Wynnton General and the results of the breathalyzer. I already knew they were in order, did my song and dance about my client's clean record, and got him a suspended license with permission to drive back and forth to work, take the class for drunk drivers, and a hefty fine in addition to the cost of driving school. He was ecstatic.

"Can't thank you enough, Ms. Jefferson," he repeated outside the courtroom several times, pumping my hand up and down.

"My pleasure, Mr. Howard," I murmured. He was a good guy with a wife and two kids. He'd made the mistake of celebrating a good-sized bass that won him a tournament but also got him a record for DUI. His wife told me he'd had two six-packs of beer by himself. He'd lost count after three bottles.

"You're lucky no one was hurt. Don't ever do this again. Remember what I told you, the recidivist law kicks in with the third conviction, and you can go to jail for a lot longer than you've lived on this planet so far." I'd already lectured him, but it never hurt to remind clients that life could get a lot more unpleasant. Say, a lifetime in prison.

I watched him stroll to his car, hand in hand with his dumpy little wife who adored him, envying her, envying him. Then what I'd said about the recidivist law registered, and I froze in mid-stride.

The current political emphasis on keeping crime away from tax-paying folks who voted had led to the change in legislation. I referred to it as the "hopeless" law, because people caught in its net went down without bubbles and never emerged in society again. "Three strikes, you're out" was the cute baseball terminology used by campaigners.

It had led, in larger cities, to desperate acts by people

who knew they were going down for the third time. A shoot-out with the police had become almost routine when some guy was facing death by .45 as opposed to a lifetime in hell in the penitentiary. If that meant killing the guy getting robbed so he couldn't identify you, it was better than facing time again. And again.

I hadn't thought of Darryl and his accomplices as anything other than dishonorable discharges from the military. But what if they'd crossed the line in civilian life once too often? What if they'd been facing a third strike situation, and getting rid of Darryl was their only way of saving their hides?

I ran to Frank's office. He was in, sipping coffee, looking through a stack of pink message slips. He almost grinned when he saw me, but stopped himself in time.

"I called you this morning," I grumbled.

"Morning, Tal, how're you?" He tossed an eye at the department secretary, a young girl just out of high school, frowning over something on her computer monitor. "Come on in my office, take a load off."

I shoved the door shut behind me, standing with my back to it. *Here goes nothing.* I sighed. "I found some evidence out where Mrs. Coleman was discovered. Cigarette butts. Henry collected them when I couldn't get a hold of you to send out a forensics team."

I knew the forensics team was Frank and one of his men.

"How do you know they were already there when we got to the crime scene? The cigarette butts could have been put there after the crime." Frank was thinking faster than I usually gave him credit. He pulled out a notebook.

"I don't. But I do know you don't smoke, and you sure as shootin' wouldn't let anyone out there smoke at a crime scene."

He nodded appreciatively at the compliment.

"And there's something else. Something that ties them in with this guy, this guy I think has been involved in some pretty heavy shit. I can't say anything else, I know how stupid this sounds." I fidgeted. "Henry will explain it, if the tests turn out like I think they will."

"Damnation, Tal, you shouldna oughta done that." The easy-going posture had disappeared. "There'll be hell to pay, and you know it, if this is material evidence."

"It probably isn't worth much anyway, except to give you something to steer for." I doubted my own words, but I didn't want to upset Frank so much he didn't do what I needed him to do.

"What I can do is give you a name. Fitch Canuette. Can you run it through your computer and see what sort of prior convictions he has?"

"You mean here? In Wynnton?" Frank was giving me his beady-eyed look that meant he thought I'd lost my mind. "Never heard of the guy, and I know 'em all."

"Well, in this state, then nationally, if you can. If Henry comes up with what I think he will, there'll be a record long enough to get this guy in recidivist trouble."

"Ahhh." Frank was beginning to get the picture, if somewhat out of focus. "This Canuette feller killed the Coleman woman? Braidwood's not gonna like this, Tal, not one bit."

"I don't know if he killed her, but I'm betting he was at least there when it happened. Remember the guy who attacked June? The son of a bitch I swear is still going to come after her?"

He had the good grace to look uncomfortable. "Now, no need getting huffy, I got only so many men in this department, and things have been right busy lately."

"Well, if what I think is true, these guys don't stop until they get rid of anyone in their way." I could feel sweat beading my palms. This was too important for me to flub. "I don't think they have anything to lose, either. My bet is, they're both facing life in prison. Men like that'll do anything to stay out."

"Damnation." My sense of urgency must have finally broken through to him. "I'll see what I can find out. Spell that name for me."

I did so, wondering all the while if I should call June and warn her about my suspicions. Fat lot of good it would do her, I decided. She was already traumatized enough by her close call at the hands of one of the thugs Darryl had run with. They played for keeps, and no two ways about it.

In the end, I did what I usually do when I'm worried sick. I went home, figuring June would be there or she wouldn't, and that would be my answer. Lack of sleep and tension had joined forces to give me a killer headache. I wanted nothing more than sleep and peaceful dreams.

"Henry's been calling. Said something about he had to send everything to another lab, he didn't have equipment to do it." June frowned at me. "Why are you wearing one blue shoe, and one brown?"

"It's a fashion statement," I snapped. "The latest thing."

"Oh, it's going to be one of those days, is it?" Nose in the air, June pranced into her office.

"June," I groaned, "I need to talk to you."

She reappeared, chin still up, giving me the evil eye. "What about?"

I opened my mouth to give her the good/appalling news, when the phone started ringing.

"I'll get that," she snapped, as if I were her cross to bear in life.

The sound of the phone had set off another burst of pain behind my eyes. As June handled the caller, I inched my way onto the back porch and kicked off my mismatched shoes. Robert E. came running, ready to play games.

"Sorry, kiddo," I mourned, scratching his chest. "If I lean over to get a stick, my head'll fall off."

"I'll pick it up." Big as life, Travis Whitlock leaned against the railing of the porch steps.

I could have counted every blade of grass, every dandelion weed, every leaf on every tree in my yard before I wanted to see him again. Yet there he stood, looking red-headed and almost handsome, his beige shirt opened at the neck to show off the springy, russet hairs at his neck, his long, slender fingers stuffed in the pockets of his jeans.

"No need," I muttered. "He's getting spoiled."

Silence filled the space between us.

"Saw your car early this morning, flying down the road toward town, from my direction." His shoulders were riding higher than normal, I finally noticed.

I swallowed. "Yes."

"Were you planning on making a social call out my way when you decided to come back at a more reasonable hour?" His voice was teasing, but he wasn't. "Or did the thought of my morning breath scare you away?"

Sinking my head in my hands, I tried to think of some clever way out of this. But I wasn't feeling clever; I was very tired and dangerously close to losing control. I needed to do this when I felt up to it, as Miss Ena would have said. But it looked like timing wasn't on my side.

He had no right to stand there looking so good, so calm, so honest.

"Hold that pose." Reaching into his back pocket, Travis whipped out a notebook and pencil, flipped open to a piece of paper, and began sketching.

I jerked upright. "This isn't the time."

"Yes, it is. Go back the way you were." He was less amiable, his eyes intent on the sketch pad. "You had the exact hunch to your shoulders this needs."

"Bless it, I'm in no mood for these games." Slamming to my feet, I hurtled down the steps past Travis, into the lower part of the yard where it slopes into the overgrown vines and scrub oaks growing at the property's boundary.

"I didn't know I was playing any." He'd followed me too closely.

I couldn't breathe. Gasping for air, I tried to still my shaking hands by sliding them in the waistband of my skirt.

"Tal?" His hands, warm as sunshine, bits of old paint drying on his cuticles, freckled as friendship, slid onto my shoulders, pulling me toward him. "Tal, you okay?"

"No," I managed to snarl between gasps. "I'm not."

His concern would have melted Miss Ena in her frostiest state of haughtiness. "Can I get you something? Aspirin? Glass of water?"

"Damn it to hell," I spit out between panic attacks. I hadn't had one of these in years, but it was washing over me now like a tsunami. "Go away."

Not the smartest thing I could have said, but I couldn't think of anything else.

"No." Forcing me into his arms, he hugged me so hard I

could feel his heartbeat through his chest. "Not until you tell me how I can help."

At first I held myself as rigidly as I could, loath to melt into his warmth, the false safety he promised. I couldn't trust him. Too much had happened since he'd come back to Wynnton to be coincidence. To be fair, the same could be said about my reappearance in my old hometown. But I knew I didn't have anything to do with Darryl Henshaw and the bottom feeders with whom he'd done business. I couldn't say the same about Travis Whitlock.

I decided to quit running from the truth. That imaginary *T* in the middle of my chest was burning a hole in me.

"We need to talk." I barely got the words out.

"Fine. Come sit down." He tried to steer me back to the porch.

"No, not here. I don't want June overhearing."

"That bad, huh?" Reluctantly, he glanced around. "My truck's out front. Want to sit there?"

"Not in broad daylight so the whole town can see us." I felt like a teenager trying to hide a trashy boyfriend from the wrong side of Wynnton from the neighbors. "Need privacy."

I didn't think he'd kill me. He might run with a pack that turned on each other like dingos, but I wasn't afraid of him. I was more afraid of my feelings for him.

Taking my hand like a child's, he pulled me behind him to the truck. He closed the door only after he'd buckled the seat belt around me. Hopping in the driver's side, Travis started the engine with an impatient twist of the key, a jerk of gears into first, popping the clutch at the same time. I had no idea where he was taking me, and I really didn't care.

What I had to ask him lay in my gut like lead weights.

"This must be serious," was his only comment as he

steered carefully through the minor traffic of Wynnton, heading back to his house. I'd been there only hours earlier, reluctant to beard him in his den, and now he was taking me, uncomplaining, back there.

"Suppose you could say that." I'd never noticed how sweet the summer air smelled out this way. Window down, I sucked in the scent of honeysuckle, old magnolias lining the back road, a whiff of cedars.

This was the second time I'd been in the Whitlock homeplace.

"You want to sit out here?" Travis gestured at the front steps. "I'll get us something to drink."

"Yes, thanks." At least my manners were returning. If I was going to destroy a man, I could at a minimum be polite about it.

I heard the twitter of birds from the old barn, the early afternoon breeze rustling the pine trees in the back of the house. Tucking my skirt under me, I perched my fanny on the edge of the top step, legs tucked under me like a girl afraid a boy's trying to look up her skirt to see her undies.

Travis sat so close to me that our shoulders touched. I held myself still.

"Why'd you really come back? To Wynnton?" Despite all my years of legal training, of knowing the way to lead a witness is by asking questions that will net a "yes" or "no" answer, I couldn't treat him like some hostile witness on the stand.

"Told you, I wanted a break. Needed to paint my own stuff for a while, figure out where I'm heading with my work." He turned to stare at me, his nose slightly red and peeling as if he'd been out in the sun too long the day before.

"Or did you need a place to hide out? Somewhere to," I

swallowed hard, "sell the stolen stuff from, where no one would think to look for you? Somewhere Canuette, Henshaw, and anyone else you used to get rid of the guns, wouldn't be noticed?"

His eyes seemed to sink into his face as he listened to me. "What on God's green earth are you talking about?"

I couldn't sit there primly any more. Jerking up, I ran to the front yard and faced him, ready to run if I had to.

"You're the link here. Your client, Epps? The guy you said was an expert on antique weapons? Well, lo and behold, he'd been ripped off. His weapons collection somehow turned up in the hands of Darryl Henshaw and the creeps who probably killed him." A thought came to me.

"Unless you killed him."

Travis's face lit with anger such as I'd seldom seen. "Don't be an ass, Tal. I didn't know Epps had been robbed. And I sure as hell didn't kill anybody."

Trying hard to breath and think at the same time, I laid it out for him.

"Your name and phone number were in Canuette's trailer when June and I got in it. The Colt that killed Darryl came from the Epps collection. You've got a weapons permit. Why in hell does a portrait artist need a weapons permit, unless he's trying to sell the guns legitimately? What better cover, huh? Respected painter?" I managed another breath. "Coleman's wife, married to the guy who lent his truck to Darryl, was killed right near your place. My God, Travis, practically in your own back yard.

"And what about the van you said you'd take Cilla and all of us to dinner in? I've never seen it. Is that because it's the van Darryl Henshaw told his wife he bought in Germany, the one with the fancy alarm system?"

Springing up so quickly he frightened me, Travis grabbed my wrist and jerked me behind him.

"I can do something about that one," he snarled. "Even someone as dumb as you can figure this out."

Hauling me behind him toward the old barn, he never looked back as I stumbled on my mismatched heels in the tall grass. Jerking open the barn door, he shoved me inside.

"Voila. The infamous van."

I stared at an old GMC model with farm plates.

"My father used it when he needed to pick up extra hands to get in the crops. Still runs, but it sure as hell isn't some fancy German model."

Crossing my arms on my chest, I glared at him. "You still don't fit in here, Travis. You show up, trouble comes with you."

"For God's sake, I have a weapons permit for the one reason I gave you before. I lived in the big bad city. In a dangerous neighborhood, which was the only place that had an old warehouse I could set up as my studio. The only reason I got it was in case someone tried to kill me when I worked late. I've never even fired the damned thing at anything, much less a person. My father worried about me, I got it to keep him happy."

"Oh." I couldn't think of anything else to say.

"If the gun that killed June's husband came from Isham Epps, well, that's really weird. Epps owns a lot of crap, has houses all over the world. People like him collect for the sake of collecting. I don't need to steal from my clients, they pay me more than enough." He sighed, adding a figure that about rocked me to the ground.

"That much?"

"More, sometimes, if it's a client I'm not particularly fond of. I charge for the nuisance factor."

"Wow."

"Precisely. I don't need to steal anything from anyone, much less kill anyone." He sounded sad. "But there're all sorts of ways to kill, aren't there?"

I'd ducked my head as I listened to him recite his innocence, feeling the heat of his outrage pour over me like molten lead.

"Killing trust, killing friendship, how about love? Joy? Happiness?" Ticking off the litany, he kept his voice from cracking, but I could feel he was close. Each word was like a blow on my back.

"I never promised you any of those." I was incapable of ninety-nine percent of what he'd listed.

"No, you sure didn't. Guess I assumed too much." Turning from me, he wrapped his arm around a beam and pressed his forehead into the wood.

I don't give up easily. But if I'm wrong, as I was with Parnell Moses, I own up to my mistakes. Trouble was, I wasn't sure if I was being conned by one of the best, or if I'd blown it big time.

"Come with me." Before I could make a move, Travis was hauling me behind him again like a sack of meal.

Back to the house, up the staircase with walls covered with his work. I concentrated on not stumbling. He'd have hauled me face first on the floor if I didn't keep up. My hand hot in his cold one, his skin rough from all the washing with turpentine, we were locked together like an unbreakable link. I didn't want to think of what I'd done to him if I was wrong.

Throwing me in front of him into the studio, he grabbed my shoulders and steered me to the center. A medium-sized canvas, covered with a cloth, faced the north windows. Jerking off the covering, he twisted me so I saw the canvas.

I was on it, sketched in pencil on the surface, holding a skull in one outstretched hand, my chin propped in the other. Although it was just a rough outline of what he'd paint later, I read the sorrow in my eyes as if I were looking in a mirror.

"What is it?" I wanted to wipe the sketch away before anyone else saw it, unfinished or finished.

"You. The Magdalene. Contemplating death, a life wasted. Sin, past wrongs, the unforgiven, the forgiven. Love lost."

He'd gotten it all. I felt naked.

"How did you know?"

"Takes one to know one."

"Damn you." I was close to tears.

He threw the cover over it. Turning, he locked his hands behind his back as if he wanted to strike me, but was restraining himself.

"Now, do you really think I would try to hurt you? Or do anything to jeopardize my place in your life?"

I shrugged. "I didn't know you had a place," I mumbled.

"You damn well did. Don't play these games with me, Tal Jefferson. I've known you since we were kids, watched you half my life." Catching me in one stride, he kissed me hard.

I wanted to believe him. I truly did. My body did those melting-into-him things I couldn't control if I'd wanted to.

"I can't," I gasped, pummeling his chest to get away before I fell into his eyes, his blue, blue eyes that saw right through me, and never came up again. "Let me go."

He didn't try to keep me. As I flew through the studio door, all I could think was that I needed to be alone.

Alone as I'd been all my life.

Chapter 22

I didn't want to think. I just moved one foot in front of the other, shuffling like an old man with stiff ankles and tender knees. I refused to let my mind work. Hard as it was, every time I thought of Travis's shocked expression, the hurt and betrayal deep in his eyes, I blocked it out. Well, I tried.

He couldn't be that good a liar. I'd accused an innocent man of killing another human being.

When I finally realized where I was, late afternoon had become early evening and I was on a road I vaguely recognized. Stopping, I checked around for some landmark so I could get my bearings. I wasn't far from Wynnton, if I cut through another corn field or two.

I worked my way through a row of corn to get closer to the road.

Filled with rocks and rubbing me raw, my shoes were torture. Tossing them away and tearing off my panty hose, I hiked up my skirt to forge my way through the last of shoulder-high corn stalks. The afternoon was so quiet, I could almost hear the corn stretching and growing. Their luscious green was too bright for my eyes. I realized I'd been crying as I stepped into a road.

I heard the vehicle coming fast around the curve to my right. Hopping into the ditch, I hoped no one saw me in my current state. I could hear the rumors now—Tal Jefferson was wandering around the Warm Springs Road loaded as a moonshiner, drunk as a skunk, soused as a flea on sarsaparilla— circulating in Becky's tomorrow at the latest.

"Damn it to hell, get in here." A door opened with a creak and a thud, as Travis jumped out the passenger side of his pickup.

"Go away." He was the last person on earth I expected to see, and I would almost rather have had the rumors.

"Cut it out, I'm taking you home. Been running these roads for hours, looking for you. I'm in no mood, Tal," he added warningly.

"You don't have to escort me home," I snapped in a prissy voice I hoped would piss him off. "I can make it by myself."

"Damned right. But I'm responsible for you being out here, and you'd better believe it, girl, I take my responsibilities seriously. Now get in the damned truck."

Grasping my hand, he pulled me out of the ditch. I felt like a feather flying in his hot currents.

"All right. But only because my feet hurt." I surrendered less than gracefully.

Clambering in, I leaned as far away from him as I could. I wasn't good at apologizing, hadn't had much practice at it. It'd take me a while to work up my nerve to give him his due. We Jeffersons have a surfeit of pride, and it goes down hard.

He drove as if he were in the lead car at Talladega, the silence between us as thick as any concrete wall waiting to eat a fender.

I swallowed hard on the first bit of pride. "Sorry."

He ignored me, his beak-nosed profile facing forward, his eyes as stuck on the road as if it were made of magnets to his iron.

"I said I was sorry. For accusing you. I should have asked you first for an explanation."

Still silent, he clutched the truck into a lower gear. The engine whined. At least he wasn't driving eighty now on this gravel and dirt road. The sun, low on the horizon, slanted straight into my eyes through the windshield.

"It's not that easy." His voice was thick as if the words came out in spite of himself.

"Know that. All I can say is, when I make a mistake, I do it big time. Nothing halfway about me, no sireee." That was the truth, plain and simple.

He didn't have a chance to answer if he'd wanted to, because a dark green van hauled out of nowhere onto our side of the road. Throwing his right arm in front of me as he slammed on the brakes, Travis jerked the wheel with his left hand, sending us careening into the brush and drainage ditch on our side of the road. Bouncing like a bronco, the pickup landed on two wheels and hung there, precariously balanced before it crashed onto its side.

The whole thing must have taken seconds, but I could see every detail as if it took years. Travis turned to me as we jerked to a stop, his mouth open to ask me something, the question in his eyes one of concern. I'd banged my head on the roof of the truck with the first jolt, then flown sideways with the crash against the opened window. My right shoulder had hit dirt. I thanked God it wasn't glass. Hanging against his seat belt, Travis leaned on my legs, splayed sideways on the truck seat and astride the gear shift.

I was more stunned than hurt. He'd slowed down just before we were run off the road, and the ditch had cut down on the force of our impact into the embankment. Slowly, I pushed myself sideways so I could try to wiggle my legs into a more decent position.

"Quite a view, huh?" Fitch Canuette leered through the driver's side window, straight up my skirt.

Still stunned, Travis gave him a blank look.

"Remember me?" Smacking Travis's shoulder through the window, Canuette cackled. "Took me a while, but I got you, boy. You and the bitch."

Oh shit oh shit, I said to myself. I wished I'd had a chance to straighten it all out with Travis before this happened. Why hadn't I made my peace with everyone I'd ever pissed off in this world? Because I knew what was coming as if I'd seen the movie before.

Cranking the driver's door open, Canuette sliced Travis's seat belt with a knife big enough to gut an elephant and jerked him out. Me, he grabbed by the foot and hauled.

"Hey," Travis shouted.

I didn't know if he was protesting Canuette's cavalier treatment of me, or the guy with the dark hair and ponytail who had a death pinch on Travis's throat with his forearm.

I'd seen those hands before. Around June's throat.

I hit the dirt on my tailbone, cursing. Canuette didn't give me a chance to complain too much, hauling me up so he could give me a full view of the very impressive gun he held to Travis's head.

"Any shit out of you, lady lawyer, and he's fish food."

For once, I kept my mouth shut. Travis's blue eyes blinked once, then settled on mine with a steady gaze. I knew he was trying to tell me something stolid, like I should keep my friggin' mouth shut for once in my life.

"Come on, buddy boy, let's lead this parade." The pony-tailed guy slammed Travis into the back of the van like a sack of potatoes. Travis grunted as he landed.

"You next." He gestured at me.

I tried to walk, but my legs were made of water and my head didn't feel very solid either. I landed in the dirt again. *Damn,* I thought, *this skirt and blouse are ruined.* I vaguely remembered they were made of silk and June had ordered them from some fancy catalogue.

My collapse didn't stop Ponytail. He scooped me up like road kill and threw me on top of Travis. Bone on bone makes for a pretty hard landing. I was feeling a strange surge of adrenaline and panic, which managed to tense me up until I thought I'd fly through the roof of the van.

Only Travis's strong hands on my back stopped me from losing it. I lay on him stomach to stomach, trying to keep my head up and our legs disentangled. With one hand, Travis stroked my spine. The other forced my head down onto his shoulder.

"Breathe," he whispered in my ear. "Take a deep breath."

I tried. It helped.

"Okay," I whispered back. "Now what?"

The van door behind us slammed shut. Canuette crawled between the front seats and crouched in the opened back beside us, the gun in his hand aimed straight for Travis and me. Ponytail drove.

"Mr. Caulder and I want to thank you," Canuette drawled in his Carolina mountain accent, thick as weeds in a muddy pond. "Been looking to get you two together off the beaten path, so to speak, for a while now."

The van was a dark green paneled job, with a utilitarian interior lined with racks and boxes bolted to the floor. I wondered if it had a fancy alarm system, and would have bet Miss Ena's house that it did. I hadn't seen it around my house, nor anywhere near Travis's place any of the times I was out there. These guys were good. What a scary thought.

"Almost got you this morning, but we needed a clean snatch, two for the price of one. Ain't got time to go doing this twice," Canuette continued, enjoying the sound of his own voice.

He was just as skinny as ever, the closely cropped hair dark on his skull. Voice flat, he seemed to be talking more for his own enjoyment than to frighten us. Matter-of-factly, he turned to Ponytail.

"Make sure you burn their clothes, Caulder. Don't want any mistakes with this one, not like you did with C.D."

C.D. Cool Dude. Charles Darryl. I knew it. I leaned into Travis's ear and spoke slowly and as softly as I could.

"They're going to kill us."

Imperceptibly, he nodded.

"Hey there, no hanky-panky," Canuette snarled, shoving me off Travis with a boot in my ribs. I was going to be covered with bruises by the time Henry got to my corpse.

Vaguely, I wondered if he'd do the autopsy, or if he'd

pass. Knowing Henry, he'd do it just to make sure it was done right. *What a comforting thought,* I mused abstractly.

"Thought I wouldn't recognize you, hey, bitch?" Canuette sniggered over his shoulder in the direction of Ponytail Caulder. "Figured out the black girl when the beer wore off, you were easier. Always did have a memory for white tail. Saw you coming out of that house where Darryl's old lady lived, put two and two together. Man, did I make a mistake, thinking this dude here was after us." He toed Travis.

I tried to sit up but it hurt too much. Travis pulled me against him, then wiggled us both until our backs rested against one of the boxes.

"You mugged us at the weapons fair," Travis muttered. "Stole my wallet."

"Sure enough." Canuette grinned, exposing his bad teeth. "Asked too many questions, you did. Didn't feel right. Me and Caulder, we decided to check you out."

Caulder cackled. "Ain't it a hoot? Ain't had this much fun since, oh shit, don't know when."

Breathing better, I decided it was my turn. "So why'd you kill Darryl? Did you figure out he'd cut you out of your share of the haul?"

Leaning back, Canuette looked at me as if I were a talking dog. "Boy howdy, she ain't as dumb as we thought."

I tried to keep my temper in check, but it wasn't going to be easy. I didn't want to die angry. Besides, I needed to think.

"Was there more than the diamond ring? I'll bet there was. Maybe a whole bunch of stuff." I clicked my tongue sympathetically. "Can't let a guy get away with shit like that."

Shaking his head as if I were a sorry student who gave all the wrong answers, Canuette shot a glance at Caulder.

"That worn't the half of it," he sighed. "C.D. had an eye for the ladies. Hell, Caulder and I didn't give a rat's ass who he screwed. But he shoulda kept his paws off Caulder's woman."

Glancing at Caulder, I could see his eyes burning holes in the rearview mirror. Out the windshield, I didn't recognize where we were until a curve came into view. I knew that curve well.

"Why're you taking us back to my place?" Travis had noticed also.

Canuette laughed. "Don't think they'll find you, not where we're gonna stash you two. Dumb idea Caulder had, dumping C.D. in two places. You all get the new plan."

Oh goodie, they'd thought about this. All four brain cells between them had come up with how to kill us.

"Let her go. She doesn't have anything to do with this," Travis pleaded.

"Ah, listen to the boyfriend. Ain't he cute?" Caulder sneered in an accent as thick as Canuette's.

"Save your breath," I sighed, leaning against Travis's shoulder. I was more than tired now. I just wanted to get this over with. "These morons are just showing off. They'll run out of vocabulary in a second."

The insult sank in slowly. "Hey," Canuette protested, waving the gun around like a Fourth of July sparkler. "We had a good thing going here until ole Darryl got itchy britches for Melly. Ain't that right, Caulder?" Canuette nodded vigorously.

"Hell yes. Can't have no black guy going after my woman." Caulder seconded that one.

Aha, a woman was behind it all. Just as I'd always said, sex, drugs, or money was the root of crime. I'd misjudged this one, though. I'd wondered who Darryl had screwed besides June, but I'd meant it figuratively, not literally. June had said he was a good-looking man; I guess Darryl had thought so, too. But going after the girlfriend of one of those lamebrains hadn't been smart, not smart at all. The three of them may have shared liquor, crime, and God knows what else, but not their women. Even I knew that much.

"Why'd you try to kill June?" I spoke loudly enough for Caulder to hear me.

"Too big for her britches. Guy like Darryl always did talk too much. Cops didn't take her out like we planned, so it was back to square one. Get her next." Caulder's voice was stiff as linen soaked in starch, flattened with a hot iron.

"And Coleman's wife?" At the very least, I deserved answers before I died, and these nitwits seemed only too happy to provide them.

"Bitch was at home. Checked the driveway, I was gonna put the truck back in the garage. Her car was gone, thought we were in the clear. Figured Coleman would go down on the truck charge, so we had to give it back, didn't we, huh?" Caulder laughed over his shoulder at Canuette.

"She just happened to notice you opening her garage door and driving her husband's truck, so you decided to kill her in it?" Travis sounded sick.

"Hey, why not? Got rid of two problems, that fuckin' truck and the mouth on that bitch." Caulder cackled.

I'd have to remember the mouth comment and try to curb mine. If I lived long enough. Since that wasn't much of a possibility, I was safe.

"And guess what? We found us the perfect place to get rid of you two. Sure was our lucky day, warn't it?" His eyes dead, Canuette leaned over and flicked the top button on my blouse with a dirty fingernail. "Too bad you ain't better lookin', bitch. We coulda had us some fun."

"Yeah, well, some folks get all the breaks." I didn't squirm away from his hand, though I really wanted to slice it off at the wrist.

"Leave her alone," Travis snarled.

I wondered why they hadn't tied us up. The odds were even. If I'd been them, I'd have made sure Travis and I were knotted up like fishing line looped in a tree's limb.

"Ah, still cute, ain't he?" Canuette was enjoying this much too much.

"Look, I can offer you a deal." I swallowed hard. "We'll say this is attorney-client privilege. I can't reveal anything you've said here. Travis will go along with us. Won't you?" I gave him my best beseeching look.

He glared at me as if I'd lost my everlovin' mind.

"They know you were on the road where Mrs. Coleman was found. Believe me, you fucked up and left evidence behind."

Canuette's eyes widened. I hurried on. "You get a free lawyer when they arrest you. All they can prove is presence at a crime scene, not that you did it. You walk."

Canuette chortled. "Boy, she's slick. She this good in bed?" His eyes flicked from me to Travis.

I nudged Travis to keep quiet. "Best deal you're gonna get, guys. Game's about run its course, and you know it. Can't kill the whole county."

"Don't need to," Caulder threw over his shoulder. "Soon as the black bitch goes down, we're outta here. Mexico sounds good this time of year."

"Can't spend the rest of your life running," I argued. "What happens when you run out of money?"

I had no idea how much they'd stolen and sold, but it couldn't be enough to support them in beer and women for the rest of their lives.

"Oh, we'll think of summpin'." Canuette laughed as if he'd told a hilarious joke. "Now shut up, bitch. Caulder and me, we ain't takin' no chances. Ain't doin' time, not never again. Been there, done that." He chuckled at his own wit.

I flexed my wrist, which hurt like hell. The van bounced off the main road and I could see yellow tape fly by. We were heading for the old water tower.

"Lord have mercy," I muttered.

"That's a good one." Canuette cackled. "Stop here. Hide it in that stand over there." He pointed at a clump of brush oak and wild dogwoods. "You two get out, and no funny stuff, ya hear?"

He didn't wait for Caulder to stop before he threw open the back doors and toed us hard. I scrambled. The solid ground felt like heaven to me. Sliding an arm around my waist, Travis pulled me close. His arm was as hot as a firecracker.

"Can you walk?" he asked softly.

I nodded. Fear seemed to have given me my muscles back instead of just the opposite. I felt as if I could run a four-minute mile.

"Stay close," he added as Canuette and Caulder leveled shotguns at us.

"My oh my, new toys." I was impressed. "Where now?"

"Up that ladder." Caulder flicked the shotgun at the old water tower.

If I'd had enough saliva in my mouth, I would have

gulped. I hate heights. And enclosed spaces. Both night-mares at once, how fun.

As water towers go, this one wasn't all that tall. Built back when Miss Ena was young and spry, constructed of wood, it was maybe twenty-five feet off the ground. It'd been abandoned when the county installed a new water sys-tem in the early 1970s. High schoolers throughout the years had used it to spray paint their names, hearts, football scores, and various obscenities. No one from the county had bothered to tear it down, mostly because it had become part of the scenery, was my guess.

Still and all, twenty-five feet up a rickety wooden ladder was my idea of hell. It may as well have been two hundred and fifty feet.

"What're you going to do to us?" I sounded petulant, but I was really scared silly. If I had to look down from up at the top of the tower, I'd probably have a heart attack.

"Have some fun, sweetheart." Jabbing me in the back with the shotgun, Caulder forced me to the ladder. "You first."

My heart ricocheting around in my chest like a balloon shooting air, I grasped the first rung and tried to put my foot on the ladder.

"She's too shaken up, the accident rattled her. I'll go first." Travis shoved me aside and began climbing quickly.

Caulder and Canuette focused on his back. I wondered what they'd do with the shotguns as they climbed if they meant to kill us at the top. For a second, I considered run-ning away as fast as I could while they stared upward. But even if they didn't kill me, I couldn't leave Travis.

Not after the way I'd misjudged him. I threw myself at the ladder and, shutting my eyes, began to climb. My bare feet caught on the old, splintery wood, but the pain wasn't anything compared to my panic. At the top, Travis hooked me under the arms and lifted me onto the narrow ledge surrounding the carousel-shaped tower. The rickety wooden fence encasing the catwalk looked like toothpicks. Leaning against the wooden barrel, I opened my eyes for a brief second and felt the world spinning.

"I can't stand this," I muttered more to myself.

"Yes, you can." Travis leaned over the edge, murder on his face. The tip of his freckled nose met the business end of Canuette's shotgun.

The ex-Marine scrambled up the ladder like a monkey, the shotgun pointed steadily at us. Caulder was right behind him. Travis and I were screwed.

"Back off," Caulder ordered, holding his shotgun on us while Canuette worked his way onto the platform.

"Move your asses," Canuette barked, gesturing that we were to sidle to our left.

Facing forward, my back to the barrel, I slid my feet in a shuffle worthy of the hokey-pokey. If they hadn't shot us yet, they must have planned something more interesting. I could easily wait to find out what was in store for us, but I didn't have to wait long.

Caulder met us in the middle, a sturdy lock in one hand. The key to it was nowhere I could see. His face was pockmarked by old scars, and I could see black whiskers poking through on his chin and upper lip. Something in his expression was beyond the cold and calculating stage and deep into serious enjoyment at the prospect of hurting someone. Whereas Canuette was just plain mean and mean-spirited, Caulder got his jollies from pain.

I tried to promise myself I'd go down fighting, that I

wouldn't cry and beg for my life. I'd do it for Travis, but not for myself. I'd hauled Travis into this mess, and I owed him that much.

Caulder swung open a wooden door in the side of the barrel. In the days when the tower held water, I assumed the door had been put in there to clean it out now and then. It could only have been opened if the tank was empty.

"Get in." Caulder waved the shotgun in my face once more.

I smelled the dry, ancient scent of death and decay. Rotting wood, termites, birds that had somehow met their deaths in this dark place, all rose up to greet me.

"Fuck you." I'd been locked up once, it'd never happen to me again. They could throw me over the railing, but I'd never step foot inside that thing.

I vaguely heard Travis shouting my name as the darkness settled over me like an old friend. I sank into unconsciousness as easily as would anyone cracked over the head with a shotgun.

I really wished I'd gotten a chance to kick Caulder and Canuette in the nuts just once before I died.

Chapter 23

✤

MY throat hurt horribly. Flailing at the hands I was dreaming were crushing my trachea, I connected.

"Damn it, wake up," Travis shouted, shaking me like a whip.

"I am," I mumbled. "Cut it out, my head's about to fall off my neck."

Travis rocked back. I could barely see him. A bit of light filtered through the spots where knotholes had fallen from the roof boards, but what came through was only pale light. We were alone.

"Where'd the sons of bitches go?" I grumbled, forcing myself to sit upright. My throat still ached.

"My guess is, away from here." Travis coughed. "They locked the door behind them. Guess they expect us to die eventually. Of course, they left a canteen beside us. Three guesses what's in it, and if you're thinking Jonestown and bloated bodies, I'd say you're right."

"What?" I grabbed him by the shoulders, trying to work my legs under me. I realized I was buck naked.

"Me, too." Travis slid my hand down to his hip. "They must have stripped us while we were out."

"Charming thought." I burned all over at the image of their hands on my underwear.

I breathed deeply, trying to calm myself and block out the picture. The smell of the old wood tower reminded me of barbeques the neighbors had when I was a kid, filling Woolfolk Avenue with the sweet scent of oak and pork.

"Must have thought we'd stay here and die a slow, painful death, rather than run around naked in Talmadge County." I tried to laugh, but my ribs hurt.

"My call is they've something more creative in mind. Wanna bet our clothes end up together somewhere with a suicide note? Our bodies won't be anywhere near, of course, but it'll take whoever finds the note some time to figure that out. Meanwhile, we're fried."

"Wow, you're full of good news." I tried to stand. "They can't spell 'suicide' correctly. The note's not going to work."

Somehow, I felt safer on my feet. "Okay, how do we get our lily white asses outta here?" Good thing I don't have any hangups about modesty.

"Not the door. It's locked solid as a chastity belt."

"Nice analogy." Pressing my hands to the wall, I began hitting at it. "Think we can work some of these boards loose?"

"Got a crowbar?"

I could feel his breath at my shoulder. "Sure. Here in my hip pocket."

"This old tank was built with interlocking boards. They used nails sparingly. Like a mortise and tenon joint." He smacked a board. "It's old, but it's seasoned wood. It'll keep us in, all right. It's not going to splinter without some tools."

I envisioned Travis showing me the construction with his hands. I wished I could see him clearly.

"In other words, we're screwed." I kicked the wall for good measure. My toe throbbed.

"There's always a chance someone will hear us. It's not impossible." He didn't sound as if he believed his own theory.

"Yeah, right. Who comes out this way but you? I gave the cigarette butts I found to Henry already, he won't be out here again."

"Cigarette butts?"

"I'm taking odds they have Canuette's spit on them. Down where the Coleman truck was found."

Circling the inside of the tower, I stepped gingerly. Mostly old leaves and cobwebs, the dessicated bodies of dead bugs crunched under my bare feet.

"Maybe one of these is rotten." I thumped another board. "These leaves got in here somehow. Can you start on the other side, we'll meet in the middle?" I gave another testing thwack.

"Give it up, Tal." Travis sounded as tired as I felt.

"No," I insisted, "try it. What do we have to lose?"

"We've lost. Face it. Make your peace with God, if you believe." His voice was fading fast.

I realized he was losing hope. I didn't know how badly he'd cracked his head in the truck, either. If he had a concussion, all I knew was that I needed to keep him awake.

"I'm sorry." The words came to me so quickly, I wondered if I really was the one saying them. "I know I said it before, but I mean it. I just don't trust easily. It's the way my mind works, I always seem to see the worst in people. Always worked for me, when I was with the firm. Kept me from feeling too badly when I lost one. I always expect the worst, and I just plugged you into one of my slots and didn't give you a chance." If he wasn't listening to me now, he never would.

Standing in the dark buck naked, trying to see Travis's face while I ate a whole pie of crow and tried to explain why I was such a jerk was a new one on me. I would have passed on the experience if I'd been offered the chance, but I needed to do this at least once, and do it right. I wasn't going to die a virgin at the apology game.

I stared up at the roof, wishing I were tall enough to push it aside. I knew it had to move. It was definitely nailed together, not made of the fancy interlocking pieces of wood the sides were.

"Shut up, Tal."

I thought he was going to die hating me. What a way to head into eternity.

"Please," I started to beg. "I hate being closed up, I hate it that those poor white trash were smarter than we are, I hate what I've done to you."

Even in the last of the compressed afternoon heat, jammed into the wooden tower, I shivered.

"That makes two of us." Travis's voice was raspy.

"Do you forgive me?" If I couldn't plead for his life, I'd do the next best thing.

"Shut up, Tal. You're only talkin' like this because we're going to die." He sounded tired.

"Well, hell." Now I was pissed. "Be like that." Turning my back, I kicked the wall like a mule.

Good thing Travis couldn't see me. I'd end up with don-key ears in the portrait he was painting if he got a chance to finish it.

I slammed the wall again with my foot, pain shooting up to my knee. Next I tried a bare shoulder on wood. More pain. I'd been locked in that cedar closet once, I'd sworn it wouldn't happen again. If I ripped my nails out by the roots, I'd find a way to get a board loose.

"Help me," I commanded. "Quit feeling sorry for your-self, and do something."

Coughing and a groan answered me. He must have a cracked rib. If I could get him riled up, maybe he'd snap out of this lethargy, if his body would let him. I tried to figure out how to insult him enough to get him banging on the walls, but not enough to throttle me. I guessed he was al-ready near the throttle stage.

"You think you're so smart, so sensitive. Just like an artist, huh? Why'd you really run home, Travis? My bet is, you had wounds to lick, just like I did." I tried the next shoulder against the wood. Pain like a thousand nails drove into my flesh.

"Difference between us, kiddo, is I'm not so stupid that I'll ever give up. Never. You hear me, Travis Whitlock? I don't need you, I don't need anybody, and I wish I were alone in here instead of stuck with a crybaby like you." I was shouting by now, feeling like a seven-year-old, remember-ing the taunts of the girls who locked me in the cedar closet.

My wicked, wicked tongue did the trick.

"My mama taught me never to call a lady what I want to call you," Travis snarled as he joined me, shoulder to shoul-der. "But then, you aren't a lady, are you?"

"God, I hope not." I tried a deep breath. Bad idea. Coughed hard. "On the count of three, give it all we've got."

Hurtling ourselves at the wall, we landed with a smack that must have ripped the flesh off Travis's arm. I know it did mine. Searing pain was added to my list of woes. But I'd felt something give. Just a tiny bit, but a definite creak had answered our full assault.

"Did you hear that?" I was chortling. "Again."

"Tal, give it up." He was standing behind me. "Let me get you on my shoulders, see if you can reach the edge where the top joins the wall."

I hadn't gotten a good look, but I knew the top was way up there, farther than I could reach even if I could stand on Travis's shoulders. But I wasn't about to tell him that. At least he was thinking of ways to get us free.

"How're you going to lift me? I weigh too much for you to stand with me sitting on your shoulders."

A wry chuckle, sounding more like Travis, answered me. "Guess I should have done some weightlifting instead of all that brush-cleaning, huh?"

"I hate weightlifters. All bulk, no brain." I patted his arm, heard a sharp intake of air. "Did I hurt you?"

"No, it was probably when the truck rolled. But what the hell, it won't matter in a little bit."

"Don't say that!" I wanted him to take me in his arms and kiss it all away. But that wasn't going to happen and I knew it. "There's always hope."

"Said the pessimist to the bigger pessimist." Racking coughs hit him. The dust and dirt in this place would have killed an asthmatic.

I thought he'd lost a lung with the last one. My own

shortness of breath was increasing. Fear, adrenaline, I didn't know what had ratcheted my metabolism up a notch, but I was cooking.

"I promise, we get out of this, I'll be an optimist for life."

"Don't make promises you can't keep." His voice was a thready whisper.

To hell with the guy making the moves. Stumbling into Travis, I wrapped my arms around him. Our nudity was nothing, only the clothing of skin that held our bones in, as I pressed myself to him from behind. If we were truly going to die, I wanted to feel close to one human being before I met my maker. Strange that I hadn't thought of Jack Bland, not once, in the middle of this mess. Travis was enough for me. I just wished I could make amends and prove to him I was a changed woman.

I hadn't planned to die in the middle of a grand delusion, but it beat falling off the roof or frying myself with the rickety old wiring I was always repairing. So I dreamed, my head against the back of Travis's shoulder, that we'd made a go of it, the failed, alcoholic lawyer and the portrait painter, and that I'd never screwed it up with my suspicious mind.

I knew then I was going to die in this dark, dirty place.

Chapter 24

"**T**AL!"

   I heard the bellow through my dark dreams. I'd
been left to die in a black desert with falcons pecking at my
eyes. Sand clogged my throat. "Huh?"

"Tal! If you're in there, let me know!"

I could have sworn it was June screaming at me from
three feet away.

"You hear that?" I shook Travis. Slumped on the floor beside me, he was in worse shape than I. We'd poured the canteen on the floor so it wouldn't tempt us. Now, I wished
we'd taken the poison and gotten it over with.

"Hear what?" He was barely conscious.

"June. Calling me."

"Oh good, God is a black woman." He tried to chuckle,
but couldn't.

"Talbot Rowena Jefferson!"

I knew that time I wasn't dreaming. No one knew my middle name but the IRS and Henry. The IRS didn't sound like Henry, and unless this was a very sick illusion, he was with June outside the tower. Hobbling to my feet, I inched to the sides once more. This time, I used the flat of my hand to smack the wood. It was warmer than the last time I'd touched it. Must be daylight again. A few streaks through the roof added to my conviction. I'd lost count of how many days and nights we'd been cooking in here without water.

"June?" My throat was so clogged, it came out as a squeak. I tried again.

"Tal, answer me!" June was right outside.

"June, June, June," I chanted, praying one syllable would make its way to wherever she was.

A huge creak and a crash, and hot air blew onto my face. An apparition worthy of my worst alcoholic nightmares inched inside the tower. The angel of death wore white and blinded me with his brilliance.

"Tal?"

Two figures moved toward me. I touched the first one. Solid as my own arm.

"Get Travis out first," I choked. "Here." I leaned down and hooked an arm under him.

The white apparition threw me over his shoulder and hauled me through the opened door, though I was trying to protest that Travis needed help first. The second figure held onto me as if I were a child about to run into the path of an oncoming train.

I tried to get away. "Help Travis," I pleaded as the figure disappeared again into the tower. It came out as a garbled croak.

Staring into the bright horizon, I refused to look down.

Cool air slipped over my skin, goosebumping me. I never noticed. June grabbed my shoulders and turned me to look at her.

"Can you get down the ladder?" She was still shouting.

"Not without Travis," I muttered.

"What?" June leaned closer. Her face was glistening with sweat. Below, I heard frantic barking.

"Hurry, oh, hurry," I prayed. "Come on, hurry."

The angel was back, Travis on his shoulder. Clambering awkwardly toward me, he tugged on something and I saw his face. Henry.

"Wore a hazard helmet, in case we found a corpse." He was matter of fact about it, his eyes on mine. Just what I needed; his calm, methodical approach to my possible demise pulled me back to reality.

"Travis?"

"He's alive. Keep calm." Henry had never sounded so good to me. "We thought you were the only one in there."

"No such luck." Travis was trying to spit like an unreformed smoker.

For the first time, I wanted to weep. My eyes stung, every inch of me was scraped and bruised, and here I was, as naked as the day I was born, in front of two men who really didn't need to see me quite so plainly. I'd probably never look either of them in the eyes again.

What a nice thought, though, to be able to worry about the future. "How'd you find us?"

Henry chuckled, hoisting Travis onto the catwalk. That football build sure came in handy. I couldn't have dragged a dead cat out of that tower, the shape I was in.

"That fool dog of yours. June swore you were in trouble. Said you'd never stand a client up, not if you were on your death bed. She started looking all over town, got the idea the dog could track you. Smart dog, that Robert E."

"You're kidding." I was still having trouble breathing, but doing better by the second. Travis sounded worse than I.

Henry stripped off the white suit and began unbuttoning his shirt. "Here, put this on. Travis, step into this bio suit."

June stared discretely into the distance.

I could have sworn Travis tried to laugh.

"Yep, that dog tracked your scent all day and half the night, it seemed. When he led her to the tower, and June saw a shiny new lock on the side from the ground, she called me to bring in the troops. Only the troops weren't listening. So we took care of matters ourselves."

I buttoned his shirt carefully, my fingers shredded with splinters. Now I was so cold, I thought I'd die of the shivers. The temperature must have been well over ninety degrees, but I wasn't feeling it.

"Hey Rolfe, remember that treehouse we made?"

He nodded.

"Remind me of this, if I ever get a hankering to build another one."

Henry laughed. I felt better.

"Got to get you two down from here." June stared at the ladder. "Travis, you up to climbing?"

Inching beside Travis, I wrapped my arms around him.

"I promise, you never have to see me again, just get down that friggin' ladder."

Lifting his head, he stared at me with his blue eyes. I couldn't read his thoughts. We Jeffersons are better at action than thinking things through.

"Take you up on that one." Struggling to stand, he

leaned on Henry. "Just weak. I'll make it, once I get go-ing."

I'd said my apologies inside the water tower and before. He hadn't wanted to hear them then, I doubted he'd believe me now. But I had a boatload of thank-yous coming up, and I'd give it all I had. One of these days, he'd forgive me. Earning back his trust was going to be the hard part.

But we Jeffersons aren't quitters. The man had no idea how patient I could be. Patience had never been my strong suit before, but I'd be the queen of patience if I had to.

After all, he had a portrait to finish. Every day he'd see my face as he painted. As stubborn as I, he'd complete the work he'd started in a fever. Loose ends weren't his style.

Talbot Jefferson as Mary Magdalene. Well, the whore had been forgiven, hadn't she? I hoped Travis remembered that as he stared at my face on the canvas.

I shut my eyes and started down the ladder after June. Henry went between Travis and me, one hand on his leg to steady him. By the time we got to the bottom, I was shak-ing like someone in detox and my legs were gelatin. Robert E., bless his heart, didn't care that I smelled like rat poison. Leaping all over me, he covered my face with wet kisses be-fore Henry and June could bring him down. Burying my head in his wiry fur, I wanted to weep, but I didn't have enough fluids in me to even try.

I wanted to sleep but it hurt too much.

Everything in this life hurt too much.

At least Robert E. loved me. June and Henry came al-most as close.

Travis was another matter altogether. I wondered if he'd always think of our slow dying in that tower every time my name came to mind.

If so, I wouldn't blame him if he got a lobotomy to excise me from his mind. Failing that, however, I was going to make sure he came around to my side.

One day at a time, they say. One day.

Chapter 25

WITH the license plate number for the green van and our detailed descriptions of Caulder and Canuette, the police got them hiding out in a motel that rented by the hour to truckers outside Pink Hill. I spent that night and the next day in the hospital, getting pumped full of fluids until I could float. Finally, I put up such a fuss, they let me go home.

June drove the Mustang over to get me.

"Why in tarnation can't you do anything that's good for you? Just once, listen to someone else?" She grumbled the whole time she loaded me in the Mustang.

Settling back in the passenger seat, I was so grateful to be in its confines again I wanted to jump up and down. Instead, I decided to be polite to June.

"I'm okay. They said I needed rest. I can get that at

home." Leaning back, I praised the 1966 Ford for its lack of headrest.

She cranked the ignition. "They got the rest of the stolen guns. Stashed in the van. Some jewelry, some other small stuff stolen from all over the place."

"Good." I really didn't care at this point. All I wanted was for Canuette and Caulder to disappear from my life. "What about Darryl's death? Have they been charged?"

"Oh yeah." Hands tight on the steering wheel, June sounded savage. "Caulder's girlfriend was picked up with them at the motel. When she got threatened with being an accomplice to murder, she spilled the whole story. About how they killed Darryl because he was making moves on her, the son of a bitch."

"Don't speak ill of the dead." Since I'd almost been there myself, I felt qualified to lecture her on death and etiquette.

She pressed too hard on the accelerator. We flew out of the parking lot like drag racers.

"Ease up. This is a small eight, not a four banger like you drive." The wind in my hair was heaven. I'd lost a lot of weight, most of it water, and my skin was a strange, crackled covering. But I could smell the magnolias lining the drive to the old hospital and that meant I was alive and kickin'.

She muttered something about bossy women but she slowed down.

"Takes one to know one." I chuckled. "Took a bossy woman to find us in that tower, too. From now on, that's the highest compliment I can give. Bossy women of the world, unite."

"Oh, be quiet." She wasn't half as annoyed as she pretended. Pulling onto Wynnton's Main Street, she sped up again. "You need to get back to fightin' form fast. That Ike

Coleman's about to bother me to death, calling every other minute. Seems he doesn't like that lawyer you sicced on him. Wants you back."

I harrumphed. "A first-year law student could get him off now. Legal Aid can have him."

"He makes too much money for Legal Aid." June sniffed. "How about you charge him an arm and a leg, and we start makin' some money around here?"

"Good idea. The hospital bill alone will bankrupt me." I didn't care. I'd face all the minutiae of my life later.

Right now, I had to get going on my new road. Nothing like almost dying over three days to put a life into focus.

"Thank you. Thank you for saving my life." I was going to get good at this appreciation game.

Turning to give me a startled glance, June almost ran us into the curb. "Well, I'll be. Now I've heard it all."

"Naw, you ain't heard nothin' yet." Grinning at the blue Carolina sky above me, I reached out and turned the knob to start the radio.

WCRG was playing my song. "You've Lost that Lovin' Feelin'" wailed into my ears. I flicked it off.

It's not over yet, I promised myself, no matter what the Righteous Brothers had to say about it.

Travis still had to finish that portrait.

June gave me a look that said I was crazy.

I didn't care. I had hope, a dog who loved me, and friends who wouldn't give up.

I am a lucky woman.